GHOST SEA

ALSO BY FERENC MÁTÉ

Autumn
A Reasonable Life
The Hills of Tuscany

GHOST SEA

a novel

FERENC MÁTÉ

W.W. NORTON NEW YORK LONDON

For Candace
Who *really* stood by her man.

Contents

The Salvage	9
The Repair	21
The Hire	27
Obsession	37
Chinatown	53
Nello	63
Chow's Debt	71
Charlie	81
Hay	85
Nightsail	97
Racing North	109
Under the Kelp	119
Stars	129
That Spring	143
Bear	151
Devil's Hole	155
Canoe	165
The North	179
Capsized	193
The Village	203
Waiting	207
A Dream	213
Potlatch: The First Day	217
Potlatch: The First Night	225
Snowy Night	235
Midnight	245
The Choice	251
To Ashes	257
Dawn	261
Quotations/Illustrations	265
Acknowledgments	266

Printed in the United States of America
First Edition

ISBN 0-920256-49-X

Book design, illustrations and composition by Candace Máté

Albatross Books at
W.W. Norton & Company Inc., 500 Fifth Ave, New York, N.Y. 10110
http://www.wwnorton.com

W.W. Norton & Company Ltd., 10 Coptic Street, London WCA 1PU
1 2 3 4 5 6 7 8 9 10

GHOST SEA

a novel

I

The Salvage
1920

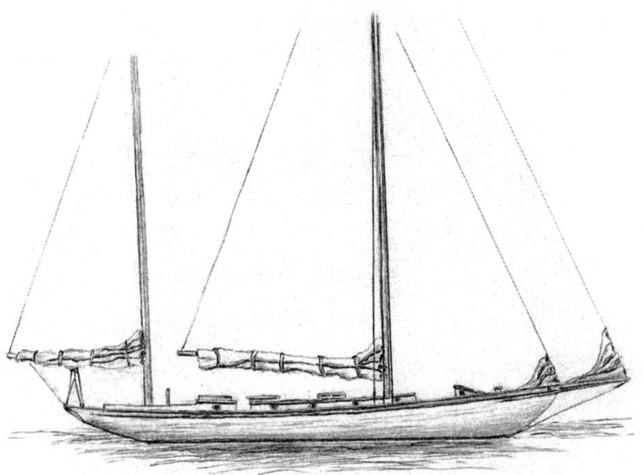

And, tell me, wasn't that the best time, that time when we were young at sea; young and had nothing, on the sea that gives nothing, except hard knocks—and sometimes a chance to feel your strength—that only.

—Joseph Conrad

It was the last of October, the first of the big storms. The glass had started falling before midnight, hesitant at first as if it might change its mind, but then it fell steadily and the gusts grew and by dawn the clouds dragged over steep seas, driving a rain as cold as snow. I rowed out to Bird Rock to pound in another ring, under noisy gulls that soared and dove in the updraft on the cliff. The old Swede was on the float of his small island, hauling out the dinghies and skiffs he was repairing, flipping them over and lashing them down. Then he stood and waited in that rain, waited until I came back from pounding the ring, and as I drifted close I saw his face drawn tight, looking worriedly out at the heaving sea, "You dance good out there tonight, eh?" he said.

I rowed back into the calm cove, in the embrace of mountains. A handful of fishermen's shacks floating on cedar logs shared the cove with a net loft, some seals, some sea otters, the odd black bear that came to crab at dawn when the tide was low, and a long-neglected ketch bobbing at anchor.

I worked out of the cove that year as a deckhand on a tug owned by a miser named Henderson, salvaging logs that came loose in winter storms out of log booms being towed down the blustery, snowy sound. All my youth I dreamt of running away to sea, but this sure as hell wasn't in my dreams. At school I stared out the window after the rain, stared at the baker's roof where a pool of water rippled in the sun, and imagined it was a vast, empty ocean—the Indian or Pacific—or the Celebes or China Sea; and my mind would drift away to atoll-strewn turquoise waters or some long sandy shore. But mostly I dreamed of clutching the wheel of a small schooner, her sails bulging, the trade winds blowing, the wooden deck warm under my feet, and as far as my eyes could see, all around me, the sea. An endless freedom.

I should have left it at dreaming. But when the sea fills your every thought awake and asleep, you can no more resist than the tides can the moon. So I went to sea. Put in two years scraping rust off a West African coaster, a year and a half shoveling coal into the furnace of a steamer, two years standing watch on a hulk that hauled rubber from a tin shed in Brazil to brick sheds in the snow, and after all that, there I was penniless in that sunless North Pacific hole, praying for a storm.

Log salvage is a profession that thrives on the loss of others, a little like grave-robbing except the law is on your side. The International Law of Salvage Rights gives to anyone the right to grab and make his own most of what is wrecked or lost at sea, and villages from Cornwall to Sumatra have eked out a life harvesting the bounty heaven sent with storms. And so did we.

North of us they were felling forests, dragging logs the size of houses to the shore with oxen or steam donkeys, chucking them in the sea, making them into floating booms with chained boomsticks around them. Then a tug would hook a yoke on, point south, and give her full throttle. And sit there. After a while the booms began to nudge, barely, like a snail. When a storm caught them and smashed a boom or popped loose logs, we'd be there driving eye pegs in them, hauling them behind our rock, fattening up Henderson's pockets and putting a few nickels in our own. Most salvagers wait until the storm dies and the sea calms before heading out, but Henderson wanted us to "get a jump," so out he sent us at the height of gales, into riptides, the darkest nights, because "that, my boys, is when the others hide under the covers, and you alone will harvest the presents from the Lord. And if by His will yea be drowned, well, hell's bells, that's your destiny."

Between storms we kept busy chiseling rot out of the tug, recaulking planks, keeping her afloat, and I would stare at the lonely ketch weathering away. Hours I spent gazing at her from the tug or rowing around her in my skiff, getting near, sometimes scooping the heaps of rot-starting muck from the corners of her decks, sometimes checking her anchor lines for fraying. I committed her every block, every line, every bit of hardware and rigging to memory. And every time we passed her as we headed out into a storm, my heart would tighten against the knowledge that she would never, ever be mine.

The sea is noble in her impartiality. She harbors, feeds, maims, and drowns with disregard for age or race or creed; the sole bias she can be accused of is that she won't tolerate a fool.

The ketch belonged to a man called Block—a fool. The year before, he'd owned whorehouses in Vancouver and Victoria full of Kwakiutl squaws sent by their husbands to earn extra cash for them to throw great potlatches and impress friends and relations with their nobility. To get the freshest squaws, Block bought a double-decked whore boat for nine whores, ran it along the coast, plucked the ripest and sent them off to logging camps, mining camps, fish camps, homesteads, and even the odd missionary, for training. The whore business flourished, so he sold it off at a fine profit, and to fit in among respectable people—those who had sold off their whatevers before—he bought himself a tugboat line and a mansion, and had Hoffar-Beeching Shipyards build him the best and fastest ketch on the coast. She was modeled after the East Coast racers, forty feet on the waterline, full-sterned, a sheer to break your heart, bronze-fastened, Port Orford cedar-planked on oak frames, teak decks, spruce masts varnished like a grand piano, sails of the finest cotton, but when her inside was still as hollow as a barrel, Block went unexpectedly and irreversibly broke. He lost everything except the ketch. While the lawyers wrangled, she lay anchored in our cove, sat there for a year. Leaves and needles piled up in drifts, rust wept from her fittings, moss grew on her decks in the shade, mildew bloomed on her folded sails, her paint cracked, varnish peeled, and long beards of tube kelp streamed from her rudder in the currents of the tide. She was rotting alive.

I rowed past her on the way back from the Swede's, checked

to be sure her anchor lines led fair over the rollers, to make sure she'd ride out the coming storm. The rain had eased but the clouds stayed low and a hard wind whipped the sea against the tide, carving six-foot waves as steep as tombstones. A mile south of the entrance, a tug dove and bucked, fighting the waves with a three-section log boom behind it. It was dusk. We got ready to go out. We donned sou'westers, tied the cuffs tight with line hoping to keep out at least some of the sea, laid out spikes, eyes, lengths of line, a boom chain, sharpened our knives and marlin spikes, stoked the galley stove under the coffeepot, cranked up the diesel, and cast off from the buoy.

The wind gusted but the sea in the cove stayed a chop; waves could never get in. Eagle Island protected it to the south, leaving a narrow twisting channel to the east and an even narrower opening—a few boats wide—next to the Swede's island to the southwest. There was only one menace in the cove—the wind. The southeast gales would slam into the curve of cliffs and turn and funnel back out with undiminished force past the Swede's island, right into the face of inward-rushing waves. Hell for anyone trying to cross the bar.

We headed out at dusk.

The poor ketch, her rain-slackened halyards slapping against the shrouds, tacked and sailed bare-poled hard against her anchors. I watched until she melted away into the rain and the fading light.

The tug reared as she slammed into a wave, and her saw-toothed bow pointed at the clouds. She hung for a moment at the crest, tipped forward, and hurled herself down the back. The propeller lifted clear into the air and its vibrations rattled the iron plates of the stove. I clung to the galley sink and when we hit the bottom of the trough with a bone-jarring thud, the kerosene lamp went out and green water ran a foot deep past the cabin. Then the next wave came and the bow lifted and we surged out of the safety of the cove. Jordan the skipper laughed, loud and self-satisfied. He was still too young to get angry at life, too young to worry about death right there beside him, so he stood cheerfully at the helm in his swaying pilothouse with a smile on his creaseless face. He was never perplexed by the violence of a storm, piloted the tug as if he didn't notice, and in no way felt threatened by the fact that the ocean was trying its best to send us straight to hell. He loved the sea. Loved the creaky tug, loved his dumb but cheery wife, his dough-ball baby daughter, his modest little house under the cedars near Dundarave which he spent every spare moment reshaking, patching, painting, beautifying. He was blessed.

I relit the lantern. We were out in deeper waters now and the waves were longer, their faces more climbable, and the tug had an easier time of it. The clouds broke and the moon lit patches on the sea. Jordan eased the throttle, slid down his side window, and smiled out at the night. I went out on deck and gazed over the moon-silvered froth, searching among that chaos for incongruous straight lines—loose logs.

WE SHOT DOWN the back of a wave, leaving behind the looming bulk of the Swede's island where a window glowed with reassuring light. Then we turned west, taking the seas abeam so that we both rolled and plunged. All we had to do was wait and not be blown ashore. The logs were coming; they had to, we knew the winds and currents; we knew our sea. The booms would be breaking up soon and the logs drifting north by northwest, pushed shoreward by the wind, herded by the tide, and they would come like cows home to the stable, toward the jagged bluffs of that nameless bight ahead, where the bottom suddenly shoaled and the waves rose up in rage before shattering into foam. But not before hurling everything they had brought: driftwood, floats, nets, lost boats, halfway up the bluff to lodge in crevices and crags.

Jordan had turned the tug bow into the seas, kept the throttle low, and braced himself against the cabinside with his shoulder to have one hand free for his coffee. When he spotted the first log, he eased the tug alongside, and I waited knee-deep in breaking sea with a pike pole. Then harpooned it. I clung to the pole for dear life, waiting for the tug and log to bob in harmony. In that moment of calm at the bottom of a trough, a mere blink of an eye, I yanked an eye spike and lanyard from my belt, threw myself down on my knees to hammer in the spike, yanked out the pike, fed out line, and cleated the bitter end.

By midnight we had done well; we were towing our fifth log toward the safe lee of our rock. The wind still raged, but the moon peeked out and threw shreds of light on the churning sea. Rounding the rock, Jordan slowed. I hauled in the line to prevent it from slacking and fouling the prop, uncleated it, and lashed it to the boom chain that linked the other logs to shore. I was just snugging the bowline when Jordan threw open the cabin door. His smile was gone—an imbecilic amazement took its place. He must have been saying something because his mouth was moving, but it was lost in the wind. He stared at something beyond me. I turned to look. I think I let out a laugh, then the tug lurched and the line I held snapped tight, almost yanking me overboard. For a moment the moon hid behind a cloud and the scene vanished from sight as if it had never been. Then the clouds thinned and in that eerie light I saw it had been no vision; it was the ketch.

She came darkly, a ghost ship through the foam, with the tips of her masts white against the night, sailing under bare poles without a stitch of sail aloft. She was propelled at a curious angle by the tide and heeling slightly from the pressure of the wind, heading toward open water with her bowsprit high. Coaxed by the currents, she turned a few degrees and drifted past Bird Rock. With the wind and waves now adding to the pressure of the tide, she gained speed, and with her quarter angled slightly across the seas, she headed toward the nameless bight where crashing breakers hurled against the bluffs.

For a moment I thought: This is how it should end: better than rotting away in the cove.

The moonlight sliced a crevice in the clouds and lit her path across the sea. Jordan had forgotten the wheel and the tug drifted into open waters, gave a roll, and slammed us hard against the cabin. The slamming cleared my head; I had to save the ketch.

Jordan was shouting into the gale, but I understood nothing and could think nothing, only that the ketch of all my dreams was heading down the last half mile of her life, to become kindling for the cottagers to find. I lashed a line to the pike pole, cleated the bitter end, and sent the pole hurtling through the gloom. It fell laughably short. If I could get a line hooked on her I could ease her away from the rocks into open sea.

"Get close!" I roared at Jordan, and he roared back something that I couldn't understand. But he jammed her into reverse and we rolled and pitched slowly toward the ketch. Then I thought of just getting near in the heaving seas without smashing her to bits, to climb on a line aboard her and let out the anchor rodes, to flatten the scope and the let the anchors catch and dig deep into the bottom.

"Get close!" I yelled again. "What the hell are you afraid of?"

Lit by the compass light, Jordan's face looked fearful, his movements hesitant. We were less then a boat-length from the ketch. I was ready. Jordan throttled down. I raised the pole and aimed at the bowsprit where the whisker stays, head stays, and bobstay formed a web, where the pike pole was sure to tangle in something. Even an idiot couldn't miss from this close. We drifted closer. I leaned back and threw. And in that very instant of release, when I had timed a fleeting lull in the lurches of the sea, when all my hopes and dreams shot like a current through me, just then, inexplicably, Jordan thrust the gear in forward and throttled hard. I lost my balance, my strength, my hope all at once; the pole fell stupidly into the sea. The tug roared ahead, leaving the ketch in the gloom.

I thought I had gone mad. I grabbed the hatchet we kept on the aft deck to hack fouled lines, and lurched toward Jordan. God only knows what I intended. The tug barreled at full speed through the uncertain light. I flung open the cabin door and raised the hatchet. Jordan turned, smiling again, that old confident, content-with-life smile. I can't remember how long I stood there.

"Shut the door," I remember him saying. "You're letting in the cold."

I shut it, lowered the hatchet, but didn't put it down. The moon burst through blindingly bright. With the silver light upon them and dark shadows in between, the waves looked even more menacing than before. Jordan spoke crisply but hurriedly and I had trouble getting the gist. I heard, "Henderson . . . his tug . . . salvage rights . . . all his . . . the ketch . . . his . . . ." I clutched my hatchet. Then we were at the Swede's island and Jordan spun the wheel, turned the tug, and stopped her but still bounced into the dock.

"I'm the captain," he barked. "You mutinied and threatened me. I could have you arrested. But I'm merciful. You're fired. Get off my ship." I was dumbstruck. "Now!" Jordan roared. "And give me the damned hatchet."

I was too stunned to do anything but obey. I scrambled onto the old Swede's dock and tripped over the skiffs. I was barely off the tug when Jordan gave full throttle, threw a wake, pulled away, then stopped. He stormed out of his cabin and, glaring at me, shouted, "What the hell are you waiting for? Launch your skiff! You want your goddamn ketch to be smashed on the rocks?" I fumbled with the knot of the line that held my skiff down.

"Cut the fucker!" Jordan bellowed. I glanced up. He was smiling. A wave broke over the dock and soaked me to the waist.

I came to, sliced the line, and, with one desperate lunge, launched the skiff and jumped in.

"The line!" Jordan howled. "Throw me the bloody line!"

He cleated it and gunned the tug. The skiff skipped from side to side on the towline like a colt trying to get free. It began to rain. Hard.

When we swept past Bird Rock the skiff started shipping water, but Jordan kept the throttle down and the skiff went skimming, now burying her bow, now rolling from gunwale to gunwale, but surging ahead. I listened with all my concentration for the sounds I dreaded, the sounds of the ketch grinding, breaking up against the bluff. Then the tug and skiff rose from a trough onto a crest, and just ahead of us through the sheets of rain I caught sight of the ketch, her bow held high.

Jordan opened the throttle wide and we bore down on her. A breaker caught us and threw us sideways. We were in the shoals now and the ketch drifted on. Something was wrong. Why the hell hadn't she slowed? Why hadn't her anchors caught? Then, just before the tug's steel teeth gored the ketch's side, Jordan spun the tug away. He shut the throttle down, ran on to the aft deck with the hatchet, and cut me free. The skiff flew loose and rammed into the ketch. I was thrown onto the floorboards. A sea broke over us, half filled the skiff, and pulled her sluggishly away, until the next sea lifted us and tossed us back. I grabbed the gunwale of the ketch with both hands and hung on.

I had her.

The tug bobbed near. Jordan cupped his hands over his mouth and roared, "All yours, you poor son of a bitch!" And kept on yelling but the rest was drowned in the storm. All mine—all I had to do was let out anchor line. The ketch rolled hard and the rail went down and the sea closed over me, but I hung on. She rolled back. On the next rising wave, I scrambled aboard clutching my painter, cleated it, then slid and lurched on the mossslimed deck forward to the samson post to ease the anchors out. We were less than ten boat-lengths from the bluff.

I knelt down thinking, By God. I *do* have her!, clutched the post, and reached for the anchor lines. But there were no lines. There was nothing near the post. Dangling there were short cut ends of the ropes. I stared at them stupidly.

Jordan was gone. He had guided the tug out of the shoals to the safety of deep water. There was only one escape. If by miracle I could raise the sails in time, and if by miracle she didn't run aground, I'd sail her out. And if I couldn't, if she was hurled against the bluff, masts snapping, decks buckling, the sea rushing in, pulling her under, at least she would have died with sails aloft, having tried to sail out to the open sea.

But the dirt-hardened knots of the mainsail lanyards wouldn't give—I gored them with my marlinespike. The drumming on the cliff was now louder than the waves. The knots opened; the sail was free.

Five boat-lengths.

I had memorized the halyards in the cove over the year and now yanked one in the dim light, watching for a movement in the sail, but nothing budged. Bloody lines. Found the right one at last, and the soaked mainsail began to rise toward the moon, pouring filthy water from its folds, rose to the masthead. I cleated it and was scrambling aft to sheet it tight when a wave broke over us and sent me sliding, banging along the deck, but I tightened the mainsheet and the sail filled and the ketch heeled—lurched ahead—and I turned the wheel but the bow barely swung.

Three boat-lengths.

We needed more sail. With the tail of the mainsheet I lashed down the wheel, then back to the mast to raise the jib, but there seemed to be ten times as many lines as before, whipping and arcing in the wind. I found the right halyard, and the sail flew up, with the bronze hanks screaming on the wire.

Two boat-lengths.

With bleeding fingers I cleated it, jammed the jib sheet through the block, and, with the cliff right there beside me, winched it tight.

One boat-length.

The sails were full and pulling, and the ketch moved ahead and I was sure now that we'd made it, saw the cliff drift slowly by—then we hit. With that deep, dull thud that breaks a sailor's heart, the ketch came down and shuddered on a rock.

No boat-length.

The keel ground. She shuddered but stood still. A statue with full sails; waiting for that last wave to lower her to her grave. I stumbled forward on deck—it was like walking on firm ground. I groped for the last halyard, clawed it loose, and hoisted the staysail. It was small; and flew fast. Then back to the cockpit. The ketch rose and thudded. I flattened all sails, and she heeled hard but stood still. I kept winching and the sheets vibrated and the blocks creaked from strain but I had nothing else left, so I winched some more. Then the wind gusted and a big wave slammed her and the bow fell, the stern rose—ready to go under—when suddenly her keel scraped and she began to slide.

Sideways.

She slid free. Free to drift leeward to be shattered against the cliff.

The next wave hit her broadside and threw her at the cliff, and the skiff, trapped between, exploded into splinters. I was watching the water vanish beside the hull when, almost imperceptibly, she heeled for the last time, and moved with a feeble desperation, *along* the cliff—*sailing*—away into the waves, toward the wide-open, glittering silver sea.

One boat-length.

I clutched the wheel.

We sailed.

2

The Repair

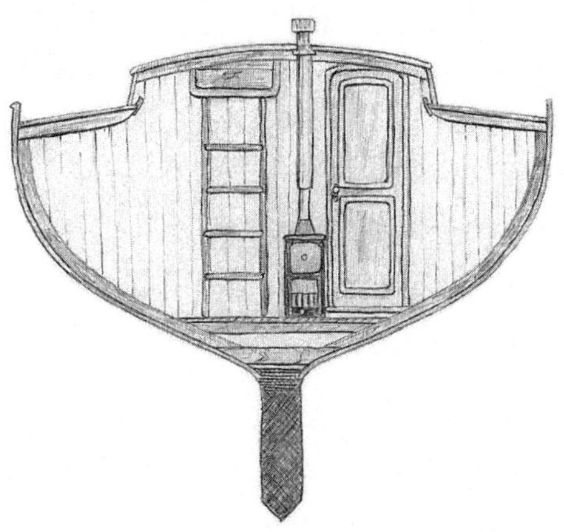

No man will be a sailor who has contrivance enough to get himself into jail; for being in a ship is being in a jail, with the chance of being drowned.

—J. Boswell (1759)

I held the wheel as tenderly as I ever held a woman. The drumming on the cliff faded behind us, and the waves now rolled more gently under us, then broke with a complacent hiss along the shore. I kept the rudder still so as not to disturb the flow of water over it, lest we lose what little speed we had and be left again to the mercy of the waves. When we gained more speed, I nudged the wheel and eased us away from the rocks, then let out on the sheets and the sails swelled, and we surged through the open sea. The storm eased; we were in its eye. With a suddenness that always surprises, the wind fell and the seas sagged, and spreading like a smile across the bottom of the heavens came the dawn. It came with a deceptive pink light and shepherded the storm-worn moon out of the sky.

Some people change little when they die; their unused faces, their expressionless eyes stay intact. Block was such a dead man. He lay plump on the rocky shore, the torn kelp around him like a wreath, the painter of his dinghy fouled around his ankle, and his eyes so much the same that I almost said hello. He had floated dead around the cove all night.

The old Swede had been kept awake by the storm, wandering through his dark house on his dark island, staring out at the besieging sea, then through a rear window at the cove to check his skiffs, and to look around the bay like some admiral at his fleet—the fish boats, the floathouses, the big ketch bobbing there, and he could hardly believe his eyes when he saw someone moving on its deck. When the moon peeked through, he recognized Block's plumpness—there was no mistaking him for a gaunt fisherman of the cove—and although he deemed it strange, he thought Block pretty decent to have come to check the anchors that could drag in the storm. He watched for a while as Block fumbled on the foredeck, stumbling, grabbing to regain his balance in the swells. Then the old Swede went smiling to bed, his faith in humanity a tiny bit restored.

A hollow drumming woke him. He sat bolt upright—it was nothing like the sounds he was used to in a storm. He went out to look. The moonlight shone on the tormented sea, the wind still bowed the trees, and he almost lost his footing on his porch when he saw the ketch ghosting, slowly but well guided, toward the entrance of the cove. Block hunched at the wheel. A dinghy was tied tight alongside and, with each surging wave, slammed with that ungodly thud against the hull. When the waves of the entrance were too much for Block's nerves, he untied the dinghy and clambered in and, almost falling overboard, shoved himself away. He struggled setting the oars, then with clumsy jerks rowed back into the cove and, when the clouds swallowed the moon, vanished in the darkness. The ketch too disappeared. The Swede rubbed his eyes, then, chilled to the bone, went back inside. He took a long slug of rum and, when he looked out again, saw nothing but the dark. He crawled back under his still-warm covers and didn't even bother to get up when he heard the roar of the log boat and our voices in the storm.

He rose, little rested, after dawn and saw the dinghy circling in an eddy in the cove. Block bobbed up behind it like jetsam, not all of him, just one foot poking, toes first, at the sky. There was a kitchen knife on the floorboards, and with the sliced anchor ropes on the ketch, it seemed that penniless Block had gone for the insurance. And the old Swede, who most of his life had trusted boats more than people, lost his faith in humanity for good.

There were no next of kin to squabble with, but I still spent the next month climbing stairs from one airless office to the next. The people in them, accustomed to more mundane events, perked up when I mentioned salvaging a ketch, perked up with a dreamy look in their eyes. As I left, some of them offered their best wishes, others just stared longingly through the walls. The police had me tell them the story three times. One with dedicated eyes came up to me and said softly, "Son, I'm still convinced you killed that bugger for his boat."

"Why?" I asked, swallowing hard.

"Because I sure as hell would have. " The room broke into laughter.

They had me sign a pile of affidavits, the Harbormaster's Office had me do the same, the Office of Registry of Shipping puzzled over the reports and told me to come back in a week, and Navigational Waters made me wait all morning for a hearing where three people sat and listened to my story while another snoozed. I signed more forms. Next week the ketch would be mine.

I went to talk to Jordan. I rowed out to the tug, where he was polishing brass in the pilothouse, whistling. I told him that of course the ketch was half his. He told me, smiling, to go straight to hell.

"I hate sailboats," he said. "Who in his right mind would strain like a beast when there are engines you can start with a finger?" I said fine, if he didn't want half the boat I'd pay him for his part. His smile faded. A crease of sadness furled around his eyes. "You barely have a dollar to your name," he quietly said. "And for a whole damned year I had to watch you pine. Night and day, stare at that bloody thing like some schoolgirl in love. Not an hour went by that you didn't talk about it, and when you didn't talk about it I could hear you think about it. The best gift to me will be never to hear words like 'halyard' and 'turnbuckles' again." And he splashed some goop on the copper pipes and rubbed with fury, mumbling, "How can a grown man utter 'baggywrinkle' with a straight face anyway?"

I was too moved to look up, so I mumbled something and went away.

At a toy shop on Granville Street, I gazed at the window and felt about in my near-empty pockets, then went to Henderson's to collect the pay he owed me. He didn't say much, just counted out twenty-two dollars for three weeks, then took back two for the pike pole I had lost. In parting, he wished me luck and—I got to hand it to him—he didn't say a word about my being on his tug that night. I spent every penny in that toy shop. Three dolls and a carriage to push them in, and a dollhouse and some tiny furniture. I swear they cost more than the real thing. I hauled it all down to Jordan's cottage and gave it to his wife. "A Merry early Christmas," I said, and left before she could reply.

Next day was the big day: the Office of Registry of Shipping. I was there an hour before a man came to open up. He looked over the papers, then furled his brow.

"There is a hitch," he said. "We can't register a ship without a name," and looked at me as if ready to say goodbye. I was dumbstruck. With all the goings-on, I never thought of one.

"She didn't have a name before," I protested.

"She wasn't a registered ship before," he said.

I stared out the window, where gulls whirled and ships filled the harbor.

"*Terrence Jordan*," I said.

He dipped his pen in the inkwell and wrote with pretty letters.

The next few months were the happiest of my life. I took the poor ketch, her rudder post bent, three planks split, the lead of her keel distorted and gouged, back to Hoffar's big shed where she was built, for repair. Out of the goodness of his heart Hoffar signed me up as a shipwright's helper, rough-cutting, planing, cleaning up the shipyard ten hours a day, and let me stay on to work and sleep on my boat at night. "My boat"—what a beautiful sound.

I stripped her bare. I pulled the masts, took off the rigging, unbolted her hardware so I could clean and paint below it, sanded the hull, the cabin, the deck, stripped the peeling varnish off the masts and trim down to the wood, then put on nine new coats, recaulked her planks, and painted every inch with two coats of the best. And in the small hours of the morning, when I had finished some small task, so tired that I could barely lift a hand, I would sit and stare at the cabinside I'd painted or the curved and beveled cabin sole piece I'd made, sit and glow with as much pride as if I had just completed the Eighth Wonder of the World. And when I launched her in March with her resewn sails, new running-rigging, her winches gleaming, she looked as good as new. I was in seventh heaven—but up to my eyes in debt. And down below, except for the bulkheads and the cabin sole and a roughed-in berth aft, she was still as empty as a barrel. I kept working at Hoffar's during the week, and on weekends began hauling goods and people with the ketch. In a month I had contracts running all over the coast. I added the word "Captain" to my name.

3

The Hire
1921

Dr. Franz Boas of the American Museum of Natural History has just returned from an expedition along the extreme western coast of British Columbia, where dwell the Kwakiutl, a race of anthropophagi, man-eating savages, who, isolated from the rest of the world, still practice the bloodthirsty customs. They are fond of festivals and devote a large portion of their time to ceremonies, dances, feasts and orgies of the wildest sort, during which terrible tortures are imposed on members of the tribe.

—*New York Herald* (October 31, 1897)

The masks of the Kwakiutl blend the contemplative serenity of the statues of Chartres and the Egyptian tombs with the gnashing artifices of Hallowe'en. These two traditions of equal grandeur and parallel authenticity reign here in their primitive and undisturbed unity. This dithyrambic gift of synthesis, the faculty to perceive as similar what all other men have considered as different, constitutes the exceptional feature of the art of British Columbia.

—CLAUDE LEVI-STRAUSS, *Gazette des Beaux-Arts*

Ghost Sea

It was a cold, dank, foghorn-riddled morning, with just a patch of water visible around the ketch. I was alone on board, tied to a tilting wharf at the bottom of an alley in that helter-skelter, gap-toothed boomtown of slapped-together sawmills, canneries, and shipyards, just gouged out of the wilderness but already falling down. The fog was as wet as rain; it streamed down the masts, dripped out of the rigging, puddled in the furled sails. The tide was out and great clumps of mussels crackled on the pilings.

There I was, shackled by debt—I felt richer when I was penniless salvaging logs—waiting for the fog to lift so I could run up coast to Squamish with some medical goods; it wasn't life or death but I was anxious to go because the ten-dollar fee would pay off a bit of debt. Just a few more dozen trips like this and about the same for Meschie's gold mine way up coast, and if in all that time—a year, maybe two—I managed not to run aground and rip the bottom out of her, saved every penny, barely ate or drank, my debts would be paid off, and then—freedom. I'd sail out of this dungeon-of-a-climate and not stop until the Marquesas or Cook Islands—fool's dreams never die—where the water is so clear you can watch your anchor touch bottom, and the air is warm and the sky blue enough to hurt your eyes, and you can get lost in some archipelago for the rest of your life. Dreams. When debts are paid—all kinds. No use leaving a port for good until they're paid, because you'll just carry them around inside you all your life.

Damned fog. Like a prison.

But mostly I was anxious to get away from her. There was nothing worse than being so near her and not seeing her, not having her look at me with those daring, frightened eyes. I stared into the fog and thought I saw the outlines of their yacht.

I leaned on the wheel, and stared at my empty hands. Bloody fog; closes you in and turns you on yourself. "Self-cannibalization," Nello, my half-Kwakiutl first mate, called it, "except you can't see the bites." But you sure as hell could feel them. I paced the deck some more. A patch of light brightened the fog and for a minute I was certain it was her, the sail of her small dinghy coming toward me, but then the light faded and the fog closed.

Cautious footsteps sounded in the distance. Then stopped. A rope strained as the wharf shifted on the tide. Then a voice called out and drifted, "*Terrence Jordan*. Ahoy."

"Over here!" I yelled as cheerfully as I could—it might be a client. An older man with a bowler hat and careful mustache popped out of the mist. He held a cane in one hand and a damp business card in the other and looked at me through his misted glasses.

"Captain Dugger?" he asked politely.

"Yes," I said.

"Hopkins," he said, and looked quickly over the ketch, clutching one of the cards I had old Mr. Chow, who ran the Chinese paper, print for me: *Captain S. V. Dugger. The ketch* Terrence Jordan. *Denman Street Docks. Coastal transport. Anything. Anywhere.* I know that last bit was pretty short on class, but when you owe as much as I did.... I went and stuck those cards in chandlers, hotel lobbies, beer parlors, social clubs, the seaman's home on Pender, the steamship terminal on Main, the railway station, boardinghouses, whorehouses, and even the Salvation Army. You never know.

I invited Hopkins to join me below for a cup of tea—I don't offer rum early, in case they think me a drunk and take their business elsewhere—but he stood and eyed the ketch knowingly: her hull, her sheer, the masts, even tried to see under the water, checking, I guess, for growth.

"Newly copper-sheeted," I said. "Fastest on the coast."

At that he seemed to ease and I slipped back the companionway hatch and we went below. The embers still glowed in the galley stove, so I heaved in some scraps of wood while Hopkins looked around the cabin.

"Wonderful," he kept saying. "A wonderful little ship. Remarkably Oriental, all this joinery." I let his comment go; it was a long story. He opened his coat, sat himself down on the starboard settee, and made himself at home, running his hand over a varnished sea rail. "Captain Dugger," he said, "we would like to engage you and your ketch for a period of time." And just as I felt the South Sea's breezes blowing on my face, he pulled out a business card, and I read in disbelief, *L. W. Hopkins, Royal Canadian Mounted Police. Retired.* I stared dumbstruck. The law and I never mixed; not that I felt myself beyond the law, but rather that the law seemed always beyond me. Suddenly the South Sea's breezes seemed farther than ever.

"I don't have room for horses."

Hopkins didn't laugh. When he saw I wasn't going to say any more, he said almost bashfully, "Captain Dugger, your name was something different off San Francisco that foggy afternoon."

I had a good mind to bolt then and there, but my legs wouldn't move. I froze half risen, with my back arched like a cat. Thank God the kettle rocked. "The tea." I struggled to the stove. It took all my wits to figure out what to pour into what. Took my time. "A bit of rum?" I offered, while pouring a long slug into mine. Through the portlight I saw the fog close in as if it meant to stay there for the rest of my life.

We sat quietly sipping tea-laced rum, the fog sending tendrils down the hatchway. For the first time I looked closely at Hopkins; his eyes were furtive—he was the type that knows a lot more than he lets on. He ran his eyes over the cabin, making polite remarks—how much he liked the doors, the bookcase, the inlaid table—and all the while, on every pass, his eyes lingered for a second on the rough-carved cedar mask hanging on the bulkhead.

"Fascinating piece," he said, nodding at the mask.

"Kwakiutl," I offered.

"Do you mind?" And he got up for a closer look.

It was plain, simply carved, the white paint thin and splotchy from age, the features smooth, the brow high, the nose thin and upturned, cut short—a skull. The square white teeth were bared, gritted tight. There were no lips. Scruffy tufts of horsehair were stitched above the brow. The eyelids drooped half closed, one eye stared out in horror, the other bled a long, crimson tear.

"A skull rattle," I said. "Keeps you safe from cannibals."

Hopkins smiled. "Could come in handy in this town."

There was a thud against the hull. It was her, I knew the sound of her dinghy bumping.

"I better check," I said, and ran up. The fog was empty. A piece of driftwood rolled on the tide and banged the hull. I took a deep breath and went below.

Hopkins was still looking at the mask. "Brilliant, don't you think?" he said in honest appreciation.

"Except it doesn't work," I said. And when he looked at me quizzically I added, "Not when you most need it."

He looked away; he knew when it was best to let things go.

"From up the coast?" he queried.

"Way up," I said. "A couple hundred miles."

"You hear a lot of stories about up there: Desolation, wild islands, wild people. Unimaginable rites."

"Stories," I said.

"You know the place?"

"Not well."

"But your first mate, Mr. Nello, was born there."

There wasn't much old Hopkins didn't know. I pulled in my limbs as if not to give anything more away.

"End of the earth," he went on. "Barely charted. Rocks and reefs, towering mountains with inlets like corkscrews, hundreds of miles of wild emptiness."

"And fog," I said. "Even more than here."

"Kwakiutl," he sighed.

The rum didn't do its work; in fact, I was getting jittery. But not Hopkins. He sat calmly and stared at me. He asked for a bit more rum, took a gulp, leaned forward, and said in a quiet, confiding tone, "Captain Dugger, you know what a potlatch is."

"Only so-so," I said.

"All summer long the Indians fish: salmon from the sea and streams, herring from the shallows. In the tidal flats they pick oysters, clams, sea urchins, mussels. They dry or smoke everything to preserve it for winter; even dry seaweed, berries, mint, everything in the summer, everything before the rains. *Bakoos* time, they call it. Then winter comes, and the rains come, and they pull back into the villages into their great cedar houses and it begins—Tsetseka, it means Magician. It all starts innocently enough, days of feasting, some mourning songs for those who died since spring, singing, joking, all very nice, very noble. But then day-by-day things turn ugly. They say that spirits come out of the sea, the woods, wild spirits; 'Dog-Eaters.' And worse."

His voice dropped. "There are rituals. Frenzied women are stuffed in cedar boxes and thrown on a bonfire. Alive. Others are hung from ropes by their skin. Everyone watches. Young men are dragged off into the woods for weeks and are left there alone; they come back wild animals—they attack their own people and . . . . They're called Hamatsa. Cannibals. We've tried to put an end to all this." I poured him some more rum.

"How long would it take to get up there?" he asked.

"With good winds, timing the currents in the passes, and not pushing your luck, maybe ten days."

"And back?"

"Depends."

"On the winds?"

"On whether they eat you or not."

Hopkins straightened up, annoyed. "This isn't easy for anybody, you know," he blurted. "I have great respect for these people, their traditions, their knowledge of their world. They're generous, caring, they look after the sick, the old, each other, even strangers. They're a noble people. But these potlatches, this savagery has to end."

He took a deep breath, calmed, and began again.

"There was a law passed against these rituals over forty years ago. But to enforce it out there, my God! It's the end of the earth! So they went on. Until last winter. An informant warned us in advance of the place, the time. A boat took in the Indian agent and police, ran aground twice, but went on and arrested the worst of them. Poor buggers. The fog thinned for an hour at midday so the boat got in . . . . Poor sods."

"I read about it," I said. "You took everything they owned."

"Just the things used in the potlatch," Hopkins objected. "Things used for the horrors; just the masks, things like that."

"Just the masks? They have no written language. Those masks are their history: deeds to property, records of marriages, stories of their creation, even their names. Christ! First you take their lands, now this. What the hell did you leave them?"

Hopkins wasn't prepared for that. He stared at me almost meanly but went on. "The Indian agent took the masks; that was within the law. Then he sold them to a private collector; *that* was not."

"What does this have to do with me?"

"The potlatchers were tried and sent to jail," Hopkins went on with a forced calm. "Thirty-two of them. Last week they feigned a riot and in the commotion two of them vanished."

"Maybe they got eaten."

"Captain Dugger!" he snapped. "They escaped, then killed a man! Left his head in a bowl."

I don't remember what it was I had tried drunkenly to say, but whatever it was, it made Hopkins's fist hit the table so hard the mugs jumped, and he roared, *"Dammit, Dugger! I can ship you back to Frisco and have you hanged!"*

My nerves had had it; my ears were ringing and I made out only phrases drifting in the cabin. "An important artifacts collector . . . family of insurers . . . broke into his yacht . . . took back masks . . . killed a crew . . . ." Hopkins talked on but it was all choked by the fog until a cold draft of it shot down the hatchway and my head cleared and his voice came back. "They stole a canoe and headed up coast. We'd like you to find them."

I must have looked pretty strange, because he asked, "Did you hear me?"

"Can't you go find them yourselves?"

"*Our* hands are tied, Dugger. They took a hostage. The collector's wife. He made us promise not to jeopardize her life." Then he leaned close to me and said slowly, with as much accusation as I ever care to hear, "Katherine Hay; I believe you know her."

I think my breathing stopped. It must have, because I passed out. When I looked up, Hopkins was gone; only his card and a stuffed envelope rested on the table. I thought I heard his footsteps die off in the fog. I had a slug of rum. A long one. It did the job. I lay down on the berth, and in the codling warmth drifted off into painkilling sleep. And dreamt of Katherine Hay.

4

Obsession

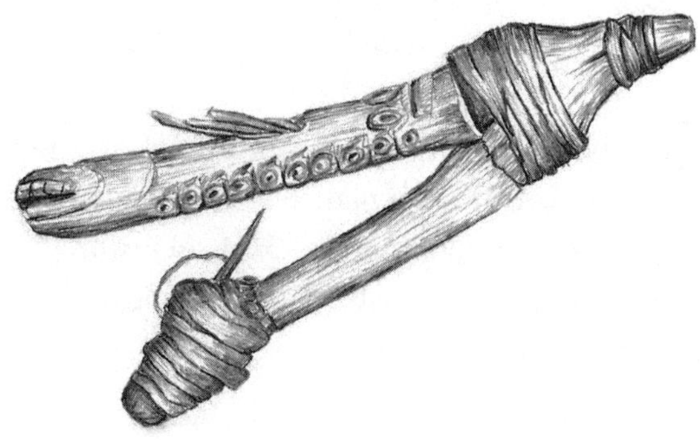

The Indians live in an atmosphere of the supernatural; not only are the forests tenanted by mythological animals, but the birds, the animals and the fish, all are capable of assuming supernatural form.

—T. F. McIlwraith, Anthropologist (1922)

Whenever I drink I drink the pain of your love, mistress.
Whenever I get sleepy I dream of my love, my mistress.
Whenever I lie on my back in the house, I lie on the pain on your love, mistress.
For whenever I walk about I step on the pain of your love, mistress.

—Kwakiutl love song, transcribed by Franz Boas

I'm not some dreamer who believes a woman to be his sole salvation. Women have come and gone in my life, some leaving an emptiness, others just the door open behind them, and I lived through them all and mostly kept my footing. But for some inexplicable reason—and I had been around, I was past thirty then—the first time I saw Katherine Hay on a street, in a crowd with the July sun on her auburn hair, eyes aglow, her steps so full of life, I was shaken. I ran after her and almost under a tram; what I would say when I caught her never crossed my mind.

She stopped on a corner, waiting out the traffic, and I landed beside her, out of breath. She glanced up surprised and I stared into her eyes, before forcing my gaze away, whistling weakly at a cab down the street. A shrill whistle ripped the air behind me. I turned. She stood there, smiling, fingers at her lips—I was a goner.

I sound like a schoolboy smitten at first sight, but when in this sorry world a face still passionate, still bursting with life appeared, believe me, it kindled something close to hunger, like a desperation. If a shooting star hurtled toward you from the heavens, would you turn away? Would you not throw open your arms—reason, fear, and tomorrow be damned? I didn't see her for a while after that. Looked for her, asked for her. For who? A frail woman, dressed too well for my empty pockets, with auburn hair and a deafening whistle. I found her practically at the ends of the earth.

I was hauling a coil of anchor rope, pouring sweat in the August sun, resting at every chance along the waterfront. At the Great Northern docks they were loading lumber bound for Mexico onto steamers. In an outside berth lay the last of the four-masted schooners pointing her proud bowsprit at the land; but she was old. Her crew toiled with care among her shrouds, decking the enormous weights gingerly. Her ends sagged, her sheer had lost its sweep; across her once-white planking, each fastener eked tears of rust, and with her patched hull and wavy bulwarks, she looked too infirm ever to leave port again.

At Hastings Mills the great saws screamed. Perched on a thousand pilings, shrouded by smoke and steam, were sheds, rickety cranes, and tar-seamed water towers; skids, horse carts, and gas trucks; dry-docked scows and dry-rotted boathouses, and a heap of steam-donkeys condemned to rust in the mud. And in that infernal din, weary, noise-silenced men loaded, sorted, tugged, and hauled, awaiting the salvation of the beer parlor. I was at the stinking cannery, where turbaned Sikhs on scows stood knee-deep in dead fish, when I saw her.

A blindingly varnished launch swung into view below me. She was sitting on the coamings in a plain white dress, hair glowing—she was the only one outside that day without a hat—sitting next to somber-suited men studying a map. She gazed detached at the smooth wake of the launch, then looked beyond toward the open sea.

I asked about her around town: the docks, beer parlors; asked Mr. Chow in Chinatown, who was kept current on everything, asked at the ship terminal where all the steamers disembarked, and the Hotel Vancouver where I knew the concierge because I took him and his mistress on a cruise once overnight. Nothing. Little by little I pushed her from my mind.

I busied myself with a load of gears and spare parts for steam-donkeys up the coast, when early one evening a rowing skiff, perfect as a violin, pulled up alongside the ketch and hailed. It was a deckhand all in white, asking politely if I would consider a small job for the captain of a motor yacht. The man pointed to a gleaming eighty-footer anchored near the woods up the bay. The owner had bought a sailing dinghy for his wife, and there was no one aboard who knew how to rig it. Would I be interested? Those days I would have eaten a boulder for a dime.

The yacht—up close—was even more perfect than its skiff. The captain, a kind-faced man with life-worn eyes, greeted me as we climbed the ladder. He complimented me on the ketch, and how well she maneuvered in light airs in tight quarters; he had seen me these past weeks.

The dinghy was on the aft deck, its rigging coiled, blocks, cleats, and turnbuckles scattered about. I laid everything out close to the final placement, stepped the mast to find the angles for the shrouds—they hadn't even mounted chain plates—and was just checking the leads for angles, when I saw her.

I had backed down the side deck to sight the rake for the mast, and looked through the windows into the main salon, where the long, gleaming table, with its silver and crystal, reflected the red glow from the sky. She sat at one end of the table, listening to a man at the other end with his back to me. I shuddered. Felt hot or cold, I can't remember which. The decks were unlit, the sun just gone, so she could not have seen me on the dark side in the dusk. The cabin boy brushed by us, lighting gimbaled lanterns on the cabinside as he went.

With the deck now lit, my movement caught her eye. She looked up. She continued to speak to her companion but her gaze rested on me, and I swear I saw her blush. Her eyes stayed riveted on me, with the urgent look of a fellow conspirator.

"Cotton," I said hoarsely to the captain. "Cotton line for sheets. This hemp will be too rough on her hands." I couldn't think of another excuse to stay. They said they would return for me tomorrow.

In the morning, I felt as if I'd been drinking all night. I scrubbed, shaved, dressed, slicked, as if going to a ball. Didn't realize just how nervous I was until I took a last glance in the mirror.

I rowed humming "Sloop John B." to calm myself. The

dinghy gear I had requested awaited me. I went to work, not daring to look up even when I heard footsteps. It was always just the crew. Then, when I had almost finished, her shoes stepped into my sight. I looked up. She stood smiling, her light dress fluttering against her in the breeze. She thanked me for my help, and said how eager she was to get out in the boat. I managed to say, "Just don't forget to turn back at the narrows. It's a tough little boat, but China, I don't know." She laughed. Such an open heartfelt laughter, with her head thrown slightly back, that the whole crew laughed with her. Infectious. And her eyes. Great dark pools. Unguarded, dancing, sparkling with life. I had to look away. Another woman came and they boarded the shining skiff and the kid rowed them ashore. "Thank you again," she called. And waved. I kept rigging. They were walking along the shore when the air was rent with her whistle. Then her laughter.

Rowing back to the ketch, I felt nothing in particular, nothing that I noted, not until I pulled alongside, cleated the painter, and clambered back on board.

Everything had changed. The brightness of the light, the richness of colors, the grain in the wood deck, the reflection in the polished brass—the world. The evening was awash with a transparent pink glow, and everything—the texture of ropes, shapes of blocks, the curve of the sheer—all seemed to have assumed a mystical intensity.

The ketch—my first love, until now—seemed suddenly to stand apart from me. I went below. The flecks of sunlight bouncing off the water, rippling in slow waves between the deck beams overhead, seemed a magical event. And the silent shadows deep in the forepeak, seemed to reach onward, endlessly forever. I needed air. I rowed ashore. A creek flowed from the forest into green pools on the rocks. The water splashed, gurgled, foamed a brilliant white, exuberant, full of life. And the mossy rocks around it—even *they* seemed to breathe. It was as if a veil had been lifted—behind which I had cowered all my life.

In Chinatown that evening, instead of hurrying past people as was my habit, I felt myself slow and let them sweep me onward. Like sailing through a pass, where the current grabs you and the rudder no longer steers because it no longer bites; you're just being swept away. But it wasn't frightening; it was almost reassuring that some great wild force now had me, and hurtled me along. And in the open-fronted shops of Chinatown even the badly plucked duck carcasses, hanging by their necks, looked beautiful.

I didn't dream about her that night. I lay half awake and thought about her. Her dark eyes filled the night, enormous and enigmatic.

The simple repetitious chores of daily life—lighting the fire, making a ten-word entry in the log book, tying a knot—became unsolvable puzzles. I stared dumbly at a rope or the empty page. When I was alone I talked to her. Aloud. Even around others I had to catch myself sometimes.

The next two afternoons I saw her in her dinghy, fumbling with the sails, just out of the shadow of the yacht. I hardly slept those nights. The third night I slept but woke up at dawn. The light soft; all calm. I felt much better. It was over. Back to normal. I thought of hauling the anchor chain onto the dock, checking it and repainting the fathom marks, a red stripe at ten fathoms, white at fifteen, two red at twenty, two white, and so on.

Four days later, when I sailed back from the islands, I almost killed her.

There was a rickety floathouse on logs anchored near the woods at the entrance of our bay. To sail up to my dock, I had to sail close to it, almost touching, then make a sharp turn into the wind and drift up to my float. Preoccupied with looking for her near the yacht, I didn't see her little boat coming out from behind the floathouse. I almost ran her down. My boom slammed her shrouds and knocked her over. She clutched the gunwales, but had the good sense to leap to the high side to right her boat. There was fear in her eyes, even more beguiling than before. I veered hard short of the dock and had to go back out and try again. The yacht's skiff rushed out and towed her home.

The next morning the cabin boy rowed over as soon as he saw me on deck. The lady sent profound apologies. He handed me an envelope with much too generous a payment for the half day's work of rigging. Then, just as he pulled away, he looked up and said, "The lady would like to know if you could teach her how to sail."

We began the next day at ten. I must say I owe God an immeasurable favor. Can you imagine being with her in a small boat, *a sailboat* she barely knew? Anywhere else I would have been at her mercy—on the street corner, I couldn't think of a word to say—but here, it was my world. I knew every damned thing: a hundred names, a thousand tricks, how to get her into danger and how to get her out. In a sailing dinghy at sea, she was mine.

I rowed over with enormous pulls, then long glides—childish, I know—and reached the yacht in a dozen pulls, each so forceful that I almost ripped the oarlocks out of the wood. She arrived in a thin dress, no sleeves; just her bare arms glowing like some goddess statue in the sun. We pushed off.

There was no wind near the yacht, so I skulled with the rudder to get us away. "No broken masts today," she said with a laugh.

"You never know until the day is over."

When we were out of hearing distance of the yacht, I stopped. She was sitting on a narrow fore-and-aft seat to starboard, I in the stern-to-port at the helm. Her eyes were attentive.

"Everything on a sailboat has a particular name," I said. "Do you know them?"

"Try me."

"What's this?"

"That's the rope that you pull to tighten the little sail up in the pointy end."

"Jib sheet."

She laughed out loud. "You're kidding."

"No. Jib sheet."

"What's wrong with 'the rope that you pull to tighten the little sail up in the pointy end'?"

"When we're in a typhoon, and the mast is about to break and crush us, which do you think more likely to save our lives, me yelling: 'Slack jib sheet!' or 'Would you mind unraveling the loops from the little horns and letting out a foot or so of the rope you pull to tighten the little sail in the pointy end?"

She laughed heartily. "Touché."

"We'll do the names another time," I said. "Now. At sea only one thing counts: the wind. You always need to know where it's coming from. Do you understand?"

"Yes," she said, but looked as if the word "wind" had never crossed her mind.

"Where is it now? Can you tell?"

"There is no wind," she said, after surveying the bay.

"There is almost always some. Land people don't sense it, but there's some."

She looked at me with hurt and admiration. I turned away. "Look at the water there. It's just a little darker. Not perfectly reflecting the light. A breath of air. Once you know what you're looking for, you'll find it."

I thought she turned away from me, but she looked around and pointed with much enthusiasm. "And there."

It was there, all right, a breath pushing a shadow over the sea.

"Very good," I said. She turned back to me, basking in her

triumph. I looked her in the eye. "Lift up your hair," I said.

She blushed. Her long hair draped over her shoulders, and she touched it, slightly unsure. The gust of wind reached us then and tossed her hair like a veil across her face. "There's a spot on your body," I said softly. But she pushed the hair off her face and turned her head away. "The back of your neck. That's the one spot that always feels the wind."

She gathered her hair and raised it slightly, baring her shoulders. "More," I said. "Lift it more." It came out like an order, and she obeyed. The tide was ebbing, pushing us imperceptibly out to sea.

"Most people would give up now, " I said. "They'd get out the oars and row."

"We have no oars," she said.

"So we find the wind."

She concentrated.

"Close your eyes." An order. "Now, always thinking of the back of your neck, turn your head." She did. "When you think you have it, turn it ever so little back and forth until you're sure."

"I have it," she said.

I crouched past her to the mast, my leg brushing hers, pushing her dress above a knee. I hoisted the sail.

The wind strengthened. Tossed the boom, darkened the sea. We surged ahead. I slipped to the side. "You steer," I said.

"Where?"

"Wherever you want to go."

She held the tiller firmly and, with the wind behind us, headed out to sea. Then she said in deadly earnest, "Except China."

It took me a while. "Nothing wrong with China."

The wind and current pushed us out, but we turned into it and fought our way back, tacking and beating, tacking, beating, against the wind and sea.

For the next four days we sailed; starting later each day to catch the strengthening sea breeze. She learned fast. We concentrated, as if we knew we hadn't much time. It helped to keep my mind from wandering, my eyes from looking at her. I inundated her with sailing terms; clew, tack, luff, leach, spreader, snatch block, gooseneck, gudgeon, pintle, and when I wanted to make her laugh: baggywrinkle. She learned every one. When I couldn't avoid it, my bare arm pressed against her naked shoulder. I felt her stiffen but she didn't move away.

By the third day, she was able to sense the movement of the waves. When we tacked or gybed, we moved together well, in harmony, without speaking. It was like sharing a well-kept secret; an intimacy. By then I knew. Wasn't sure how, but I felt it from her lingering smiles, and by a brief moment, a defenseless look in her eyes. I had been explaining the need for a captain. "Sometimes you have to obey on faith," I said without chiding. "There will be rogue waves, gusts, when you'll have to trust me blindly."

"I know that," she said softly, without her brashness, her humor—the armor that had kept her safe all her life.

The last day it blew hard. As soon as we passed the point and headed toward the sea we took constant spray over the bow. Little by little we were soaked. She wore her hair tied up to free her neck but loose tufts were now plastered across her face. She steered flawlessly. A rogue wave burst and surged toward us and, without time to explain, I grabbed the tiller, her hand with it, and yanked it hard toward me to head us into it. I had pulled her off balance and she slid toward me, grabbed my arm, and fell against me. In all that wind I felt her warm breath on my face. We stared, her eyes deeper than ever, a shadow of doubt around them. But her voice was tender, barely a sigh. "And then what?" she said.

I gybed the main, slacked the jib, and headed back into the bay. We didn't speak. Where would we begin?

I had to sail to the Gulf Islands on the dawn tide.

When I came back from the islands, I stayed aboard all day waiting for word from the yacht, or for her to sail up alone. But she was nowhere. By evening I hated her, hated her for not coming, hated her for not giving a sign, hated the hand she had put on mine while I held the tiller, hated her smile, her laughter that she must now be giving to someone else. She might be lying with him now, his hand on her, on her neck, in her hair, all the places where I had dreamt my hands to be. I rowed over.

It was past midnight, and the yacht was dark except for the anchor light dangling in the bow, the ports open in the warm night. I rowed along the portside, then back on the starboard, hoping to hear her. The next day I couldn't stand it beyond ten. I rowed back to ask if she would like some more lessons, but was told by the cabin boy that Mr. and Mrs. Hay had gone inland for a few days.

That night I slept in peace.

The evening of the day she returned, there was a large gathering on the yacht. By sunset, the aft deck was crowded with well-dressed people. It had been so hot I had anchored out to catch a bit of breeze. I was close enough to them that I could see her clearly through the binoculars, her bare shoulders among the suits and gowns, smiling here, nodding there, laughing, reaching out and touching an arm fleetingly, but occasionally her smile faded and she glanced toward the ketch. When I couldn't stand it anymore, I rowed over to Hoffar's to play cards with some fishermen on a crate on the docks. And lost. The yacht was dark and silent when I returned after midnight.

I slept restlessly in the cockpit until I was awoken by a thud. Stars filled the night; the mainmast loomed like a dark road among them. A sliver moon hovered near the horizon, with a fainter glow behind it where its darkness ended, and I watched, bewitched by that curve of light, when a pale, ghostlike shape swam suddenly before it. A sail. A small sail.

She moved awkwardly, trying to hold on to the caprail of the ketch with one hand, fending off the slowly weaving boom with the other. I could barely see her face until she looked up and the anchor lantern reached her with its glow. She looked thrilled having sailed in the dark, but it was mixed with a fragile, captivating fear.

I sat on the deck with my hand on the caprail barely touching hers. She stood there with her face close to mine. "I just came over to . . . ." She fell silent and said softly, "I just came."

As gently as I could, I held her head in my hand; felt her cheekbone, her hair, the bone around her eyes, the hollow of her temple, her heart beating there. With the heel of my palm I touched the corner of her lips, and she closed her eyes and tilted her head, let it weigh in my hand.

We stayed unmoving for a long time. When she raised her eyes, they sparkled with tears.

After a while she said, "I'd better go. Someone might notice that the sail has stopped moving."

I swung my legs out over the gunwale.

"What are you doing?" she asked.

"I'm coming with you. Move over."

"I don't want you to."

"As long as the sail is moving, no one will see me in the dark."

She remained silent.

"I'll sit on the floorboards if you're afraid."

"It isn't just that," she said.

"What, then?"

Instead of answering, she looked away.

A sudden anger filled me. "Then why did you come?"

She turned back to me, her face confused. "I don't have to

justify everything," she said. "It's my boat."

"But I'm its captain. Now shut up and move over. And why don't you learn to button your blouse." She had miss-buttoned at the bottom and skipped another at the top.

She gave a nervous laugh, and moved toward the stern. "I almost came in my pajamas," she said.

I pushed us away from the ketch.

"Sit down before you tip us," I said.

"Yes, Captain."

The breeze filled the sail and the dinghy heeled so I had to crouch quickly onto the floorboards at her feet.

"Spread your legs."

"What does—"

"I have to sit somewhere; just shut up and spread your legs."

She spread her knees but only enough to give me room to sit and lean back barely past them. I put my hand over hers on the tiller to head us up into the puff of wind.

"I like it when you tell me to shut up," she said softly.

"Good. Then do it. And watch where you're steering."

We were beating away from the ketch and the yacht—tacked twice unnecessarily to give whoever might be watching a good show—and headed toward the far tip of the bay, where the great firs blocked the moonlight, darkening the sea. In their lee, the wind softened and we ghosted in the dark. The sail shook; the wind was on the bow—we were in irons.

She slowly eased the muscles of her thighs and let me lean back. I felt her breath on the side of my face; then her lips touched my cheek—hesitant, like a child stealing a kiss. Then she drew back. I took her hand from the tiller and kissed the delicate skin of her wrist. I pushed up her skirt and kissed the long hollow on the inside of her knee. She ran her hand across my neck, wrapped her fingers around my throat, and pressed. "I could kill you."

I bit her thigh. She cried out softly. Her mouth ran across my neck, kissing and biting hard into the muscle of my shoulder, higher in the back, into the nape, where the Kwakiutl say the soul resides.

I turned. She leaned away but kept her arms around me. I could only see her teeth, the whites of her eyes, and her white blouse. I unbuttoned it. She lowered her forehead onto mine.

I kissed the sweat from the bone between her breasts, kissed her breasts, her stomach, then pulled her skirt up to her hips. She was naked under it.

"You..." I said.

"Me," she whispered.

I pushed her back against the transom, raised her knee, and kissed and bit the topmost part of her thigh.

"Damn you," she murmured.

"Damn *you*."

"Oh, shut up."

The moon had already set when I sailed us back toward the ketch. She was down on the floorboards, with her head in my lap, her legs curled up like a cat, her skirt hiked high, and her white breast and naked shoulders pale in the darkness. She slept with long, even breaths. I pulled down her skirt and covered her with her blouse to keep her warm.

I could have stayed in that dinghy all my life.

I sat on the caprail of the ketch and held the dinghy's shroud. She stood in the dinghy, did up her buttons, then tried to press the creases in her skirt with her hands. "Look at me," she said. "I look like I've been run over by a train." Then she slowly and patiently combed her hair with her fingers. "May I have a glass of water?" she said.

I reached down to help her aboard but she shook her head; her eyes seemed to be looking far away.

"I better not," she said.

She drank, holding on to the shroud for balance, then handed me back the glass. She took my hand from the shroud, kissed it, and then put it against her face just as it had been when the night began. Then she lowered it and, as I turned to put the glass on the deck, she let it go. By the time I turned back, she had pushed the dinghy off. She sat and filled the sail, eased the sheets to get up some speed, then hauled in and accelerated as she sailed around my stern.

"What time for the lesson tomorrow?" I said in a loud whisper.

A block squeaked as she let out her sheet and began a dead run toward the yacht before her reply came out of the darkness. "He doesn't want me to see you again."

The eastern sky had a thin blush of dawn. The yacht, dark except for the anchor light, stood black and immobile against it. On its aft deck, a small flame flashed then ebbed and flashed again, as a match does when someone is trying to light a pipe.

KATE
The Wilderness

I feel myself less than a beast, without dreams or aspirations. I don't need sleep and I don't care if I never eat again, all I want is to be warm once more in life. I sit in the canoe and shudder. I feel colder inside than out. I can't help but wonder if it is really only the cold. I should be afraid of what they might do to me, especially the young one with the icy eyes, but I'm too cold to care. I believe in fate, or God, or whatever it is that does these things to you. I longed for you but I got him instead. I wonder if it's too late to make amends; if I promise to be good forever, would the world let me go home and just stay by the fire? The sun is coming up; at least it will warm my face. What wilderness and silence all around me. It is as quiet as a graveyard.

5

Chinatown

Slowly, slowly, catchee monkey.

—Chinese Proverb

By the time I woke up, the stove had gone cold and the fog hung dark over the skylight. I counted the bills from the envelope Hopkins had left—I hadn't seen that much money in a long time. There was also a note about a passenger: Katherine Hay's husband was coming along.

I went to look for Nello.

In the gloomy alley, the smitty's fire glowed, and lantern light came from the cobbler's shack. The door to the shop of the frail Welsh beauty was ajar, and she sat by the fire knitting sweaters as thick as armor. And the Gypsy woman, who patched and darned, came out and hung a lantern on her sign, and beckoned to read my palm, always the same: I would live and be in love forever.

In the street, the gaslights burnt yellow through the fog, and the drizzle dripped from wires overhead. Horse carts and rickshaws popped up like apparitions, then just as quickly disappeared again. My head still swam from the rum; I sucked in cold air but it did no good.

I kept along the docks. Smokestacks of steamers jutted from the fog, and the rigging of the last clipper ship, which, hogbacked from weariness, still managed to sail the coast. More than a thousand of them were built on the west coast in fifty years—clippers, schooners, brigantines—but less than a hundred still survived; the rest had been wrecked, burnt, abandoned or sunk, or run on rock, or were simply and forever "lost at sea."

The *Sunshine*, a three-masted schooner, was found bottom-up off Cape Disappointment in 1875—the year she was built. *Aida*, a four-master, "vanished" out of Shanghai in '96. *Rosario*, a schooner, was crushed by ice in '98; *Parallel* blew up in San Francisco a year later; and *D. H. Talbot*, whose skipper fell ill, and his sixteen-year-old daughter steered her, broke up on the Chinese coast—only two of the crew survived. Oceans of dead ships. God rest them all.

I asked after Nello but no one had seen him for a while.

Someone heard he'd gone on a Jap fish boat, but fishing was tough now, the fish all gone, didn't sound to me like a place he'd hang his hat.

Water Street swarmed with the drunk and nearly dead. Stevedores jostled in the road, hungry immigrants cowered in doorways, Indians from up coast, with heads down, lumbered on; and the dead drunk curled up like curs beside the boardwalk or splayed out devil-may-care where they fell. But some were resurrected when coins spilled on the boards, slipping through the cracks, and they dove and clawed about in the gloom below.

I found a lodged penny, and from a stall with mounds of sauerkraut bought myself a pickle.

I turned uphill to ask Mr. Chow. He supplied Chinamen to everyone in town—had a cousin or nephew in every sawmill, cannery, beer parlor, and hotel—no one sneezed without Mr. Chow hearing about it, so if he didn't know where Nello was, Nello had left the planet.

I left the wood-blocks of the road and turned down an alley into Chinatown. Planks formed haphazard bridges in the mud, and the air was a stench of fermenting things, smoke, spices, burnt meat, and sweat. Lanterns dangled in the steam of noodle carts whose owners called or whistled, weaving among people lugging nets, pots, children, bamboo cages, or sacks of coal, all searching for a small space in the mud among the vegetable stalls, and butcher stalls, and stalls where fish hung, still alive, cut clear in half, their head on one hook the rest on another. A goat head with dangling tongue hung on a hook and one with lonely eyes sat in a bowl—and I wondered who they got: the captain or the cabin boy. In a wicker cage, puppies whined. A cleaver thudded and a hammer beat a rivet in a pot.

I swung a door open. At a long table strewn with dishes sat a mob of Chinamen of every age, size, and description, all chopsticking noodles as fast as they could. Old Mr. Chow, tiny and gaunt at the head of the table, waved me over and the others slid along the bench to make me room. I sat and was handed a bowl of soup with a chicken foot and a seahorse bobbing in it. "Good for cold night," Mr. Chow said in greeting.

I slurped down the soup and tore the chicken foot with my teeth. It all tasted just right after the rum.

"You look tired."

"It's just the fog," I said.

"Fog good," Mr. Chow said. "Indian say fog breath of rain. Rain wash you outside, fog wash you inside."

"I could use a good wash inside," I said.

Mr. Chow laughed, held his bowl to his lips, shoveled and sucked in some noodles. "Sorry about Missis Hay. She nice lady."

Chow was running way ahead of me but I wasn't surprised; that's why I was here.

"Me too," I said.

"No worry; you find."

"First I have to find Nello."

He said something to the old woman beside him, and she to the kid beside her, and so it went down the line.

"You're a lucky man, Mr. Chow," I said. "Nice big family, like happy tree in forest."

"*You* are lucky man, Captain Dugger," he retorted. "Alone, like bird in sky. Question is"—he smiled coyly—"which mo' happy?" He laughed and chased his last noodle, "Me old man. Dream many night go home. To village. Big sky. Fish. Old man need quiet. Need peace."

"Maybe we're all old men."

He gave a gap-toothed grin. "You be good old man, Captain Dugger."

"I've always been old man."

A plate of sliced-up roast duck came with a bottle of plum brandy, and we chewed a piece—all skin and grease—and washed it down with long slugs.

"Mr. Chow," I began politely. "Kwakiutl men escaped from jail."

"Nephew take picture. You want see?"

I wanted see. He spoke to the old woman again.

"And that night on the yacht?"

Poking, whispering. The place quieted; I could hear the old lady gum her greens. Someone laughed out nervously and I looked up. It was a fleshy girl beside me clearing the table: pretty, flushed from the stove, sweat on her face and naked arms, smelling of ginger. People started to leave. A young man came in with photographs, bowed to Mr. Chow, and slipped them before me. The first was a group of Indians, mostly men, all ages, all short-legged, broad-shouldered water people who seldom used their legs but had paddled all their lives. Some wore pants, some blankets, one a polka-dot shirt, and all wore caps or bowlers or straw skimmers.

"Which one?" I asked.

The young man pulled out a photograph taken closer, all broad-faced, fleshy, thick foreheads, staring in cold defiance, or anger, or bitterness, and an older man as calm as a stone. One—young, bare-headed, big eyed, and hollow-cheeked—could have passed for a European with that cleft chin and slight smile.

"Which you think?" Mr. Chow asked.

I pointed at the European.

Something passed between the boy and Mr. Chow, something private, then Mr. Chow politely laughed and the boy poked his finger at a face I hadn't noticed, but now that I saw him I couldn't look away. I held the picture closer to the lightbulb. Straggly hair framed his face; he wasn't old—the forehead was lined not horizontally from age, but with lines curving downward from the center to the outer corners of his eyes. His eyes were fixed, unyielding and shiny as ball bearings. A thick, graying mustache and haggard beard rimmed the tight-set mouth, around which, from the flare of his nose to where the mustache ended, ran deep furrows—as if from smiles.

I didn't remember ever having felt such a strange unease.

"And the other?" I asked, surprised by the tightness of my voice.

He pointed at a man who seemed about to die. The huge-hooded eyes were nearly shut, just dark slits, but it was his parchment skin that held my gaze. Between the eyebrows were deep creases that could have been gashed with a claw; and below the jutting cheekbones and the mouth, the dark skin hung in folds and pleats, as if the muscles that held them had surrendered long ago.

"You sure?"

The young man seemed offended. "Cousin cook on Mr. Hay yacht. He see Indian men come. See cabin boy with knife. Big fight. Lady hear noise so she come. Men take her. Cousin see. He hide, he see."

The kitchen noises ended, the place fell quiet. We sipped the plum brandy without the duck to absorb it. It was hot in there, and when I got up to leave, my head swam. "Could I keep this?" I asked. They both said yes at once. I thanked them for everything and was pushing down the door handle when Mr. Chow called after me.

"Young Indian, dangerous warrior. But old Indian, he from other side. Have much power; from other side." And he indicated somewhere over his right shoulder.

I tried to smile. "You believe those tales, Mr. Chow?"

"Captain Dugger," he said, "land is land, sky is sky; other side is other side."

A shaft of light fell through the doorway into the fog. Something scurried out of a barrel and under a plank and when I stepped down, it gave a gurgling squeal. With the door shut, the alley was dark; only the coals of a noodle cart lit the face of the noodle man.

I was at the top of the alley when I heard steps hurrying after me. I stopped. The steps stopped. I turned into another alley, then another. The steps followed. I pulled out my knife, crouched down between two crates, almost losing my drunken balance, reached out, and, with the heel of my hand, thudded softly on the plank, softer and softer, like fading steps. A small figure came slowly up the planks. It stopped right before me. I lunged against the side of his knee and he staggered but grabbed my wrist as he fell and pulled me with him into the mud. I thrashed, grabbed his arm, and held the knife against his throat. The flesh was soft, and smelled of ginger; I held the arm of the plump girl from Mr. Chow's.

"Jeezus," I burst out angrily. "You fight good for a girl."

"Fight good for boy too," she said. "Chinagirl no get work; Chinaboy do."

I pulled her up. We were drenched in mud. "What the hell did you follow me for?"

"Uncle send message. Mr. Nello in cannery in river."

"You had to sneak up to tell me that?"

"Uncle say to be sure you get home okay."

I felt bad; dug around in my pocket counting my change.

"Come on," I said. "I'll buy you a bath."

THE LOTUS GARDEN was full of the sound of splashing water and the smell of wet cedar. An old bent woman finished wiping down the shower walls in our room and turned on the tap in the soak tub in the floor. I asked to have our clothes washed and pressed dry. The steam rose.

The girl took off her coat, went and hung it on a peg, then stood there—an honest face. She undressed. Didn't hurry, didn't tease. Such pretty breasts. She unbraided her hair; smiled at my watching, then went to the shower. So young. So pretty. She soaped her hair, scrubbed her head with spread fingers, and the bubbles ran down her shoulders. She soaped herself all over, then rinsed off, turning to one side, then the other and, seeing me undressing very slowly, she smiled; an old smile for her age. She wrung the water from her hair, then, covering herself with her hands, went to the soak tub in the floor, felt the water with her foot, and waded slowly down the steps into the steamy water.

When I came out of the shower wrapped in a towel, she was sitting deep in the tub, her breasts floating on the surface. Damn life. Damn stupid life—everything at the wrong time. If only this had been yesterday. Or better still, before I even met Katherine Hay. I sat on the bench against the wall. I was so drunk I could barely sit straight.

"You're very pretty," I finally said.

She blushed. Cupped her hands and poured water on her face to hide it. Then looked up into my eyes. "Uncle say you much in love," she said softly. "No have to say; I see your face in house."

It was my turn to blush.

"Is she very beautiful?" she asked.

"No more than you."

She leaned back, her face full of confident warmth.

"Does she love you?"

Her directness was a shock. "I don't know," I said. "Wish I did."

"Always same," she said a bit sadly. "One love much; other not sure." Then she cheered up. "Uncle say you go save her. When you save her, she will love you."

We sat on the bench wrapped in towels, waiting for our clothes to come.

"Uncle say old Indian have power of other side."

"Yes."

"Cousin say her husband have much power this side."

"So it seems."

Slowly she sorted the tangles from her hair. "You not afraid they kill you?"

"No," I said.

"Not afraid to die?"

"No. Too busy being afraid of everything else."

She stared at me with motherly concern. Then she moved close, leaned her head on my shoulder. In a few minutes her breathing was even. She slept. It felt comforting having her against me. I closed my eyes. When I awoke it was dawn.

The streets were empty; only a milk wagon came slowly up the hill, the horse snorting steam, the bottles clanging softly. I went to find the horse cart that hauled new cans to the canneries. The tide was so low that mussels crackled on pilings and the air smelled as if everything had died.

6

Nello

The young men dive (t!e'qwa), carrying heavy stones about one hundred and fifty pounds in weight . . . . They walk into the water . . . to a depth of one or two fathoms, to see who can carry them farthest.

—Franz Boas

Oi vita, oi vita mia, oi core 'e chistu core, si' stat'o primm' amore; o primo e l'ultimo sarai per me!

—Canzone Napoletana

A mile away you could see the sun glitter on the new tins. Old Nagy took the feed bag off his horse, checked the net that held the mound of tins, and told me to get on for the ride to Steveston, on the river. Nagy loved company; would never accept anything for the rides—well, maybe a bottle of rye at Christmas—but you had better know how to listen because he could talk your brain to mush. This time he railed about the price of oats, how horseshoes don't last, the long wait at the whorehouse, and the goddamn Pakies who didn't net the tins tight so they'd clink and clang and drive you out of your mind.

I mostly ignored him, but he never noticed because I threw in the occasional "damn right" or "you said it," then with the clap clap of the horseshoes I drifted off and had a nap. I was startled awake in the stench of rotten fish, to the shriek of gulls.

The great cedar-shaked cannery leaned darkly over us. Steam engines hissed and a fish boat engine roared as it made a tug-turn on the spot. Anxious voices yelled in every language you can name but over it all rose Nello's melodious, *"Donato, Donato, sarebbe stato meglio se non fosse nato!"*

Nello and I went back a long time; we slithered in the same mud in the war—on opposite sides, but then mud is mud. He was the best sailor I ever shipped with; it was in his blood because his father had been a sailor from Pisa, and he also knew the northern coast, and that was in his blood too because he was born there to a Kwakiutl mother, in a village called Karlekuies. It was at the end of a narrows Cook named Beware Passage.

Except for the odd run with me, Nello had quit the sea a year ago; no explanation, just threw up his billet on a clipper ship that sailed lumber to New Zealand and took on odd jobs on the waterfront. Now he was filling in for the dock foreman unloading the listing fish scows, organizing the chaos of Hindus, Chinamen, Dutchmen, and Bushmen on the fish-slicked docks. Nagy blew his horn so loud his old horse startled.

I crossed the vast shed where soldering irons belched acrid clouds and a monstrous machine named the Iron Chink clattered. Chinamen hosed down the floors, and women, with their infants on their backs, stood in water slicing, gutting, and throwing; the same motions in endless repetition from the first light of dawn until the place went dark.

I saw Nello coming up the ramp through the spraying water. He was a couple of inches shorter than me, but his feisty stance coupled with what he used to call my "condescending stoop" made us, in my mind, similar in height. He had his mother's skin and straight black hair, but his father's frail bones, held together by a flesh so hard that his veins only found room by bulging through his skin. His face was gaunt, making his blue eyes even more startling.

His movements were quick. Aboard the ketch, he would always fidget with blocks and lines, making minuscule adjustments to sheets and halyards until the sails were set to perfection, without a ripple. He was the perfect first mate except for his mouth. He would say whatever crossed his mind, consequences or reaction be damned. And he would say it to anyone's face with his eyes riveted, softening the blow only with an occasional, "Don't you think so too?" even when the unsaid answer was obviously no. And having embarrassed or offended, he was never apologetic. "It's the Tuscan in me," he'd say with a shrug, as if that somehow justified all.

He came leaning slightly forward, a worn, narrow-rimmed black hat pushed back off his forehead, in a dark seaman's sweater with the sleeves ending halfway down the forearms to keep away from fishhooks and winches. His strong arms and big hands made him look heavier than he was. He was all of forty but his movements made him younger.

He seemed glad to see me and was about to extend his hand for a shake, but something on my face must have made him uneasy, for he suddenly diverted his hand to his shirt pocket and yanked out the stub of a cigar. He lit it, took a puff, and blew out the smoke with an agitated force as if trying to blow away a bothersome insect. "Good to see you, Cappy," he said.

"You too," I said.

"Something eating you, am I right?" he said, studying my eyes.

"You're always right," I said.

"When you're this congenial, I'm in trouble."

"No trouble, I promise. Just came to offer you a cruise. A vacation from flying fish guts."

"I don't need a vacation; I need money."

"There's that too. Lots of it."

"Like the last time. You still owe me half my pay."

"This time it's different. Here's what I owe you," and I handed him some bills. "And when you step on board I'll give you half of your share in advance."

"You rob a bank?"

"Just got me a good trip, that's all."

He snubbed out his cigar. That was a good sign; he was calming down.

"How long a trip?" he asked guardedly.

"Can't tell for sure. Maybe a week, maybe more."

"How much more?"

"A month."

"Forget it!" he blurted as if someone had slapped his back. "A month's too long."

"Two weeks' pay in advance."

"Still too long."

"For what?"

He looked embarrassed. "For me to stand."

"Stand what?"

"Your cooking. Last time you cooked flapjacks morning,

noon, and night. Twenty-two goddamn days; sixty-six plates of flapjacks."

"And sausages. The first days we had sausages. "

"Burnt to charcoal."

"All right. A whole month in advance."

"I'd rather be crucified. That only lasts a few hours, then you get to die," and he turned to walk away. I had to grab him. I yanked a bunch of bills from my pocket.

"Okay. A month's wages now and you do the cooking."

"Tuscan men don't cook."

"But you're half Indian."

"That half don't cook either." And he was leaving.

"I'll get a cook," I blurted. " A Chinaman. The best cook in town, from Mr. Chow. You know he owes me." Chow had already paid me back generously but this much he'd do for me. Nello turned. Considered.

"A Chinaman cook. You swear."

"On my mother's grave."

"And real food; no flapjacks."

"Not one."

He counted the bills. "When do we sail?"

"The tide turns at noon."

"Tomorrow?"

"It's life and death."

He thought about it and sucked the cold stub more. "I must be nuts," he said. And turned and walked away. But before he took three strides he came back. "What kind of a mess are you getting me into? You didn't get all that money in advance for honest work."

I told him the story. Most of it: Hopkins, the Kwakiutl, Hay, his wife, without mentioning a word about her and me.

"You want me to hunt down one of my own tribe?" he said in disbelief.

"Nobody's hunting anybody. The man just wants his wife back."

"And the masks."

"I don't give a rat's ass about the masks."

"Just you and me and the Chinaman."

"And her husband."

"Poor bastard," he said. "Must be going through hell. Unless she's ugly and stupid."

"She's not."

Nello went quiet on me.

"What's the matter?"

"How long you known her?"

"A bit."

"Since July?"

"I don't remember."

"Well, I remember. July. This is the one you taught how to sail, right? Jesus Christ. You haven't stopped talking about her since!"

"That was someone else. The Welsh girl from the alley. The one who knit your sweater. This cold rich bitch would be the last on my list, believe me."

He didn't and he said so.

"You think I'd be stupid enough to take the husband along if it were her?"

"You'd take the devil if he paid you!"

"She's lifeless and cold."

"You sure?"

"I'm sure."

"*Ficca fredda*, my *nonno* used to say. Cold cunt."

"That's her."

"Thank God. For a minute I thought . . . . But even you wouldn't sink so low as to drag me into such a mess."

KATE
The Nights

The nights are long and the night winds sharp, but I lie in the bottom of the canoe, keep out of the wind, and I wrap myself double in blankets over my pajamas. Very stylish; apricot silk with rotten gray blanket. So I'm all right. The canoe is old and it stinks of dead fish or dead something, but it's safe and with the blankets I'm warm. I'm all right.

We move all night. And all night I lie there, not sleeping much. Just lie there looking at the stars. I never knew, never even dreamt there could be so many. Layers and layers. You can see them if you look long enough. So dense there's no darkness in between them. The whole sky. All my stars. I know a lot of them by now: their brightness, their names. I don't mean the names in the books, I never did learn those, didn't mean a damn to me—I mean, what exactly is an O'Ryan's Belt? A triple shot of Irish whiskey? So I named them all myself: Uncle Harry, bright and smiley; Fat Joey Miller, kind of lumpy; Mary McLean, because sometimes she'd show up and other times she'd be hard to find. And Dull Sue. Dull but reliable. And that means a lot in this stinking world. She was reliable and very nice, once you got to know her. But few people ever bothered to take the time. George didn't. He was busy traveling; collecting things. And did he ever get to know me? Though I was right there, traveling with him. Did he ever know even one of my fears? Or my smallest secret?

Oh, well. Dull Sue sure was reliable.

7

Chow's Debt

Heaven took my wife. Now it
Has also taken my son.
My eyes are not allowed a
Dry season. It is too much
For my heart. I long for death . . . .
Once gone, life
Is over for good. My chest
Tightens against me. I have
No one to turn to. Nothing,
Not even a shadow in a mirror.

—Mei Yao-ch'en (1002 - 1060)

I had once done Mr. Chow a favor.

One morning, I was loading the ketch with empty herring cans at Ballantine Pier destined for a family cannery in Sooke, a quiet hole on Vancouver Island where the strait empties into the ocean. They were lowering baled cans through the skylight—down below she was still empty; just the bunk and a woodstove—when Nello yelled out to come up and have a look. From seaward comes this wreck of a tramp steamer limping in, beat-up, patched, belching ghastly smoke, listing as if battling a hurricane, down in the stern full of who knew how much water. Rust bled from every fastener, and her sheer was so distorted by years of pounding waves that her back, if not quite broken, was forever deformed. She seemed to undulate as she moved, barely alive, and not only would she never cross an ocean, but I wouldn't have bet on her making it to the dock.

The stevedores stood among their hills of coffee sacks and bales of stinking hides and stared at the dying ship. A shiny new police car, bell clanging, weaved along the pier, followed by a horse cart full of cops, and out they all poured, forming a wall along the pier ready to defend the continent.

One shouted through a megaphone at the ship that showed no life, ordered the invisible everyone to remain on board, and some even pulled their guns ready to fire at her dented smokestack, her swaybacked bridge, or maybe her limp flag, unrecognizable from soot. Then the enemy appeared: two lean Malays or Siamese clutching dock lines looked at all the commotion with the detached interest of monkeys watching their watchers at the zoo. A few more scruffy seamen crawled out of the hatchways. A pack of cops scrambled down onto her deck and shouted through the megaphone at the poor buggers, ordered them—still as statues—not to move. Then the cops vanished down a hatchway in the hold. The stevedores took her lines and tied her to bollards as if this kind of wreck landed every day.

The cops suddenly reappeared, some gasping, others running to the gunwales and retching over the side, all of them scrambling back onto the dock as if chased by fiends. An emaciated pair of Chinamen came half-naked into the sun, holding by the ankles and under the armpits a nearly weightless corpse. Then others came with similar burdens. They laid the corpses side by side on the foredeck: five, ten, fifteen, and still they brought more. When they ran out of room, they stacked them like cordwood.

From the hold they hauled up seven coffins—some light wood I didn't recognize—and stood them against the deckhouse ready for the lucky winners among the thirty dead. Somebody laughed aloud; a big stevedor cried. But the cops stood their ground; nobody was getting off alive or dead. There was a prohibition of colored people coming into the country: a shipful of Pakies had been put back out to sea, and they rounded up eight thousand Orientals into a fenced camp on the island ready to stuff them into the next steamer, and shove them off for home.

And they were the lucky ones; the others had died for a king they never heard of on a continent they didn't know existed, died serving "real" soldiers, clearing mines or burying the dead. But now the war was over and the Pakies and the Chinamen had to go.

By nightfall the stiffs began to reek. The sergeant wanted to cut the lines and let her go. "That's the way, O'Hanlon!" Nello yelled beside me. "Kick their slant-eyed asses back where they belong. It's what we should have done when you whities came and ruined the neighborhood."

"You got a lot of good things from us whities," O'Hanlon snarled.

"All I got was the clap from your sister."

"If I had a sister, your nose would be busted."

"If you had a sister, you would have her clap."

"Get him out of here, Cappy," O'Hanlon said, beet-red. "Before I stain my hands with his blood."

A man with a long pole lit the gas lamps on the shore. Later, Chinamen came with lanterns, steaming pots dangling from their shoulders—roast pork, and tea, and a big cauldron of rice. They filled bowls and handed them down to the bony hands that shone white in the dark.

I went back to load and put things in order below. When I came back near midnight, the pier was deserted, the ship gone. I looked over the edge, sure that it had sunk, but there were no dock lines, no jetsam. "So what did you do with the yacht, Harry?" I asked the dock foreman. "Sailed for parts unknown," he said. "How about we go get us a beer?"

I sailed alone for Sooke on the dawn tide. The sky was clear, the nor'westerly fresh, and by early afternoon I had sailed across Georgia Strait on a reach and was riding wing-and-wing past Saturna Island, keeping to the north side of Boundary Pass so I wouldn't end up on the gallows in Frisco. At sunset the wind eased, and in the warm fragrance of firs I dropped anchor off a spit to catch an hour of sleep.

When I awoke, moonlight lit the cans.

I sailed with just the main, doing about three knots plus the tide so if I bumped into a deadhead, I wouldn't bump too hard. The night air cooled, and I bundled up in the cockpit. When the first swells from the ocean passed under us, the ketch rolled gently. Near midnight the wind fell. The fog came in and bit me to the bone. A shudder rippled through me. I thought at first it was the cold. I gybed the main and headed higher northwest.

I was hungry. I lashed the wheel a good half mile off Vancouver Island and went below to get a hard-boiled egg and sausage. Huddled in my big coat, I leaned against the mizzen and hummed to keep myself company and to keep from getting queasy in the lazy rollers. Eat and sing, especially at night. I felt content, and for a moment considered just sailing right out of the damned strait into the Pacific, the thousands of miles of empty Pacific, with the boatload of empty tin cans and all. I went down below to fill the mug, heard the sea rush past the hull and the tin cans give a rustle as we rolled, and I was just coming up the companionway into the splash of moonlight when I heard the first thud: muted, almost shy, as if not wanting to disturb the silence.

The moon glowed through the fog like a candle through angel hair. With the shores now hidden, I lit the compass light. The reddish flame seemed curiously alive. Then the thud came again. Too soft for a log, not hollow enough for driftwood. Soft; like someone tapping in the bow. I went forward on the starboard deck; the moon lit brighter there. The bow wake rose a black fold and trailed off into the night. Tap. A swell raised the bow and lowered it with a whoosh. Tap, tap. I lay over the bow, hung on to the whisker stay, and looked down into the water. Foam flowed from where the bobstay split the sea, for a moment blurring what trailed beside the hull, but as the bow rose again and the bobstay rose free, I could see—so close I could almost touch her face—a black-haired mermaid staring up at me. Her body long and white, only her sharp-boned face and long, streaming hair were etched by the silver light.

They had wrapped her in a white sheet, frail as a child, but her hair was free to snag the bobstay pin, so she swung in the swell and her knees banged the hull. I climbed down; a swell came and put us both half under. As gently as I could, I untangled her hair and set her free. She floated off into the night.

The swells grew and the tin cans rustled. I went below for dry boots but settled for more rum.

The next one came when I stepped back into the cockpit. A man this time, on his belly, head turned like a swimmer taking breaths. The wind picked up and the fog thinned and I could see now, some close, some far, the pallid shapes floating slowly by. We drifted through a sea of the dead. I stared so hard I almost hit the wreck.

Noiseless and darkened, it came out of the fog directly in my way. She made no sound. Her stokers must have given up long ago, for there was no smoke rising from her funnel. She lay lifeless beam-on to the swell, and rolled just far enough that, at each starboard roll, another white-wrapped shape slid across her foredeck and splashed into the sea.

The not-yet-dead had gathered on the aft deck, clinging to the cabin top or with their legs over the rail. My port lantern in the shroud cast a red glow over them. They gazed with stony eyes, not a word, not a plea.

I sailed by.

As suddenly as it had appeared, the wreck vanished from sight. It was a while before I got my thoughts together enough to trim the sail. I took a slug of rum. The fog thickened. The sea was empty; the dead had had the decency to leave. Son of a bitch; why me? Why, in this immensity of empty sea, did those damned faces have to be near me? Hadn't I seen the bastards enough before? Fine. I'll stop the first fish boat coming down the coast to get some help from Victoria and get them on their way. Back to bloody China. Or at least toward China, which they'll never see again because the first gale is going to tear that rat-ass wreck to shreds. Serves 'em right. Should have stayed at home. Why come anyway? Greed, that's why. "More," they wanted "more." Well, there's no "more." The "more" is all gone.

Son of a bitch. Another fifty feet and I would never have seen them. Those eyes in the lantern light. I cursed and flung the empty bottle at the dark. Then I tightened the main and threw the coiled sheet on the deck, uttering a curse I didn't know I knew. I turned the wheel and fed the main out again. Turned back. The compass rose spun in the sputtering light. This was madness. Back where? What course? How far? Probably sunk by now anyway. For a moment I hoped they'd sunk.

They stood where I had left them, every one of them. This time the green starboard lantern lit their eyes. I yelled at them, my voice breaking with anger, but no one moved. I luffed up and slowed. "Throw me a line, you bastards! Throw rope!" Nothing. I yanked the mainsheet loose and hurled it at their faces. Not a blink. "Grab it, you morons! Grab it!" And I waved a violent motion toward the ketch. Dead as doornails. "This is your last chance, then I'm gone!" I was sailing right by them, within reach, but the sheet kept sliding off the stern rail into the sea, when I saw something shift. Someone moved enough to put a skeletal foot on the rope. A kid, even frailer than the rest. I threw him the stern line. He raised his stick arm and caught it. Others stirred and helped. The swells rose; the ketch and the wreck rose and sank more or less together. I kicked the fenders over as we rubbed against her stern. The kid leaned awkwardly down and lowered his bundle of bones into my arms. One by one they came, I could have sworn I heard their bones clattering. Over the rail they came and scattered on the deck like pick-up sticks.

I herded them into the bow. There must have been forty of them. Good thing I was only running empties. In the engine room of the wreck, I found water up to my knees. I hacked at a sea cock with the fire ax until it gave, and the water rushed in, swirling around me as I climbed back out.

We sailed off. In the pale light the wreck pitched steeply aft.

The dawn broke. On the pink horizon, only the bow of the wreck now pointed at the sky, then it was gone. Some of them watched the empty sea a long time. I sailed into a little bay, fetched up, and stopped a couple of boat-lengths from the point. "Go on, get off," I whispered, to keep from waking the fisherman anchored up the bay. The kid was first to rise. He eased his legs over the side but hung on to the rail, then he slid a bit farther. When he let go, he sank like a goddam stone, didn't even know enough to struggle. I had to save him with the boathook.

I launched the skiff, cleated a long line, then rowed ashore and tied it to a fir. I waved at them to come hand over hand along the line. One by one they slipped into the sea, but they were too many, and when the line went under, they went with it. I hauled on my end to pull them up again and saw the ketch begin to head for shore. I rowed back and dropped anchor; didn't set it, just dropped it. I hauled the line tight again but not all of them were on it. Some made it and lay like drowned seals on the rocks. The last of them sank a few steps from the shore, but there was no one strong enough to help.

The kid had sense enough to untie my line and I sailed the hell out of there and didn't even look back until I cleared the point. The dawn had spread and there they were all along the rocks: some standing, some kneeling, some leaning on each other, each one of them bowed as low as their last strength let them.

WHEN I GOT back to town, neither the papers nor the beer parlor gossip had anything to say about the wreck. Some weeks later I was crossing Chinatown with a handcart of lumber to build some berths when a Chinaman politely touched my arm and asked me if I could step into his shop. What the hell? I thought. Might be a customer. We waited. A frail old Chinaman came in and up to me. I thought he'd give me hell for drowning some of his kin, but instead he looked at me and quick tears filled his eyes. "Grandson," he managed finally; then bowed. The door opened and in walked the kid, looking a lot better-fed now. He stopped beside the old man, who said more strongly, "Grandson," and they bowed.

Next Monday a horse cart pulled up to the head of the alley with a load of the best damned boat lumber I'd ever seen—mahogany and teak boards, some a good foot wide—and asked where to unload it because it was all mine, no charge. And next morning down came a couple of pigtailed Charlies with boxes of the weirdest saws and chisels. One of them spoke some English and said they came to build my boat. I told him to turn back around because I couldn't pay them. He smiled his worn-toothed smile and shook his head. "No pay," he said. "Honorable family."

That's how I knew I could count on Mr. Chow.

8

Charlie

There is such an abundance of animal life in the sea that the Indians live almost solely upon seals, sea lions, various species of salmon, the halibut, cod and herring.

The oil of the eulachon, a herring-like fish containing iodine and many vitamins, is most prized. Caught in the spring—a lone fisherman can bring in 10 canoe loads—they are left to "ripen" in pits covered with logs. In a great bent-wood box or canoe, water is made to boil by putting in fire-heated stones, then the rotted fish is added and stirred until the rendered oil rises, then is skimmed off and stored in long tube-kelp. It is used year-round, poured over dried salmon or clams, or dried berries pressed into cakes.

—Franz Boas

So I went and asked Mr. Chow for a sea cook, then left a note for Hopkins telling him I was sailing the next day. At Palotai's I bought a string of hard-dried smoked sausages that lasted a month at sea if you wrapped them in brown paper; then I stopped at the purveyor for a small keg of rum.

When I got back to the ketch and stepped into the cockpit I almost squashed him. I was about to give him the back of my hand for sneaking aboard my boat when he cried out, "No hit, no hit! No hit cookie!"

Jesus. He couldn't have been a day over fifteen. Small-boned, with those mischievous eyes only kids have before they grow old and dull. "You good cookie?" I asked.

"Charlie best cookie whole world," he said, and beamed so brightly that I would have kept him just as long as he could flip a flapjack. I was making a list for provisioning the galley when someone knocked on the hull. It was Hopkins, all smiles, wishing me a safe trip and handing me another stuffed envelope. Then he was gone. Charlie was polishing the brass binnacle so hard I thought he'd start a fire.

I asked him if he knew Sam Ling at Sunshine Market. "Yessir, Captain," he said. "Sam Ling uncle." I should have guessed. I told him to provision for a month and he wrote while I rattled off the list: tinned biscuits, eggs, slab of bacon, tea, syrup, jam, lemons, apples, sugar, flower, rice, onions, cabbage, carrots, prunes, tinned beef, lentils, beans, lard, and he repeated everything so clearly I almost understood him. Then I told him to tell Uncle Ling no horse meat, no cats, and no puppies, and I asked to see the list in case I missed something. He went beet-red and handed me the paper, beautifully written—in Chinese. "Perfect," I said. "Tell him I need it by tonight."

He ran up the floats, his pigtail flopping. I began to fill my water tanks, checked the little one-cylinder engine that had only enough power to get us in and out of harbors in a calm, went over the rigging, and got ready to work all night. I barely sleep the night before a long voyage. Especially this one, with her at the end.

KATE
My Keepers

The more I watch the old one, the more I'm sure he can see in the dark. Long before dawn he stops paddling and we drift and he stares at the pitch-black shoreline, silent as a ghost. He paddles a bit, then stares. And he always finds us a perfect place to hide: a creek mouth, the cleft of a rock, a hollow, brambles, something. It's different every day and it can't be just dumb luck.

The young one is just eerie. He's very good at hiding us during the day, flipping the canoe in just the right spot on shore, in the shade, then he covers it with moss and branches until, even close up, it almost vanishes. Then he tells me where to hide so I can sleep. Well, he doesn't actually tell me—he hasn't said a single word to me, although he seems to be talking a lot to the sea, the rocks, even the canoe. Sometimes at night he stops paddling and he talks, to the stars, I guess. Sometimes I think it's a prayer, at others just demented sounds: moans, clacking, warbling.

He is so calm it makes me nervous, and he moves differently from anyone I have ever seen. On foot he almost floats. And he rarely eats, has four bites of dry fish at dawn and four drinks of water and that's all for the day. Never does he utter a distinct word, just drones, song-like but faint and distant. He aims the sounds at every blessed thing around. He even muttered to a slimy green fish he caught yesterday. He talks to everything. Except me.

And today I thought I heard the wind answer him, and the sea.

9

Hay

When a hunter sees that another hunter goes to hunt on his hunting ground, they fight. The mountain-goat hunters do the same. And when one of them is beaten, he is pushed down the mountain.

—Franz Boas

It was a windless, misty dawn, awash with that pink light that could restore hope even in the dead.

I got to know Hay's footsteps before I met him. I was checking the rigging with Nello when they thudded on the rickety wharves, so full of assurance and vehemence that I thought he'd walk right off into the sea. He wasn't as big as he had seemed sitting with his back to me that first night on the yacht; looked intelligent, with a most amenable expression and only the slightest hint of that uncertainty one has in a new place. He seemed propelled by some irrepressible energy that kept in movement not only his limbs but more than anything his eyes, which had an elegant ferocity—not openly voracious like a feeding shark, but their irritating alertness left no doubt that he was, in some indefinable way, gobbling up everything around him. And it was contagious; it made you reach for something, anything, to do, so while we exchanged pleasantries, I nervously uncoiled and recoiled what had already been a perfect coil of rope.

He stood courteously on the wharf waiting to be invited aboard, showering compliments on the ketch: her construction, her Bristol condition. "What a self-contained world," he said, and for an instant, and it was to be the last until Devil's Hole, I saw a twinge of jealousy in his eyes. He carried a big leather bag and a rifle in a leather case—both with just the right amount of wear—and he was dressed so ideally for a sea voyage that he seemed like an actor in a play.

While I set him up in his cabin—only a berth with some drawers below but he was grateful for the privacy—I gave him a short version of what Nello had told me: that we should assume the Kwakiutl were well ahead and we'd head north as fast as we could, stopping only to make inquiries. He agreed.

We were late catching the tide. Nello cast off while Charlie finished putting away stores, then he came on deck anxious to help but without the least notion of what to do. We slipped past

Prospect Point, shooting the center of First Narrows to catch the full power of the ebb. The wind came out of the northwest, and we beat under main, the staysail, and the jib, heading west into the open but mist-choked sea. Blowing against the tide, the wind whipped up steep waves and, with the short trough between them, the ketch buried her bow and green water shot down the deck and fountained out the scuppers. The ropes strained. Then, shaking off the seas, the ketch sprang ahead.

The canvas bulged, the sheets quivered, and a halyard slatted keeping time against the mast, and I braced my foot in the cockpit corner, clutched the spokes of the wheel, and for a moment forgot about Hay below and Katherine up ahead, forgot my debts and even the South Seas—I was sailing.

Past the narrows the steep seas eased and Hay slid back the hatch and stuck out his head. The fire had left his eyes. He looked gray and sick. He clambered out awkwardly in an oilskin buttoned for a hurricane with a pair of fancy binoculars dangling from his neck, crept along the sloping deck clutching now the grabrail, now the gunwale at his feet, until he reached the cedar skiff lashed amidships on the house, where he made himself into an inconspicuous bundle by the mast. Once in a while he'd raise the binoculars and peer into the mist; other than that he was as inanimate as dunnage.

The wind picked up but the mist wouldn't rise. It made no sense—the nor'wester always brought cold air and clear skies, but not today. I could see no shoreline either north or south and steered using only the point behind me. We short-tacked four times to keep off the southern sandbanks, tacked with quick shouts and scurrying, and Hay had to defend his head against the flogging lines, then we settled into a long beat, into the blinding haze ahead.

Nello trimmed and retrimmed the sails, tidied up the sheets, then sat in a corner of the cockpit with his legs gathered under him like some holy man. He began whipping the frayed ends of lines with a palm and needle and waxed line. He never once looked up, absorbed in the precision of his toil, his big square fingers making delicate whippings, lacings, knotting off.

I stayed alone at the helm, checking our speed by watching the foam wash by, dead reckoning through the unyielding mist, steering with as much conviction as if I actually knew where I was going. North, was all I knew; to look for her. We were to search hundreds of miles of coastline wilderness for a piece of hollow log, a hollow log that didn't want to be found in that immensity that mocked the arrogant and killed the fool.

I banished from my mind the thought that they might be off to the west among the reefs of the great island, or east in the archipelago hauled into some creek mouth. "North," I repeated, like some magic word.

Besides, as Nello said, they had to be heading home; they knew it was too dangerous to try to hide on the southern coast. If they had managed to escape from jail, find Hay, grab the masks, grab her, they weren't stupid.

At noon I plotted us to be in the middle of the gulf. The nor'wester picked up, whitecaps sprouted, spray flew, but the blinding mist stayed. Nello, came aft. "We're hexed," he said.

"Meaning what?"

"You ever seen mist this thick in a nor'wester? No. Besides which I dreamt last night that we sailed through sand. No water. Hexed."

Hay's lifting of the binoculars began to irritate me. If he did it one more time, I'd head straight into a wave and soak the son of a bitch.

"How many hours can your relatives paddle a day?"

He knotted a whip and slapped it hard into his palm. "That depends on how scared they are. One time, a war canoe full of them was chased by the Bella Coola. They paddled nonstop all the way home from Rivers Inlet; eighty miles in fifteen hours.

"Jesus. They'll be home in three days."

"No one can paddle nonstop for three days."

"If they take turns; there are two of them."

"Three if she helps."

"Why would she help?"

"I don't know. I don't know her."

"The young guy looks tough enough to paddle home by himself," I said.

"Oh, he's tough, all right. We're all taught to be from the day we're born. No pants or shoes summer or winter, and from October till spring it rains or snows every day. And we play tough games. We hook middle fingers and see who let go first with a bunch behind each pulling. Some guys had their joints torn loose before they gave in. Or we stick a short stick in the ground near a fire and pick it up with our teeth, move it closer and closer—no fair shielding your face—the one who got closest won; scorched hair, bubbled lips, and all. Older boys play war games with dry nettles; no shirts. Or with spruce branches; you ever grab a blue spruce? Tears your skin to shreds."

"And I bet those two are the toughest of the lot. You think they sent mamma's boys to get back the masks?"

"Lemme finish. We had to be tough for falling in icy water or getting a fishhook in the thigh, but we were taught one main objective: not to die. Those two know someone's gunning for them; and the southern tribes hate them, so they only move at night. That slows them by half. Then there's the tide. They're not stupid enough to waste strength going against the current; so there goes another three hours. Leaves nine hours a day."

"Even then . . . ."

"The third thing are the passes; three of them, one running at thirteen knots, Cappy—that's three times faster than your average river. But they don't run—they break, like cataracts, except they're full of whirlpools. Big ones: a hundred feet across; that suck down giant scows, never mind a shit-bit canoe. You go through right at slack tide—got maybe half an hour—or you don't go through at all. The fourth thing is Johnstone Strait; when it blows twenty knots in here, it's a gale out there. When it's a gale here—forget it. One last thing: they don't know these southern islands, so they might get lost for a while."

"If they get lost, we sure as hell won't find them."

"What do you care? You get paid by the day."

"Take the helm, will you? I'll go check the chart."

I tried to plot our position by dead reckoning, but instead kept thinking of her out there somewhere in the mist. Wouldn't they be better off dumping her in some back bay and going on alone? Sure they'd lose a hostage, but they sure as hell would look less suspicious and be more mobile without her weight. Dump her on some miserable island; the wilderness would kill in three days.

I plotted us over Halibut Shoals, then slammed the parallel rules down hard because our course put us right over the White Islets: flat rocks white from bird shit that blends in perfectly with the haze. We could keep going farther out in the gulf but the currents are fluky there and who knows where we'd end up. And past Merry Island the sea is so full of rocks that in this mist you'd be wrecked before you know it. To be safe we had to short-tack; waste time.

Back topsides, I thought I heard waves crashing on rocks. "You hear something?" I asked Nello.

"Only you worrying."

The bloody mist was getting on my nerves.

"We have to short-tack past White Islets," I said, and took the helm. "The current might be taking us for a ride."

"I'll get the anchor ready," and he headed forward.

"In case I get to close to shore?"

"In case we're hexed."

With the mist still thick, the lighthouse keeper blared his foghorn on Merry Island where the strait is split in two by the great mass of Texada Island just beyond. His light could blast into the night for fifteen miles, and the foghorn was enough to keep you off the rocks that littered the sea. The fishermen called him Rolf the Precise, and many thought him a saint for keeping his cogs and gears in perfect order, keeping that light aglow even on gale-torn nights, even though breaking waves swirled around his house and his island shuddered as if in an endless earthquake.

Between his island and the mainland, the pass was so narrow that the light would turn the darkness into day—he could see a duck pass, never mind a canoe—and he stayed awake all night, not just to keep the light, but because he loved company, was on the lookout for someone to save or hail over for a hot rum; even Indians. He had little use for them: couldn't tolerate their approximate lives, not when he checked, adjusted, regulated with absolute precision the angle of cogwheels, the balance of counterweights, kept spotless the hundred sides of his giant prism, while they drifted about more or less by the moon, the tides, and the seasons. And their villages—rotting fish, garbage, excrement cleaned away only by the currents—deeply offended him. But he plucked them from stormy seas, often at night; the sick and injured he nursed for weeks, and watched sadly as they left.

We dropped our sails in the lee of his island and drifted downwind until the anchor dug in. Rolf was already on his dock hollering invitations. I rowed ashore alone. He was as glad to see me as if I'd just returned from the grave. In his spotless kitchen—*zittzen, zittzen*—he chatted on about a recent shipwreck—two dead, three saved—and a logging camp that burnt—one dead and the rest in their underwear in the rain—and only when he finally came up for breath did he ask where I was headed this time.

I told him the story briefly and Rolf leapt to his feet. "Paah!"

he grunted like a wounded beast. "Women go to hell!" and with a flick of a hand dismissed half the human race. And told me again how he was married once to "one of those Eastern races" that for him included everyone from Berlin to Japan, so in love that even now his big hands closed with a tender longing, until he got to talking about their wedding day. The day after the wedding she was gone, with his Canadian citizen name, his gold watch, and the shoes he'd bought for the wedding. "Why take my goddamn shoes?" He calmed down and poured me some more rum. "This man sure his wife no running off with Indian?"

"Pretty sure," I said. He got up and watched a burst of light blast into the dusk, then, satisfied, came back. "If she not run off," he said quietly, "why she row like one sonovabitch?"

"You saw them?"

"Sure I saw them. Last night; after dusk Indian try to fool me. Made her paddle when the light hit them. The woman's face was blackened—but I have binoculars of German army so I see her in moonlight—wrapped in blanket look like squaw. But white woman never move like squaw."

A cloud of garlic and frying pork drifted up from the galley. We left the lighthouse far behind, passed between an island and a point, then turned east along a rocky coast and entered the long cove in the gloom of dusk. The wind had eased and we ghosted in under the main, past a kerosene lantern hanging from a pike pole to mark the shoals, edged up to a log boom, and tied her bow and stern.

The floathouses huddled in a row and the clanging of pots and pans echoed from the bluff behind them. A bulky shadow herded a group of white oxen toward an enclosure on a flat point. Across the floating logs, with a lantern swinging in his hand and stepping with the ease of a gentleman out for an evening stroll, came Ernie the foreman in his slippers, to greet us. He didn't have to be coaxed to stay for dinner.

We ate in the salon. Nello savored every bite of sliced pork with hot peppers and shrimp and noodles smothered in garlic. Only once did he look up to say, "Charlie, you're a godsend." Then he saw me push my food around on my plate. "You miss your flapjacks, don't you?"

Now that the ketch stood still, Hay had regained his confidence and played the perfect host. After some slugs of rum he and Ernie were old friends; after dinner they sat back and had their pipes, and Hay questioned Ernie about logging up here in the wilderness with as much interest as if he had nothing else on his mind.

They had built a skid road up into a valley where there were cedars ten feet across. Took two men two days to saw one of them through, and fourteen oxen to drag it down here. The oxen had stampeded down a slope with one of those logs chained behind them, and he had kept driving them as hard as he could because if they slowed up, the log would have made chopped meat of them all.

Ernie asked Hay about his trip.

"Very fine," Hay offered. "Exhilarating. But to be sincere, I'm not used to a boat being on its side. Had quite an ill effect. I prefer motor yachts that stay flat on their bottoms. My wife, on the other hand—"

"Even more so," I cut in.

"Oh, women." Ernie laughed. "Solid land is what they like."

"No, no," Hay insisted. "More than anything she loves sailboats."

Nello's cup froze at his lips.

"Especially," Hay continued, "since Captain Dugger so very patiently taught her how to sail."

I couldn't look at Nello.

There was no air in the cabin, just pipe smoke and rum fumes, so I went above. A land-breeze had blown away the mist, and the moonrise was so bright I couldn't see a star. Saturday night laughter came from the floathouses and through the windows I saw the loggers "climbing wall"—running full speed at it in their cork boots to see who could get highest before falling to the floor.

Nello came up into the darkness and walked past me without a word. He pulled out his cigar stub, lit it, took two long drags, then blew a cloud of smoke into the moonlight.

"So. You gave sailing lessons to the Welsh girl. Right?" he said. "The one that knit my sweater?"

There was a lull in the laughter and I heard Hay's voice from below. He was talking about Indians and their artifacts, masks especially. Had Ernie heard of a Kwakiutl from way up coast—with a white squaw—passing through here in the last few days, loaded down with masks he might want to sell?

"You were right." I finally said. "About her paddling the canoe."

He was too angry to answer.

"Rolf saw them," I went on. "And you were right about them moving at night. They came out after dusk."

He sat down on the coaming and sucked on his cigar.

"Why didn't you tell him?" he said, blowing his smoke toward the open hatch.

"I don't know."

He picked up from the deck one of the lines he had whipped that afternoon, squeezed the dew out of it, then hung it on a spoke of the wheel. He stared at me hard. "You met her just once, right?"

When I didn't answer, he said, "It *is* her, isn't it?" He turned and spat a bit of tobacco in the sea. "I knew we were hexed, but I never thought this bad."

There was a huge thud from the houses, followed by laughter.

"It's not serious," I tried to assure him.

"Who are you kidding? I know you. For *you* even flippin' a flapjack is serious."

Lanterns began to go out in the bunkhouses and the night fell silent. Ernie swayed up the companionway ladder feeling no pain. "What a night, gentlemen, what a night. Lovely food, lovely company." Hay came up behind him. Ernie brimmed with gratitude; he wanted to host us for a Sunday breakfast with a real surprise here at the world's end, *genuine* maple syrup. Then he bade goodnight and walked home over the log booms with his unlit lantern creaking as it swung.

"What a beautiful moon," Hay said softly.

"Mr. Hay, we have some news," Nello said with as much calm as he could muster. "The lighthouse keeper thinks he saw your wife. Last night. After dusk. They were catching the tide."

Hay just stared in confusion.

"They were a distance away." I said. "And it was pretty dark. He might be guessing."

"Was she all right?"

"Seemed fine. Sitting up."

No one spoke for a while. Even the wind fell still.

"Thank God," Hay said at last.

10

Nightsail

It is lucky for children to be born at new moon. It is unlucky to be born at nighttime. Then they will not live long.

—Franz Boas

Lost in thought, Hay pulled out his pipe, struck a match to light it, but forgot to suck and the match burnt down and he threw it in the sea. He clambered over the lifeline down onto the logs and ambled away into the night.

Nello puffed hard on his cigar—I had never seen him take more than two drags at one lighting. From the bunkhouses came the sound of a fiddle playing a slow tune.

"Mr. Hay, sir," Nello called out firmly. "Please don't go too far."

"I'll be all right," Hay replied.

Nello looked at me, and when I didn't move, he snuffed out his cigar on the chainplate and, as the breeze scattered the sparks, said, "It isn't that, sir. It's just that we'll be setting sail any moment now."

I stared at him but he went on without looking up. "Because Captain Dugger has calculated that they're about twenty miles up ahead, and the captain thinks that if we don't catch them before Devil's Hole, the first set of big whirlpools, we might not be able to catch them at all before they reach their village. In that case, we might have a nasty problem on our hands. Isn't that what you said, Captain?"

I nodded in agreement. But he was crazy. To sail here at night! With the eastern strait littered with rocks and islands, and the waters full of deadheads that could hole a hull better than a rock.

"There is moonlight and a light breeze," Nello went on. "And the current is with us. Isn't that what you said, Captain?"

"Word for word."

Hay seemed suddenly clear-headed. "But shouldn't we have left hours ago?"

I began to say something but Nello's words came first. "The captain wanted to be sure the wind stayed up," he said. "And that the mist didn't return and block the moon. To sail safely, sir, we need good moonlight."

I sounded like a ventriloquists dummy. "Need moonlight."

Hay picked his way back toward the boat. Nello went forward and began untying the main.

The fiddle played and a voice sang along, "Midnight on the water, so steady and slow / Pour us another drink, set them up Joe."

With no lanterns lit and only the sails shedding moonlight, the ketch sliced across the sheet of silver sea. We had even gutted the lanterns down below and turned off the chime on the ship's clock because sound carries a long way over calm water. We spoke only when we had to. They might be just ahead; why alert them? The stern wake sighed below the transom, then shone long and white, bent northward by the current. Hard shadows lay on deck; the world was black and white except for the faint flame of the harbor-entrance lantern far behind.

To the west, Texada Island rose like a wall; to the east, snow-capped mountains shone white on an indigo sky. We were crossing the tide line with its trail of torn kelp and sea grass, and Nello went into the bow to watch for logs and deadheads up ahead. Hay sat in a corner of the cockpit holding his unlit pipe. There was no sea running, so our motion was slight, and he seemed all right, if a bit pale in the cold light. We were doing less than four knots, so we tacked often to stay in the middle of the strait and let the strongest part of current take us north. Once clear of the tide line, Nello came back to announce, "So far, so good."

My neck was tightening from staring hard ahead, or maybe it was the night air, or maybe nerves. Nello was right: I took things seriously. Too damned seriously. Had to learn to enjoy what I had: the wind, the moonlight, the ketch. If only she sailed faster. My mind had drifted and I had gone off course and pointed too high, luffing the sails. They slatted loudly until I fell off again.

"You have good eyes, Captain," Nello said, looking over the

side. "I wouldn't have seen that deadhead to save my life." I turned back and saw the round, dark shape bobbing in our wake. But it bobbed too much for a deadhead—it was just a flimsy sawn end of a log and Nello knew that. I took a deep breath.

The breeze stayed steady, bringing warm air from the land.

"Mr. Hay," Nello began. "After the Kwakiutl left your yacht, you didn't notice a piece of your clothing missing, did you?"

"No," Hay replied. "Why?"

"Because when we Kwakiutl want to hex somebody, bewitch 'em, we take a piece of his clothing, and some strands of hair."

"Yes," I said. "Have you counted your hair lately?"

"I'm afraid it's serious business, Captain."

"I quite agree," Hay piped in. "I studied many of Boas's field papers. Years he spent with the Kwakiutl; and witchcraft was the thing they feared most. If you were found out putting a spell on someone, you could be put to death. Isn't that so?"

"Sure is," Nello said. "At least in my village."

"Which was that?"

"Qa'logwis. Crooked Beach."

"I heard it's a beautiful area," Hay said wistfully. "Tiny islands in a gentle inland sea."

"Islands everywhere," Nello said, "Like a maze. Some are just rocks, some with a few twisted spruces, others a tangle of salal bushes so dense you can walk on them. Mist and rain, fall and winter." He paused. When he started up again it was like someone telling a story to a child.

"That's when the spirits come. And that's when your soul wanders off in the mist and you get sick. That's when a hex works best. If you go down to the water, you can sometimes coax it back inside. If not, a *pexala,* a shaman, comes and gets it back for you. Sometimes not. Then you die. Then we take you over to the little island across the way and lay you on the salal bushes."

He fell silent and stared at the waves. "Sorry. Didn't mean to bore you."

"On the contrary," Hay burst out so loudly I had to tell him to keep it down. "I am an anthropologist. I collect Indian objects not just to have them but because they tell stories. It's part of the science. But objects are only second-best story tellers, when there's no one left alive to tell them; nothing can replace an oral account. The most precious are personal stories. My respect for your people is profound; nothing fascinates me more than their stories." Then he added almost as an afterthought, "Even under the circumstances."

"Mine aren't what you call scientific material. Just stories."

"They might be that to you, but for me it could be a gold mine of information. Take one of your creation stories. They tell not only the mythology, but hidden in there is so much ethnography, from foods to clothes to habits."

"Well." Nello laughed. "I have one of those. Of our *na'mima*, our big house. *Na'mima* means 'one of a kind'—family—wives, kids, brothers, uncles, cousins. There were eight *na'mimas* in our village; our tribe. Our tribe was called Kwexa, Murderers. We had a bastard of a chief and one of the *na'mima* chiefs put a knife in his neck. The tribe broke up. Some moved away. We stayed. Some call us Kwe'xamut, Those Who Stayed After the Murder. Charming name.

"Anyway, each big house too has its own name, its own fishing grounds, hunting rights, berry grounds, and—believe it or not—its own creation story. Myth at the end of the world, we call it. I guess we mean the beginning end. Our name was Echo of the Woods and you'd never guess in a million years why.

"They say the Great Inventor had a beautiful stepdaughter—so of course he wanted to make love to her. He told her to prepare for a feast with a nice bath in the river. So off she goes, naked except for the tiny cedar apron between her legs. He ran into the woods and cut some yellow cedar—it sparks like hell—and set it by the fire. Come by the fire and dry yourself, Inventor called to her. She came and squatted and then he threw the yellow cedar in the flames. Well, sparks flew and her apron caught fire and burnt off the hair between her legs. Off she went, moaning, to her sleeping house, moaned all night that she was so hot she couldn't sleep. Inventor went to her and whispered, 'My dear, I know who can help you. He's called Echo of the Woods. You go and call his name and he'll answer back, "Yaa. Yaa." Like that. When you are near, be silent, just feel around. You'll recognize him from his magic member. You lie down on it and it will ease your pain.

"The girl went out into the woods and called, 'Oh, Great Echo.' 'Yaa. Yaa,' came the reply. When she found his member, she lay right on it and in the morning her mother found her in her bed sleeping like a baby. And from her were born the first people of our *na'mima*. Now, doesn't that beat some old guy breathing onto a lump of clay?"

Hay snickered with laughter. "That's the best creation story I ever heard. But you are half Italian. Catholic. What do you say about God creating man?"

"I say forgive and forget. I, for one, have forgiven Him. We all have our bad days, don't we, Cappy?"

"I wouldn't know," I said. "Lately all my days have been bad."

"Yaa. Yaa," Nello said, and got up. "Should we tack?"

We came about and the sails slatted and sprinkled us with dew. A light burst right behind me in the night.

"Dammit, Hay!" I hissed. "Put that thing out!!"

Hay froze, his face lit red by the clump of flaring matches he held above his pipe; but he kept the clump of matches flaming until his pipe was lit—then he threw them in the sea.

"I'm very sorry, Captain," he said. "I thought aiming the light behind us wouldn't do any harm."

"We don't know for sure where they are. No more matches. And no pipe. Please!"

Nello went forward and pretended to check the headsails. When he came back he sat and seemed to be studying Hay's face.

The moon shone clear in the middle of the sky. Nello sucked his cold cigar.

"Must have been a wonderful place to be a child. Your village," Hay said, trying to sound cheerful.

"It was okay," Nello said distractedly. "No one bothered us. We believe kids are relatives back from the dead. My mother called me 'Grandpa' because I could hold my breath underwater just like him and sink to the bottom like a rock.

"So we just played all day, or helped haul hot rocks to steam the sides of the canoes, carried boards, dug clams with the old women—it was all a game. In the summer for the salmon run, the grown-ups let us help build weirs across the rivers out of poles and twigs. Haul stones for the traps—dams, really, all shapes and sizes. The fish would swim into them at high tide, and at low tide they'd be high and dry. When the weather was good my big brother let me steer his canoe, hold it in the current, while he knelt in the bow and speared fish."

"Shhhh," I said. "Look at two o'clock!" and pointed at two small islands dark on the silvery sea. "A flame flared there just now. Who the hell is out here after midnight?"

"Fish boat, maybe," Nello said without conviction. "Anchored for the night."

"I'll check the chart," I said. Down below, I lit a lantern and held my hat over it to shield the light. The chart showed the water around the islands full of rocks; no boat could get in there, unless it was small, with very shoal draft. I blew out the lamp and sat in the darkness. They couldn't be this close. And why would they be so careless as to light a fire? Maybe they thought it safe so late at night. Or maybe they had to. Had to why? And why the hell would they have made less than ten miles since last night, unless something happened to them? Or to her? It was hard to breathe down there; I went above.

"It's all rocks in there," I said. "You can't get near those islands, unless . . . ." I didn't have to say more, Hay stared at me so hard I had to look away. "There's a reef this side of them. We'll drop the headsails and ghost. No anchor—the chain makes too much noise. You two handle the ketch. I'll row the skiff in."

"I'd like to come along, if you don't mind," Hay said, but he wasn't asking.

"I don't think—"

"She's *my* wife."

"Fine. But not a sound."

"Sailors say," Nello cut in, "that flames on the sea are an evil omen. A spell. They draw boats into waterspouts, onto reefs."

"St. Elmo's fire," Hay said. "Or *ignis fatuus*, fool's fire."

Nello went on as if he hadn't heard. "Some sailors say those ships came to a bad end all because the captain or helmsman who saw the flame was deranged to start with. Went and followed it and sailed the ship to its death."

"Barroom gossip," I grumbled, heading down the companionway. I unwrapped the Winchester from the oil-cloth and loaded three bullets. I didn't need more. I'd probably only get one shot.

When I went back up, Nello was on the foredeck silently lowering the jib. Hay held the wheel. He froze when he saw the gun. "What's that for?"

"I don't speak Kwakiutl," I said, and took the wheel from him because he had almost brought us into irons. I fell off and headed for the islands. When Nello came back and he saw the gun leaning in a corner, he looked silently at me. His eyes said nothing. With only the main up, we had slowed—we were less than a quarter mile from the rocks.

"Another thing us kids used to do," Nello said in a hard whisper, "was to try and help people who had been hexed. My brother had a woman almost kill him. Didn't mean to, just wanted him so bad. We would be out fishing, then he'd suddenly get the shakes and say "I gotta go," And he went. She lived at Gilford Island, a good ten miles, and he'd paddle his canoe as if the devil had him by the balls, then he'd run across the island through the salal, sweating and bleeding, and he'd grab her and off they rushed to do the work. He'd stay a few days, then come back and fish. Then, wham, off again. He was down to skin and bones. Our aunt lived in the woman's village and spied on her. One day when she went swimming, the aunt went through her clothes and found it. Tiny, wrapped up tight in the belt of her skirt. Our aunt ran home and put it in water to take it apart, otherwise the spell might have killed him. It was all wrapped in hair—his and hers—and there were two clay figures inside: a man and a woman. She had her tongue in his mouth and he had his pecker inside her. With great care, the aunt took them apart and threw her in the fire and sank him in the sea. My brother never thought of her again."

"He had some good times, though, didn't he," I snapped.

We were so close in, I swear I felt the reef rising below us. I signaled for Hay to take the wheel.

We lowered the skiff stern first over the rail and Nello handed down the oars and rifle. He held on to the rifle and pulled me so close his face almost touched mine. "Be careful," he whispered. "Something's up."

"I know," I hissed. "We're hexed."

"Hexed, I don't know. *Him*, I do." He jerked his head toward the companionway. "A bonfire to light a pipe?"

Hay neared and Nello pulled away. We pushed off.

I rowed in short, even strokes to keep the oars from banging the gunwale. The ketch began to melt into the darkness. As I glanced over my shoulder at the islands, a fish jumped with a loud splash behind us, and Hay, turning to look, slid to one side, nearly tipping us over. I had to grab him to keep him from falling overboard.

"Sorry," he whispered.

I rowed on. How suddenly life could change at sea. All the way to death. A roll of the skiff, a helping hand a bit too slow in coming, and another name struck from the ranks of the living. Who would miss him? How badly? And who knows; he might just be glad to go.

A shadow of panic raced across Hay's face and he grabbed inside his coat and yanked a silver flask into the moonlight, untwisted the cap, and took a slug. Then, smiling dumbly at me, he whispered in an absurdly casual tone, "Do you hunt?"

"Only people," I said, and concentrated on keeping the oars from splashing. I pulled hard, held, glided. The wind lulled and the night was so still I could hear the droplets from the oars splash into the sea—they left ringlets of phosphorescence on the black water.

I had just broken a sweat when I saw the flame. It flared for an instant, then vanished, but I had the spot marked—a saddle on the larger island. "Hold these and don't breathe." I cocked the Winchester as gently as I could, but it still made an awful racket. Laying it across my knees, I took back the oars and did a silent pull. Pull, glide, pull, glide, when something grabbed the blades of the oars. The kelp undulated in the swells with a sickly motion; the long stipes trapped the oars—we stood still. I handed the Winchester to Hay, had him hold one oar out of the water, then I knelt in the bow to push and pole my way ahead.

With his free hand, Hay grabbed the stipes and pulled. We both strained hard but it was the current that pushed us free.

I stayed in the bow and paddled. We slipped through the pass suddenly into darkness—the shadow of the islands. There was no telling black island from black water. We drifted. I turned back toward Hay to signal for perfect silence but I couldn't see him in the dark. Somewhere up ahead I heard a voice, low, guttural, Indian. I lowered the blade into the water and pulled, making phosphorescence but no sound. Something splashed ahead. I froze. My left leg cramped. Nerves. I looked back, but if Hay was still there, he sure as hell didn't stir. "The gun," I whispered. The steel was slippery with sweat; I was wiping it with my shirt when, with a great crunch, we hit and the Winchester went off with a deafening blast. Flames filled the night, and there, lit by the fire that burned on a pile of sand in its bow, was the canoe. An old Indian woman—her terrified face contorted—held a long-handled fishing net with a bullet-splattered wild-goose in it. A soaked cedar basket, which must have covered the fire, lay on its side. Bobbing on the waves, blinded by the firelight, a flock of wild geese stretched their gangly necks. In the stern sat an old Indian with an immobile face and calm eyes, eyes that had seen so much that nothing more surprised them in this stupid world.

KATE
Sleep

During the days I sleep. I lie on the pebbles of some hidden cove covered by hemlock branches he puts on me to hide me, not to warm me. And I sleep. Not right off. I peek out at the water, hoping to see your boat coming to save me. The young one goes down to the shore to do his voodoo. He strips naked. Walks in the water. I don't know how he does it because the water is like ice. He pees in his hand and then rubs it on his arms and legs, chest and back, then goes in up to his waist and stands there. He rubs himself with a hemlock branch chanting softly something like qeqale and selwaka.

Then he whips himself with the branch of evergreen across the back. The needles make a sound shiiyupp, shiiyupp, on and on. He bleeds. Red streaks run on his dark skin. He stands and whips on and on until I can't watch anymore. I sleep.

11

Racing North

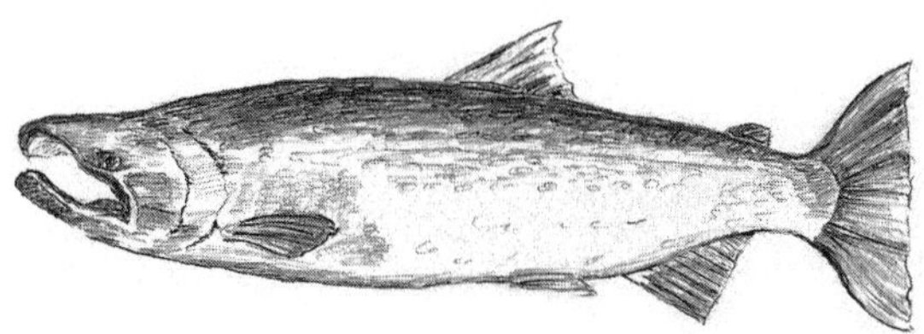

> I measured and described the skull which I had stolen and made arrangements . . . to return to the graveyard in order to obtain one or two additional skeletons. I have three skeletons, without heads . . . . Besides having scientific value these skeletons are worth money.
>
> —Franz Boas

The ketch came tacking back and forth across the moonlight. Hay emptied his flask and began to hum a Christmas carol. When close in, Nello swung the ketch upwind, and as we drifted up he called out, "Who the hell got shot?"

"A duck." Hay snorted drunkenly.

The moon beamed down a broad smile—or maybe outright laughter.

While we hauled the skiff aboard, Hay told the story.

"Jesus, I forgot about them," Nello said. "Old-time goose hunters. They blind them with the flames, then throw a net over them."

Hay laughed, made the dumb remark about a wild-goose chase, wished us goodnight, and clattered off to bed.

I took the helm. We'd lost almost an hour.

"Then there was poor old Pike," Nello said forcefully. "He paid five dollars to a Scotsman for his name. He had wanted a longer one, like O'Shaughnessy, but the Irishman wanted ten, so ol' Pike just got Pike. One day he and his wife got sick. Their heads wobbled. No strength. Burning up during the day, shivering at night. Some kids found a dead man wedged between two rocks, so the sun boiled him during the day and the wind from the ice fields froze him at night. His mouth, ears, nose, even his asshole, were all sealed up with pitch. So they lowered him into the water and scraped the pitch out of him, and found bits of Pike's hair all rolled up, and a piece of his shirt, and a piece of his wife's skirt. They washed the dead guy out, then let him drift off in the current. When they brought all that stuff to Pike, he was already feeling better. But it was too late for his wife; she died that morning." He trimmed the jib but the wind kept veering. "Hexed."

WE STOOD TWO-HOUR watches through the night. Off watch, I

slept below, but Nello just bundled up against the house with his collar so high only the top of his head showed, and snored.

By my second watch, the moon had set behind the big island and I stared into the dark and tried hard not to listen to the sounds. They can drive you mad when you're sailing in the dark, when the hiss of the bow wake becomes sighs of the long-drowned, and the *whoosh* of the stern wake whispers memories. And, if you stare long enough, the sails become ghostly faces. I closed my eyes and drifted. I smelled her skin, felt her warmth, felt her small breasts, the long hollow behind her knee, the softness of her thigh; heard her whisper, "Damn you." I had lost sense of the wheel when I heard Nello stir. He sat upright, face drawn, and said in a hushed voice, "What the hell is that?"

I heard only the sounds of the sea.

"You hear it, Cappy?" he insisted with the agitation of one just shaken from a dream.

"I only hear you."

He cupped a hand over his ear but there was only the sound of the wakes, and the occasional groan of ropes tightening in blocks as we rode gently over swells. Nello hung his head over the windward side, listening, then he crossed to leeward and did the same. "It's behind us," he said.

"What is?"

"Good question." He turned his head back and forth to center the sound, stared, shaded his eyes with his hands to block out the compass light and what little light drifted down from the sky. "How come I don't see a fucking thing?" and he went below. When he came back up, he looked gloomier than before. "I thought so. A big boat with a noisy propeller."

"I don't hear a thing," I said. "You sure you're not still dreaming?"

"I had my ear against the hull."

Near the big island the wind eased and, in the now-calmer air, I finally heard it too. Over the soft sounds of the night rose a low thudding: faint, far away, ebbing and flowing as the wind rose and fell. And nearing.

"A big boat with no lights," he said. "Why?" And he stared at me as if I should know.

"Maybe he's saving kerosene."

"Or he's sneaking up on someone. Like we are."

"With that engine?"

"He can't do much about that if he has no sails, can he?"

"What are you getting at?"

"Him." He pointed violently down the companionway. "I don't like him."

"I don't exactly love him either, but so what?"

"Did you ever meet him?"

"Who?"

"Hay."

"You kidding me? He's been here all day!"

"I mean before. Did you ever meet him with his wife, or his captain, or the guy who wipes his boots?"

"What *are* you getting at?"

"Just wondering what he was like with other people around: honest, sneaky, what?"

We were in the deepest shadow of the island, sailing blind, so we came about and settled onto a long tack pointing at the snowy peaks. He went below, rummaged, then came back up with the Winchester and sat in his corner. "I see it," he said, and pointed south.

Far behind us, at the tip of the big island, in the last spill of moonlight, a small black mass, strangely shaped, darkened the sea. It headed west toward the island's tip, then vanished. Whether it went behind the island or just into its shadow I couldn't tell, not until the thudding of its engine died away.

"Whoever they're sneaking up on, it sure isn't us," I said, "because they just rounded the point. They're going on the other side."

Nello stared at the spot the strange craft had just deserted.

"The Dutchman," he blurted. "You remember. The scavenger. The one the bear ate. Had that ugly, tacked-together tug with the cabin higher than the pilothouse. I swear it's him."

I remembered the Dutchman. I had seen him in beerparlors or on the docks trolling for jobs. A stump of a man, but ferocious. Big ears, squinty eyes, a wiry mustache, and pipe he bit down on with as much determination as others would a bullet. He had this sweater, standard seaman's thing, but with huge holes in its left shoulder and left sleeve. They said he'd been mauled by a bear, and he always kept his head down, eyes fixed ahead, as if ready for its next charge. He made friends with everyone, then he'd cut them to the bone with some vicious remark. His old tug was patched with staves and steel plates. He log-salvaged some, scavenged some; hauled old derelicts down from up coast and cut them up for scrap. Never lasted at anything. Except that sweater.

"Anyway. You're right, Cappy, they aren't following us. Sorry I got you all worried." He was silent for a while, and just when I thought he'd gone to sleep he said, "Cappy. Let's say you were following a boat on the sly. What would you do?"

"First I'd kill you to get some peace."

He flashed his teeth. "And then?"

"Then I would do precisely what that son of a bitch is doing."

"What?" Turn off your lights?"

"Yeah."

"And?"

"Then I'd go on the other goddamn side of the goddamn island. That's what you want to hear, isn't it?"

"I want to hear your opinion, is all."

"How can someone follow us if they're not behind us?"

"What's it matter as long as they know where we're going?"

"How can *they* know where we're going? *We* don't know

where we're going."

"Don't ask me. I didn't signal pretending to light my pipe."

We tacked at the mouth of an inlet that wound east for forty miles among the mountains to a thundering waterfall that some Indians thought was the door to eternal life; others of them just went there because the fishing was good. The air was colder here—the water came from fields of ice. We headed north.

The night passed. I was gazing at the phosphorescence streaming in the stern wake when Nello touched my shoulder. "My watch," he said. I went down to my berth but didn't really sleep; just lay half awake and talked to her.

I awoke to the sound of the stove lid sliding in the galley. Wood smoke, the smell of coffee, and a sleepy light filled the ketch; Charlie was frying tomatoes. Nello stood at the helm, the steam from his coffee mug misting past his face.

"Morning, Cappy. Glad you're up," he said.

The sky was clear with no mare's tails in the west, so the wind would last at least another day. We had made good time, the tip of the big island lay on our port quarter, and if we didn't make much leeway we could clear it and run the tack another mile.

"Cappy, I've been thinking," Nello began as he lay the chart on deck, putting the mainsheet over it to keep it down in the wind. "Past that flat island is a big shoal full of rocks. We can stay close to the mainland but there are no coves, no inlets, nowhere to hide, so if I were them I sure as hell wouldn't stop anywhere there. Not until I got here." And he pointed at a maze of broken water. Inlets, sounds, channels, and reaches wound among islands of every shape and size, with rocks that dried only at low water, and rocks that—even then—lay just below the surface, that you'd never notice until your keel hit them. It looked as if someone had torn a chart to pieces, thrown the bits atop one another, and written over it, *Desolation Sound.* Fathom marks were rare and there were no contour marks on the land. When Captain Vancouver charted these waters in 1792, he had written in his log that he hated this dark, dismal place more than any in the world. It showed in his charting. And no one had bothered to chart it much more since. North of Desolation Sound the land and islands were marked with broken lines as warning that they were only approximations. Uncharted. The North.

"Once they're here, they'll feel safe," Nello said, and poked his finger at a string of islands. *Ragged Islands*, the chart said. "He could play hide and seek there with us until our teeth fell out."

The sun rose without warmth over the mountains.

Charlie came up the companionway, balancing steaming plates of the fried tomatoes, bacon and eggs, and fried bread. He stayed to watch us eat.

"We could follow them inside those islands," Nello said. "But if they see us they might get scared off and hide, and that would be that. But if we don't follow them—"

"Just let them go?"

"No. We head them off. We go outside around all the shoals and the islands, sail like hell in open water, long tacks, no worries, and don't come back in until we're here," and he pointed to a narrow pass between the northern tip of a dogleg island and a place called Reef Point. "Then we reach over to the north end of the Ragged Islands, drop anchor, catch some fish, and have dinner ready for the buggers when they come up the pass. It's only a stone's throw wide. Can't miss them." When he saw I wasn't convinced, he added in a whisper, "You might just have her aboard tonight. Ah, good morning to you Mr. Hay," he said boisterously. "Slept well, I trust?"

Hay came up the companionway ladder, blinking into the sun, and plunked himself down. Charlie brought his breakfast and cleared away our plates the moment we were done.

He worked without pause, was as enthusiastic as hell, and he worshipped Nello. When his chores were done, the galley spotless, he would come on deck and watch his every move. Nello didn't mind, in fact seemed to cherish playing the caring dad, showing him how to trim sail, how to read the waves and the wind in the telltales. And Charlie would nod his head, seeming to get it all. I was convinced that the little bugger didn't understand a word until the bowline. But that came a bit later; for now he hauled the dishes below.

We headed into open water.

The wind rose and whitecaps danced in the climbing sun, when a stiff gust hit and we heeled hard and everything clattered in the galley.

"You okay, Charlie?" Nello shouted down.

"Charlie okay," the kid said happily.

We beat hard, long tacks, and by noon had logged thirty miles.

Hay spent the morning in the cockpit studying the coast with binoculars. He asked questions about sailing in general, and this place in particular, so I showed him on the chart where we were headed, explaining why. I left out the possibility that his wife might be aboard tonight. He thanked me, then he went and took up his customary post with his back against the mast, and stared motionless at the emptiness ahead.

Off to the west, a salmon leapt in desperate flight. It hung for a moment in the air, a thousand tiny mirrors in the sun, then fell back. Into the spreading rings it left behind, a porpoise burst, blew, and then dove to give chase. It didn't need to hurry. Much faster than the salmon, it would swim from side to side, guiding and herding its prey toward the shallows of a cove whence there was no flight. Confident and engrossed in the chase, the porpoise never noticed the killer whales closing in behind. It was a small herd, maybe five, a few females and an old male trailing, with a tall fin whose tip hung folded down.

The porpoise vanished. The salmon jumped one last time when the old killer whale signaled with a splash, and two of his herd shot forward, throwing swells. The porpoise now made a final leap, but fell between the killer whales, and the water turned a foamy red. The herd stopped in an arc and seemed to take turns tearing it to shreds. We didn't see the salmon again; he must have sensed his escape and made off toward the deep.

Charlie had watched it all and now stood shivering beside me.

Nello yanked a piece of line from the lazarette, grabbed him by the arm as if to shake off what he'd just seen, and said, "C'mon, Charlie, I'm gonna make you a *real* sailor. Teach you the bowline. The most important knot. You can tie it with one hand and untie it with a thumb." He wound the line around the base of the mizzen, talking all the while. "First you make a loop we call the hole, then you take the end of the line, that's the fox, and he comes up the hole, around the tree, and down the hole. You savvy, Charlie?" And then he untied the knot with a flick of the thumb and handed him the line.

Charlie took the line cautiously as if it were a snake, held it waiting for some miracle to come and tie it for him, glanced back to where the killer whales were feeding, then with a couple of soft Chinese words handed Nello back the line. Nello tied it again, slowly, patiently. "Okay, now. You try. Step one. Make the hole."

Charlie looked at him, took the line, whipped it around the mizzen, bent the loop, shot the bitter end around the tail, then down the hole, and made the most perfect goddamn bowline you ever set eyes on. "Charlie okay?" he asked nervously. Nello looked at me, looked at the knot, looked at the kid. Finally he said something in Italian or Kwakiutl, then came back to the wheel and told me to have a rest; he was anxious to steer again.

Hay, who had been watching all this, shook his head. "It would take me a year to learn that," he said.

"It took me two," I said.

Charlie kept tying bowlines like there was no tomorrow.

The wind picked up some more. By midafternoon the rail was steadily under foam, the ketch struggling, so I let the main off some until a counter-curve billowed at the head, then the ketch stood up and plowed firmly through the seas.

We were coming up on the dogleg island—the cut was still a few miles ahead. I went below, washed up and shaved just in case, as nervous as a kid. When I went back up, Nello smiled. "You got it bad, Cappy."

"Because I shaved?"

"No. Because you look bewildered."

I wandered around the deck, checking blocks and leads that didn't need to be checked, made sure the anchor was lashed, gazed at the sails as if there were something there to see. To calm myself, I sat down in the cockpit and studied the chart without seeing a thing. When I finally looked up, I had no idea where we were. If I'd been at the helm we would have been on the rocks.

12

Under the Kelp

They are doomed to extinction . . . . At almost every gathering, where chiefs or leading men speak, this sad, haunting belief is sure to be referred to.

—James Teit (1910)

Rocks littered the glittering sea ahead, their size and distance impossible to tell. They vanished behind waves, rose, loomed, then, as if falling backward, disappeared again. To starboard, the sandy tip of the island shoaled and the water paled with silt. Nello studied the chart as if trying to memorize each fathom mark, then he went to sound the bottom with the lead line but the speed of the ketch, the slant of the line, and the deep, hard pitching of the bow made it impossible to feel when the lead touched bottom. The wind rose; we pitched more. He coiled the line and went below, and plotted course lines on the chart.

The heaves and wallows of the hollow seas were much too much for Hay. He lay limply behind me on the narrow aft deck, where I told him he'd feel the least motion, lay there pale, eyes closed, looking ready for the grave.

We sledded down one wave and slammed into the next, and the ketch yawed and green water surged on deck. Hay, lying athwartships with his head high, on the windward side, had one foot wedged between the cockpit coaming and the toerail; other than that, he was free. Spray washed over us. The varnished toerails were as slippery as ice. I quietly cranked the winches, tightened the genny, then the main. The ketch pointed sharply into the wind and heeled some more. The rail stayed under. We slammed into a wave so hard the ship's bell rang and the whole ketch shuddered. I fell off a bit to pick up speed so I could bring her over quicker. We plunged, then hit with such a slam I thought I'd pop the masts right out of her. The decks were awash; the air dense with spray.

I spun the wheel.

The ketch stood suddenly upright, swung violently to starboard, and, with the genny still sheeted tight, she went down on her other side, burying the rail, and Hay—now nearly upside down—began sliding headfirst, flailing but grabbing nothing, steadily overboard into the churning sea. I lunged for the genny sheet to try to free it but we were already too far over and Hay kept going down. His head skimmed the waves, his left hand tried in vain to grip the rail, and his right reached up as if trying to catch a cloud. He never uttered a sound. Just kept sliding down—then was gone. In the cold water, he'd be dead in twenty minutes.

I released the genny and was sheeting it in starboard when the life ring flew by my head and then Nello was on the bridge deck yelling, "Charlie! Get up here! Charlie!" He lunged to release the sheets while pointing at the dark receding speck, that kept vanishing in the heaving, blinding sea. "For chrissake, Cappy! Turn back!"

Charlie came as best he could up the viciously heeled ladder, his feet catching the sides more often than the rungs. Nello raised Charlie's arm and pointed it at the dark speck.

"Point, Charlie! Point! No matter how the boat turns, point, 'cause once we lose him, we won't find him again."

I grabbed Nello's shoulder and spun him around. "What the hell are you doing?" I hissed.

The ketch teetered on a wave, then tumbled down into a trough, and we scrambled for footing. "I'm saving your fucking life."

"Who would convict me?" I retorted.

He looked at me. "Untie the rope ladder, would you," he said.

He pushed me aside, turned the wheel, eased out the genny and main, and the ketch turned slowly downwind, south, and now sailed on her bottom toward the distant speck.

With the waves on the stern quarter pushing the keel about, we slipped and rolled like a drunk on a greased floor, the genny collapsing, the main boom pumping, and all the while we hurtled violently ahead. The speck grew. It was a while before I could make out Hay's head and the life ring right beside it.

We had to swing west and loop around so as not to run him down. We threw off all sheets and let the sails rattle, and the ketch stopped broadside to the wind. We drifted down on him. Acting as a breakwater, the ketch smoothed the seas between us. Hay bobbed, his face contorted from the cold. He was slipping away.

Nello loosened the spare halyard from the mainmast, cleared it past the shrouds, unlashed the rope ladder, and kicked it overboard. "He'll never climb up on his own," he said. "I'll go get him." We were less than a boat-length from Hay. If we missed fishing him out, we'd run over him and drown him.

I took the halyard out of Nello's hand. "I got him in there," I said. And without letting him answer, I kicked off my boots and jumped in. The heat trapped in my clothes kept the cold away for now but I had to hurry. I swam to Hay. His grip was frozen on the life ring. I wasn't sure he was alive. I slipped the halyard under both his arms—he didn't seem to notice. The ketch loomed over us. I felt the halyard tighten and grabbed the rope ladder and, as they pulled, I pushed Hay, stiff and waterlogged, up along the side. My teeth chattered and my foot cramped. Then my right hand cramped. I tried to shake out the cramps but I was shivering too hard; my grip slipped on the ladder. The ketch rolled hard and its bilge pushed me under. Then the ladder pulled me up. "C'mon, Cappy!" I heard Nello roar. "Hang on!" But we rolled and the bilge pushed me under again.

The harder I gripped, the worse the cramps got, and my hold slowly loosened. The ketch was crushing me.

There were no more sounds. I let go of the rope.

I saw clouds like angel wings spread across the sky. In between them, so close I could touch it, was the face of a cherub smiling a gentle smile. "Cappy," said the cherub softly, "Cappy." Then something crushed my chest and I coughed up sea water, the echo bouncing down from the sails. Charlie leaned over me. Nello crushed my chest again and I coughed some more but this time there was no water, so he pulled me up and leaned me against the cabin. Charlie wrapped a blanket around me. Hay lay nearby on the deck, barely breathing.

The sun was behind us; we were heading for the pass again. I shivered myself warm in the sun. Once we were inside the islands, the wind eased, the sea calmed, and we sailed smooth and upright as if in a lake. A warm balsam fragrance drifted down from the forests below the snow line.

When Hay was breathing better, I told him to go below and put on some dry clothes. He stopped in the companionway, turned to me sheepishly, and said, "Thank you."

"Skipper's duty," I managed to reply.

We dropped anchor in the lee of a lone islet just north of the Ragged Islands. The peninsula rose stark, steep, and featureless—except for a slender waterfall sparkling in the sun. This was the tip of the funnel; if the Kwakiutls took the best course home, they'd have to pass between the cliff and us.

Nello launched the skiff, saying he wanted to wash the salt out of the clothes under the falls. He took Charlie and the soaked pile, and a fishing pole to do a little jigging, and the rifle, just in case, he said, they tripped over a goat. They pushed off.

"Okay, Charlie," Nello's voice came drifting back. "Now I'm gonna teach you how to row." And they glided across the waters with oars clattering and Nello scolding and the skiff trailing a snaking wake behind it.

Hay, in his dry clothes, slept on the foredeck. I studied with binoculars the waters north and west, and the whole chain of islands right from the southern tip, nook by nook, up to the last island near us. There was nothing—no movement, no canoe.

At midafternoon they fished back and forth off the rocky tip of the northernmost Ragged Islands. Nello was showing Charlie how to jig in the confused waters of the current, where the fish lose all their bearings and snap excitedly at anything that moves.

It seemed they had caught something big, because I saw Nello lean back hard and bend the pole, the skiff tipping from his movements. He pushed Charlie down to get more room or to steady the boat, or to keep him from getting snagged as he brought in the fish. But the fish must have thrown the hook, because the pole went suddenly straight, and Nello sat down in a hurry.

They rowed slowly back and pulled alongside the ketch without a word. Nello helped Charlie aboard, handed up the clothes, but he kept the pole and the rifle, and he said with a forced calm, "Could I have another lure, Cappy? They're biting like crazy there." I got a lure and handed it down but, instead of taking it, he took my wrist and said so loud even Hay could hear him, "Why don't you come and bring the boat hook, in case we land a big one?" He glared at me and motioned me to silence. I felt myself go cold in the warm sun. Don't know why. Just didn't like the look in his eyes. I clambered down. He rowed.

"You start a fire, Charlie," Nello shouted back. "We bring back nice big fish."

We moved in silence until we were out of range. He looked around worriedly.

"Did you see anything?" he asked.

"Nothing. Why?"

He didn't answer, just gave some hard pulls toward the island.

We were half-way there when he looked at me and asked, "What color is her hair?"

"Auburn."

"Nice," he said.

At the spot where they had fished, he eased the skiff along the edge of the kelp bed that ringed the island's tip, keeping watch over the side into the deep. Suddenly he stopped the skiff with the oars, turned it broadside to the wind, and created smooth water in its lee. The oar dripped, making rings, blurring the surface, so he shipped it and waited until the rings disappeared. Then he stared down. I looked down too but saw only kelp undulating in the current.

"I've never fished like this before," I said.

"Me neither," he said. He took both his oars from the locks, floated them in a V to stop the few ripples that the breeze sent across the water, then lowered his face almost to the surface.

"Cappy," he said solemnly. "We missed them. I can't figure out how, but we did. They must have passed this morning. At low tide."

"How do you know?"

"They left something." He straightened up. "How many people know we're up here?"

"I don't know. Hay swore that no one knew. Chow knows."

"If Chow knows, all China knows."

"He would never tell."

"Convince *him* of that," he said, and pointed past the guwale into the deep.

I leaned down and cupped my hands around my eyes to cut the light and slowly, slowly they adjusted to the dark.

The tip of the island was a long tongue of pale smooth granite, marked only by some gullies filled with crab claws and broken shells. The tide was in and even though the granite lay under six feet of water, its paleness lit the bottom of the sea. Both sides of the granite dropped rapidly away. On its slopes, near the low-tide line, grew forests of bottle kelp with their broad, brown leaves rippling on long tubers, waving like a drowned-maiden's hair in the lazy current. And there, in a broad cleft, as evenly carved as the sides of a throne, sat a half-naked figure. His head bobbed lightly as if keeping rhythm with the tide and his long black hair streamed with the kelp. His arms were extended as if he were trying to get up but he couldn't, because on his legs and propped against his chest, with a rope passing over it and around his limbs, was tied an enormous boulder. His shoulders were powerful Indian shoulders. The hook and flasher glittered in his arm.

I looked at Nello but he wouldn't look up. He thrust the boat hook deep into the water and hooked it under the rope that held the boulder.

"He hasn't been there long," he said. "The crabs haven't found him yet."

Around the sitter, the water was empty; only a few shiners darted between his arms.

"A hell of a boulder," he said. "Whoever put it there sure didn't do it alone . . . . Hold this tight, would you, Cappy?" He handed me the boat hook. Then he undressed and slipped quickly over the side. I felt the pole sway as he pulled himself down.

I looked around. The sound was empty. Only the ketch lay peacefully at anchor, a tuft of smoke rising then drifting slowly south.

Nello's head broke the surface. He slung his arms over the gunwale and hung there, catching his breath. His face was twisted from the cold.

"Its him." He shivered. "The old man in the picture."

He let go of the gunwale and the water closed over him.

The sun was low; the wind had died and the water was so calm, the reflections so still, that it seemed nothing could ever happen in the world. Only the current whispered as it hurried along the shore.

Nello burst out behind the stern and I helped him into the skiff. His teeth chattered. "Good shot . . . forehead . . . damned good." He climbed, shivering, into his clothes.

A breath of wind passed over the water and the reflections blurred, and below the surface the kelp fronds and the sitter disappeared.

The sun settled blood red beyond the islands.

Nello rowed to get warm but took his time. He pulled, then let the skiff glide.

"He'll want a pillow," he finally said.

"Who?"

"The one that's still alive. For him," and he nodded toward the dead man in the sea.

He held the oars and stared at them as if he'd never seen them in his life. When he spoke, his voice trembled. "Cappy," he said, then held his breath.

We sat there, saying nothing. Then he lowered the oars gently into the water. "When a Kwakiutl is killed, he has to have . . . a 'pillow.' Another dead man for him to lie on. To comfort him. Anyone will do. Friend or foe. Anyone. Nearby." He pulled and I watched him stir a ring of eddies. "Some even kill themselves. But I don't think he's the type."

Somewhere near the islands a seal chasing a fish slammed the water with its tail, and the sound echoed like a shot from the cliff behind us.

13

Stars

If a warrior sat with his legs stretched out, nobody was allowed to step over them, because this would take away his strength. The beds of warriors were on a high platform so that nobody could step over them. After a warrior had killed several enemies, he was allowed to wear grizzly bear claws on a headdress.

—Franz Boas

"Damn!" Nello hissed, and dug the oars into the water and held them still. The skiff stopped. "I promised the kid a fish." And he spun us around, rowed back to the edge of the kelp, dropped the weighted hook over the side, and jigged. On the third stroke, he caught a good-sized snapper. It writhed and thrashed on the floorboards until I took the boat hook and drove the bronze end through its skull. The fish shook. I twisted the hook until it lay still. Nello rowed, but kept looking at the blood spreading on the floorboards and filling the white around the eye.

"You don't mind killing, do you, Cappy?" he said sadly, and gave the oars a pull.

"When I have to," I said.

The evening darkened. Even the soft squeak of the oarlocks seemed an affront to the silence.

"You'd kill me too, wouldn't you? If you *had* to." He smiled. "For a woman you barely know."

I yanked out the boat hook and trailed it in the water. "Sorry," I said. "Nothing would make me happier than to forget her."

The smell of alder smoke drifted over from the ketch. She looked small and forlorn in that empty immensity. Her smoke seemed a plea in all that desolation. Twilight had erased all depth between the islands; they formed a relentless ring of darkness around the still luminous sea. In the north, where night had already fallen, the mountains stood solemn and indifferent to the descending gloom.

We ate the roast fish in the cockpit without speaking. From the dark, wooded slopes, the howl of a timber wolf rose guttural and deep, a melancholy sound but somehow comforting in all this emptiness.

Charlie washed the dishes down below, placing things gently without a sound. Nello lit his cigar stub, and the flame of the match lit his angry eyes.

"Mr. Hay," he began softly, but with a tone of menace that was impossible to miss. "Excuse me for prying, but I'm afraid our lives—and your wife's—may be hanging on the line. How many people know why we are up here?" and he sucked hard on the stub so the glow threw light on Hay. There seemed to be no reaction on Hay's face, and when he spoke his voice was calm, as if he had been ready for this question for some time.

"Very few. But why?"

"Because someone followed us. They followed us, then, when they saw us last night in the strait, they went around the outside—in the gulf—and passed us. And beat us here. There are traces on the island. Unmistakable traces, fresh from this morning."

He struck another match and put it next to some others. When they flared together, he held them up. He held them until they burnt down, then he threw them overboard, plunging us into darkness. It was much too dark to see if Hay had flinched, but I heard his ring knock against the deck.

"So who knew besides you?" I insisted before he had a chance to settle down.

"Only Hopkins," he said. "And he was sworn to secrecy."

"And your crew."

"And the Kwakiutls," Nello said. "But I don't think they went and bragged about it."

"Can Hopkins be trusted?" I asked.

"For what he's being paid—more than you can imagine, *just* for insurance—I can assure you he'll stay silent."

"Yes, of course. I forgot, you and insurance."

"So if no one knew," Nello said, "who the hell is up here?"

"What makes you think they have anything to do with us?"

"Because last night an unlit old junker passed us. And this morning, here in the middle of nowhere—right on the path that anyone could figure they'd be on—one of the Kwakiutl who took your wife is dead. Shot clean between the eyes, then hidden underwater."

This time Hay didn't even rustle.

"Look, Hay," I snapped. "We'll never find your wife if someone buggers up things ahead of us."

"Maybe the crew," he finally pleaded. "At a bar. I'm sure Mr.—" He caught himself. "Maybe the crew."

"Mr. Hay," Nello cut in calmly. "We can't defend ourselves unless we know what we're up against."

"Mother of God," I blew up. "One of your crew is short a head, I almost blasted an old squaw to kingdom come, and now there's a Kwakiutl playing fish food. This is a fucking slaughterhouse. And if you don't help us and she is killed, I swear to Christ—" but Nello cut me off.

"Try hard, Mr. Hay. Come up with something. Like who the hell this 'Mister' is you just mentioned."

It took Hay a long moment to find an answer, and when he spoke his bland piety was shocking. "There are some things in life whose explanation would serve no purpose. That should, in fact, for the good of all, remain unexplained. So things can go on in an orderly fashion. But I promise you that—as far as I know—no one, besides those mentioned, knows that we are here."

The night fell silent. Even the murmur of the current against the island had ceased. Nello sucked hard on the stub, blew out a cloud, and flicked the embers over the side.

"We better go," he said. "The tide's turned." He got up and started forward. "It's no longer against us. The rest of the world might be; but at least not the tide." He freed the main halyard, hoisted the sail, then he went to the foredeck and pumped the windlass back and forth. The chain clattered over the gypsy with a belligerent sound, an attack, on the vast peace of the night.

We sailed out the anchor on a breeze so light the water kept its sheen, so light I could barely feel it on the back of my neck. Across the sound, keeping the boomed-out mainsail full, we ghosted. To the west the islands rose like dark stairs to the sky, to the east the sound vanished under peaks of starlit snow.

Nello brushed by me in the cockpit, went below to study the chart under a wan flame. At last, he folded it carefully in four and slipped it in the drawer. He turned down the wick and blew out the flame, said pleasant dreams to Charlie, then came up. He leaned on the mizzen shroud and took a deep breath—as if something had been resolved, a worry lifted from his mind.

Hay picked himself up and said he was turning in.

When all was still below, Nello spoke so softly it startled me. "Well, that's that, Cappy," he said. "We're on our own. We've sailed off the chart."

The wolf howled again, but now very far behind.

I smiled. "Good. Now we don't have to worry about all their rocks and shoals. We just sail and if we hit, we hit."

"Just be careful," Nello said. "Or you'll run into a mountain."

There was no use lighting the compass light; I just steered by the path of stars that hung between the islands.

"How far to his village?" I said.

"A hundred miles. Maybe more."

"Good luck to us," I said.

The night was still. The ketch moved ahead but her wake was so slight it didn't make a sound. Far, far away there was a murmur or a sigh; a puff of wind in the trees, or the current against the shore. The sails stayed full without a flutter, and the current moved us north—where the dead man had pointed. There was a soft thud as Nello vanged the main boom down to the starboard rail to keep it from gybing, and put the reaching pole out with the genny to port.

The mountains closed in. The shore rose on both sides enormous and dark, and by some trick of the eye, the stars above them grew ever denser and brighter, an unnatural brilliance.

I felt I had entered a world I didn't know. Not just the islands, or the unknown sea; it was more than that—a sensation of something enormous. Not in size, but in power, in possibility. I wouldn't have been surprised if the seas had parted, or the mountains all fell down.

That's when I saw her.

She floated in the night where the pale sail had been. First just her eyes, then her face; so close. I touched her mouth, the back of her neck, held her so tight her heart pounded my ribs, her breath filled my lungs. The vein on her neck pulsed in my lips; I tasted the salty sweat between her breasts. Bit her warm thighs. This wasn't love; this was madness. And, in this world without restraint, how much worse would it get?

I don't know how long I stood there. The shores had closed in; we were sailing in a canyon.

We ghosted wing-and-wing pale in all that darkness, ghosted without a sense of motion, with a sky of stars above, and a sky of stars below. And for the first time, I felt stars *all around* me. I was adrift among fiery giants in a boundless immensity; adrift among stars aflame in a universe gone wild. And if *they* could burn with a fire that would at the end consume them, then why not I? Why not go out in a great blaze—like the stars?

"You're too far starboard, Cappy," Nello whispered. "Come back or we'll gybe."

He took the helm for the next watch. I went below, lay down, and closed my eyes. And fell asleep with her head across my chest.

KATE
Northern Lights

I awake in the bottom of the canoe but feel no movement. He sleeps behind me. The moonless night is faded, the stars look dimmed, and when I raise my head I see why. We are in the middle of a bay surrounded by mountains and along their northern rim, as bright as if a whole row of suns are about to rise, hangs a wafting ribbon of pearly light. It does not light the sky as would a dawn, but hangs there, glowing.

A single stream of green-blue light snakes slowly across the heavens, then arcs of colored light billow upward and fold into curtains: pinks, blues, golds, and violets, vast and undulating, they swell and cover the night. The curtains swirl, then dive toward the sea, and back skyward again. Starting from the center, they burst into sparks toward the horizons, burning up the last remnants of darkness. My breathing swells and ebbs with the pulsations of light. From the top of the dome of night, light pours down around me; like a circular waterfall it tumbles into the sea. Then it closes in as if to carry me away.

I feel I've been living this since the beginning of time. Or have gone mad. Or am just now being born. Or dying. Tears wash my face. The streams of light burst for the last time, and in a giant, sky-covering dust devil of sparks, they rise away—and leave me in the darkness.

Nello slumped sleepily over the wheel. The sea had opened and the snowcapped mountains lay against the night. I took the wheel but Nello, instead of going below to rest, settled into the cockpit corner and stayed. An owl lit near the shore, hooted, flapped the air, then settled with the sound of rustling branches.

"Somebody's soul," Nello said. "While the owl lives, the soul lives."

A cold dew had slicked the wheel.

"Why don't you go get some sleep?" I said.

"I better stay," he said. "He might come."

"The owl?"

"The Kwakiutl."

I shuddered as if the cold dew lay on my skin.

"He'd take on a boatload of armed men by himself? He's that brave?"

"No, Cappy. He wasn't taught to be brave; he was taught to be sly. Hard and murderous. And sly. When a father decides to raise a warrior, he begins by rubbing his newborn with a hornet's nest. Handles him roughly, bathes him in ice water. And he makes him a thing you wear around your neck."

"An amulet."

"That. Out of a toad's tongue, a snake's tongue, and a lizard's tongue—because they all have Death-bringer on their tips. Then he scrapes four pieces from a grizzly's paw to give him merciless power. Puts it all on a black pebble, and wraps it into a piece of grizzly heart. Ties that in grizzly sinew, braids the ends, and hangs it around the baby's neck.

"As he grows, he's taught to swim, run, dive, kill; with weapons or his hands. Taught how to insult men and seduce women. He sleeps on planks. Owns nothing. Rubs himself with snake's blood and the fresh heart of a grizzly. When he kills enemies, he gets to wear a necklace of their toenails. He takes their women as slaves, or fills them with eulachon oil and rapes them.

"Before going to war, he stands in ice-cold water and rubs his body with a hemlock branch until it bleeds. Eats little; a bite of dried salmon at a time. He rubs his canoe smooth with dogfish skin, then oils it, so it glides fast and without a sound. He paints himself black from head to foot with charcoal from a tree struck by lightning—for power, and to be invisible in the dark. He sneaks up on his victim just before dawn at the time of his deepest sleep. Not to fight; just to kill."

I didn't say a word. I just kept looking around on the star-littered sea for the dark, gliding canoe.

The moon rose. The night lasted forever. When I steered, I looked around more than up ahead; when Nello took the wheel, I sat in his corner, sleeping only now and then, the rest of the time keeping vigilant watch. I saw the canoe a hundred times; every rock near shore, each cloud shadow on the water, every time the current or a breath of air took the sheen of stars from the sea, I unclipped the holster and held the pistol grip. I was steering, staring at the shore, when Nello sat up with a sudden start. "Sayami," he whispered. "It has to be Sayami."

"Wake up, would you?" I snapped.

"The bullet," he whispered on. "Would have blown his head off close up. Must have been shot from a distance. From a bobbing boat. Who else? That fuckin' little Jap."

I sat down to make a smaller target. Suddenly the night felt colder. Sayami was scrawny, with a nose that had been broken a few times. He always had a red bandana tight over his head; tied back like some old washer woman, and wore a rough jacket with long sleeves that crumpled, and pants that ended just below the knees. Padded knees: he knelt when he shot. And he had big striped socks that he must have stripped off a dead clown. And faraway eyes. Carried his rifle wrapped in oil-soaked rags. Shot whatever they hired him to shoot: cougar for ranchers, wolves for sheep farmers, seals for the fish companies. They say he could hit a seal between the eyes at a hundred yards. Not from land; but from a moving boat.

A cold dawn drenched the ketch with dew. It beaded like rain on the varnish and ran in streaks down the paint. The sea was broken by loaf-shaped islands to the west and great mountains to the east, under whose vast, steep, wooded slopes long fjords twisted and vanished in the continent.

There were sounds in the galley and the smell of bacon frying. Then Charlie's little face poked out the hatch—half fearful, half smiling—and he handed us steaming cups of coffee.

"You a helluva good Charlie, Charlie," Nello said. "If we live through this, I give you nice big tip."

Hay poked his head out and bade us good morning, but glanced furtively at us: that, if I remember right, was the last time he looked us in the eye until the end. He asked if we'd seen anything, looked around, saw nothing to catch his interest, and went below to eat his breakfast in the warmth.

Sea fog drifted over the cold water. The tide had turned but was neap during the day and with the waters here more open and the land breeze still coming down the fjords, we sailed north at three knots toward a lump of land that seemed to block our way.

"The pass," Nello said, his voice flat from concern. "That's where the North begins. It runs at thirteen knots; not the fastest pass on the coast, but the bloody longest. A two-mile dogleg of reefs and rocks. There's only a half hour of slack water but with this engine it'll take us an hour, if not more. The whirlpools will be up; and the overfalls. It flows at thirteen knots, Cappy, except it doesn't flow—it boils. This whole fjord, fifty miles long and a mile wide, has to blow through a hundred-foot-wide throat in just six hours.

"Imagine a giant wave out at sea—what would it take for a

wave to move at thirteen knots? Would have to be thirty feet high, right? Now imagine that wave blasting through those narrows. One colossal wave breaking and breaking, for hours. They call this end Yuculta Rapids, the far end Devil's Hole.

"It'll be good for you, Cappy. Take your mind off things."

We were less than two miles from the entrance of the pass—we could see the cleft between the steep bluffs where it began. But slack water was not for three more hours, so Nello steered us into the only anchorage around, a sandy hook-shaped cove, huddled below the dark wall of forest. A mass of brambles framed the cove: salal, blackberry, salmonberry, some fruit trees gone wild, all entwined into a green chaos. Someone had once eked out a life here.

With our slow sail during the night, we had given up hope of catching the Kwakiutl before the rapids; even paddling alone, he would have made it through, if not on the midnight then for sure on the dawn slack.

We dropped anchor and launched the skiff. We had Charlie bring a bucket and an old knife. "Good clams, Charlie," Nello said, pushing off. "Good clams in the sand and oysters on the rocky point." Hay was given the hatchet to cut some firewood, Nello took the Winchester, and I took my pistol.

Hay had been silent all morning. His manner had changed from that quiet arrogance to almost deferential; he seemed more like a hostage than the one who paid for the show. It took him a while to understand that we were going ashore just to stretch our legs, and he had to be told twice about the narrows and the slack. As we rowed, he kept turning back and looking north toward the pass.

I jumped ashore. It was good to stand on land for the first time in days.

The sun rose behind a mountain and seemed to torch the

trees, leaving only dark skeletons against the sky. The clamshell beach glowed white. Beyond the high-water mark, where shells were packed in dense welts by the storms, the shadow of the mountain still left the forest and brambles dark. An old log sticking out of the brambles into the sun, covered in lichen, seemed a comfortable place to rest. But as I sat, it collapsed under me; I fell into its hollow. It was a rotted, upside-down dugout canoe, the once-thick cedar sides as crumbly as a biscuit. I reached down behind me to push myself out but stopped; I felt as if I had stuck my fingers through some bars. I edged to one side to look down. The sun shone into the hole, onto my hand, and onto the rib cage which my fingers were gripping. Beside it, askew, as if looking up in curiosity, was the skull. Gap-toothed. The rest of him—shinbones, shoulders, arms, all jumbled—had been scattered by animals and restacked by the tides. I backed away. I could discern odd shapes up in the salal now, mounds that had been houses, and more rotten "logs" just below a low bank of a midden. I walked along the brambles searching in the shadows and saw a drooping eye look back; a burial pole lay face-up just beyond the sand. At the end of the midden was the solitary remnant of a house: a carved post with a once-ferocious wolf's head, teeth bared, half rotted away. A fern, waving in the light breeze, sprouted from one ear. Inland of the brambles, in a great cedar whose lower branches had been desiccated by time, a half dozen boxes hung or were wedged in the crooks. Parts of them had rotted and fallen long ago, and out hung shreds of blankets, clothes, feathers, and more bones. A raven had made a nest in one of them; it now flew off cawing lowly over the cove.

"Leqwildex," Nello said beside me. "A rich village. They fished the rapids. Two hundred people lived here when the smallpox hit that spring during the eulachon run. There were nineteen left alive when the salmon came in July. Most were old—moved away, why stay? The village was dead."

Charlie was down on the water's edge, singing a little song, digging with a stick into the mounds of mud that squirted, then digging with his hands and clanging the clams loudly into the bucket.

Nello went and pried some oysters off a tidal rock. I made a fire with driftwood, and threw the oysters right onto the coals. "Come on, Charlie," Nello called, and he cut a long switch with a forked end, went to the water's edge, kicked off his boots, rolled up his pants and waded in. Charlie did the same. They stood in the water with Nello poised like some great heron, switch in hand, its fork below the surface. Then he lunged, stopped, and with a slow, smooth movement lifted the switch with a big rock crab, too dumb to let go, hanging from it. He laid it on the shore on its back. The crab's legs and claws sawed the air, and I drove the sharp edge of a rock right through his pale belly—an ugly crunching sound. The legs went limp. Grabbing both sets of claws and legs, I tore them from the shell. There was nothing left but a hollow. I stripped the spongy tissue from the legs, rinsed them in the sea, then threw them on the coals.

We sat under a cherry tree gone wild and leaning precariously seaward from the midden. We ate without a word. Nello threw the shells, clattering, on the rocks.

"They say that was the best eulachon run ever."

14

That Spring

The ravages of that most frightful disease continue unabated. The northern tribes are now nearly exterminated. They have disappeared from the face of this fair earth, at the approach of the paleface, as snow melts beneath the rays of the noonday sun.

Captain Shaff of the schooner *Nonpareil* informs us that the Indians recently sent back North are dying fast. Out of 100, about 15 remain alive.

The small pox seems to have exhausted itself, for want of material to work upon.

—From the pages of *The British Colonist*

"I had just turned five," Nello began, "when it hit our village.

"My mother got sick; she started to go blind. My grandfather paid the captain of an old steamer that hauled boom chain and steel cable to logging camps to take her down to the hospital in Victoria. He sent me with her to get away from the sickness. He had been chief of our *na'mima*, but got old and passed down the title to my elder brother, who fell through the ice the next winter and died. My grandfather had a great bird burial pole carved for him; its beak alone was longer than me. Cost him every penny he had, so with no money to pay for our passage, he offered the captain of the steamer all he had left: the pole. He had offered himself as a slave but the captain told him nicely that he didn't need one and he preferred the pole to sell to collectors in Victoria. My grandfather sat beside the pole with a lost look in his eyes and watched two sailors hack at it with hatchets.

"It was the most splendid burial pole in the islands, painted all bright colors, even the sick had dragged themselves outside to watch when it went up; now they dragged themselves out to watch it get hacked down. Those sailors were no loggers, didn't know a damn about how to fell a tree, so they never bothered to back cut, just hacked away stupidly at its front, cursing and laughing all the while. The villagers sat silent. The sailors got angry as they went on, hacked harder, cursed louder, until finally the pole made a sound of pain—leaned toward the sea, turned slightly, then splintered. To my child's eye, it seemed for a moment that the great bird took flight—flew miraculously over the sea, over the islands, its reds and yellows defiant in the mist—but then it just fell, in a quick sad arc, beak-first into the sand. Only a giant splinter remained standing. The steamer backed close to the beach, churning up the silt of the shallows. They threw a towline around the bird, then the funnel belched soot, and it surged ahead. Some of the village men began beating a slow rhythm on a board.

"The rope shuddered so tight that beads of water flew from it; then, with an ugly crunch that hurt my heart so much I still recall the pain, its beak cracked at its base and it lunged forward through the water. The beating on the board grew frantic. Women wailed. My poor grandfather stood unmoving, his head down, staring at the gash the bird left in the sand.

"Out in the bay, the steamer dropped anchor. The drumming on the board grew irregular and it began to rain, a soft drizzle. My grandfather hadn't moved; just stood and stared. He was still there as, man by man, the drummers fell silent. Night came. A bonfire was lit on the beach, in the rain, near the little house on stilts where the sick people stayed to be near the curing power of killer whales and the sea. My grandfather came and sat on a rusted sewing machine that someone had long ago bartered for a dugout war canoe.

"In the morning, they carried my mother down. My aunt held my hand as we followed; she told me not to be afraid because the raven would look after me, and to be strong like the Hamatsa and hard like our warriors. Meanwhile, she held my hand so tight she almost crushed my fingers. How could I be strong with all my fingers broken? I was watching them load my mother into a canoe in the rain. We were well away from the shore but still I could hear my aunt shouting advice. Bless her heart.

"They put us under the tarp that stretched from the deckhouse to the backstay of the riding sail, but the wind and the boat's rolling sent the rain in under it. We didn't mind; we're a people used to rain. The rain is our world. We suffer when the sun comes out and blinds us with the sparkling sea.

"The engine throbbed as the anchor chain came in. My mother's eyes smiled up at me but her face was still. By then the smallpox had made her almost blind but she tried to pretend that she still saw me as before. There was a sour smoke from the coal fire in the boiler. We moved ahead and the great bird rolled, went down, then leapt like a fish trying to throw a hook. Our village vanished in the mist. I heard a long wail, soft like the rain.

"At the bottom of our passage we didn't turn west toward the strait like I thought we would—I could see the clouds above it racing north, whipped to a wedge by the wind—instead we turned east, into the islands. I heard the mate argue with the captain. The mate said to try the strait, for the love of God, but the captain yelled back that he wasn't going where the wind could blow you off the deck, and the waves were so goddamn steep they fell on you like a wall. What would be the use anyway: the squaw would surely die. The mate told him not to bullshit about the squaw, that all he really cared about was not losing his blessed pole. I kept wondering what a 'squaw' was. The captain ruled—we weaved east and south among the islands. In the canoe passage the tide was so low the bird's beak kept hitting bottom.

"My mother lay quietly. I poured some water between her lips and pushed a morsel of dried salmon past her teeth. She chewed out of obligation. The storm started to break over the strait and shafts of sunlight shot down from the clouds. I liked that boat—I can't remember why—maybe I thought it would make my mother well again.

"WE BUCKED THE TIDE. It took us until afternoon to catch sight of Broken Islands, and beyond them the clouds racing up the strait. We swung near Hope Village. I could see the beach, the midden, the houses, all deserted; no smoke, no people. The canoes were there, all right, pulled high on the beach, black against the white of the clam shell, but there was no one—not even the old or sick, who normally stay behind when the rest of the village moves to summer fishing grounds. Anyway, it was too early for the salmon run and the eulachons had gone. Besides, the roof planks and the wall planks were all there—like the canoes.

"We headed west.

"I was looking forward to going down the strait, especially in the blow. Children have no fear, not even when their little world is ending. Maybe they just don't know that word, the 'end.' Anyway, I was hoping for a blow. Hell, I had been out there before; just me and my uncle, he was of the Killer Whale Clan. He loved killer whales. They would come into the strait in the summer, favored a bight on the big island, where the Nimpkish River brought the best morsels to the sea and attracted salmon. But my uncle didn't go to fish; he went to pray.

"He and I would paddle out to the bight just before slack tide and we would sit there, tearing smoked clams with our teeth off the yew skewers—goddamn clams harder than your boot sole—and my uncle would sit like a rock staring down at the water as if that would somehow make the killer whales sound. The air around the whirlpools smelled of the bottom of the sea.

"Sometimes he would stand up and chant; at others he'd have a pee over the side. I was never sure which it was that brought up the whales, but my God, when they came! Always from the north. Always from the north. A small female led the herd—she used to sound with a quick fling of her head—then three or four young males side by side, some more females, and at the end the 'old man,' my uncle called him, with his tall fin split from battle. He would sound and hang in the air an improbably long time, shedding sheets of water, his big black body and white cheeks aglow in the sun, the smell of the spray he shot filling the air with stink, and my uncle there with his arms open wide, beaming with pride as if he had, by magic, conjured them from the deep. Maybe he did. I wouldn't bet against it even now.

"So he'd stand chanting, and he'd never notice the wakes from the whales coming at us, always on our beam as we drifted in the stream, and when they hit, he'd be taken by surprise, lose his balance, and as often as not fall into the sea.

"The whales came every time, always together. They stick

together all their lives; like us Injuns. Not like us whites.

"The captain kept his steamer near the shore where the wind was calmer, but still we came down the strait bouncing, the bird bobbing. At the fork, instead of going on straight south to Victoria, he swung east up a sound toward the snowy mountains. We slowed, and the big bird banged the stern, and the captain came out and asked nicely how my mother was. By then she was so blind she didn't even blink when I leaned down to her. Her skin began to slough away.

"The captain said we could make better time if he went up the sound and left the bird with a friend on a homestead, then we could barrel on full speed to Victoria. But with the wind funneling up the sound, it was even rougher than the strait, so he would leave my mother and me for an hour on a sheltered little island. They rowed us ashore with some salmon and water and two blankets. Said she would eat better on firm ground. They put her in the lee of the salal, then steamed away, full speed, up the sound.

"We never saw them again.

"I covered her with the blankets, then cut some hemlock branches with an oyster shell and built a lean-to over her. I poured more water on her lips, but most of it ran down her face. I can't remember how many days we stayed there. The sun was often out but the nights were cold.

"It was a beautiful sunny morning when she died. There was a mist over the sea, and the water was so flat, you couldn't tell where it ended and the shore began. The sun was on her face. I could tell she liked it. She sort of smiled. And it stayed. That smile. After a while, I put a raven feather under her nose like I'd seen my brother do with shot bear, but the feather didn't move. I held it for a long time.

"The next morning some crows came, so I began to bury her like our people do at the summer grounds where the shore is all rock. I built a house gently over her. Rocks, driftwood, bark, and lots of shells to make it pretty.

"I can't recall how many days passed before the church boat came down the sound and saw me standing on the shore. At first I didn't want to go. Didn't want to leave my mother. They took me to Victoria, to a mission. Full of Indian kids with no parents. My father came at Christmas and took me to my *nonna* and *nonno*, near Pisa.

"They say there were eight thousand of us Kwakiutl that spring, but barely nine hundred left by the fall."

15

Bear

Now I shall press my right hand against your left hand. O friend! Now we press together our working hands that you may give over to me your power of getting everything easily with your hands, friend!

— Prayer of Kwakiutl bear hunter after the kill

The wind had shifted; it came around the point and whipped the smoke of the fire in our faces. Charlie, who had been listening with his eyes fixed on Nello, absorbing if not understanding every word, got up and looked anxiously around for something to clear away and wash, but we had eaten with sticks and our fingers, so he backed shyly toward the woods, said, "Me back soon," and walked toward a low hole in the brambles.

"Just take care you don't sit on a bear," Nello called after him.

The last of the crab claws burnt on the coals; no one wanted them. "There's water in the creek," Nello said. "And some nice blackberries." When we didn't respond, he went alone to the creek, knelt, and cupped his hands to drink.

The sun beat warmly down. I closed my eyes and, with the breeze and smoke wafting over me, drifted off.

A terrifying bellow shook the air. "Charlieee!" Nello howled. "Bear!" And he lunged head-down, like a madman, through the hole into the woods.

Pumping the Winchester, I ran after him, gasping as I got to the hole where the brambles had been crushed, where, in the silt by a stream, bear tracks glistened, sharp-edged in the sun. I splashed up the creek hearing, "Charlie! Charlie!" up ahead. The cobweb light of the brambles ended and I burst into the forest gloom. Through the wall of cedars the light filtered from the shore, and bowers of colossal firs and hemlocks blocked the sky. There was no undergrowth; the bear trail swept on across the duff of rotted needles.

A cry such as I had never heard, not even in the slaughterhouse of war, rose up ahead.

I ran, leaping over fallen trunks, slipped and fell, holding the Winchester in the air. I found them in a hollow where the air reeked of bear. Nello stood at the foot of a giant cedar, staring up like Mary at the cross, and up on the tree trunk, the body hung slack, facing out. It hung by its white arms a few feet off the ground, the arms extended, its wrists wedged in the branches, the shoulders wrenched, the long hair covering the face, head tilted sadly sideways and down. Nello didn't move. He stood with his powerful arms crossed strangely on his chest.

I was struck by how well kept were the shoes dangling in the air and how white the shirt, tidily buttoned at the collar. But from the collar down, all the way to where the belt sagged slack and empty from the hips, there was a dark and gaping hollow, a cavern of ribs and shredded flesh. Something that seemed like a part of Nello moved and uttered a strangled sob. Only then did I see he had been holding Charlie, the little face buried in his chest. I looked back up at the body and thought, Thank God it's over. Tears ran down my face. Nello, still holding Charlie, walked past me and looked up. "The pillow," he said. "You know him?" I couldn't reply. "Did you know him?" he repeated.

Whoever he was, with that stubbly beard, he looked tired. The shreds of cedar bark that the bear's claws had torn into ribbons gave the scene an aspect of festive sacrifice. Only then did I see that his wrists were tied with rope, and in his mouth what had seemed at first like a rolled-back tongue was a roll of cedar bark.

He had been gutted, the soft parts gone. The bear had left only the pelvis and the ribs, and they already swarmed with flies and winding trails of ants. The holster on his belt was still snapped closed.

It occurred to me that I should scramble up and cut him down, give him a decent burial, but the tide was turning, the pass was going slack. I crossed myself and left.

A rythnmic thudding came from the beach, an aggressive sound, like war drums. And I had both the guns. I ran through the half-light of the brambles and didn't stop until I was at the gap, looking up and down the beach. The skiff was gone; the drumming was near. I eased myself into the sunlight of the empty beach. Behind a point of brambles, I heard the thud, thud, thud. I held the rifle waist-high; at this close range there was no need to sight. As I stepped around the point, the drumming stopped. Standing with the hatchet in his hand, Hay blinked excitedly in the sun. At his feet lay the carved wolf's head, surrounded by wood chips. "If I can cut the head off, it'll fit under my bunk," he said.

Maybe it was the dead man, or the long days and sleepless nights, or the blinding beach after the forest gloom. Whatever it was, something in me snapped, and I fired the rifle, pumped and fired again and again. The cove shook with the echoes and the wolf's head flew to pieces and lay shattered in the sand. I turned the gun on Hay with my finger still on the trigger. Out there, way out there, like out at sea, things change, things can happen. One forgets that anything exists but "out there." Someone rang the ship's bell. We didn't move.

"The tide's turning," I said.

I shouldered the hot barrel and went down to the water's edge to await the skiff's return.

16

Devil's Hole

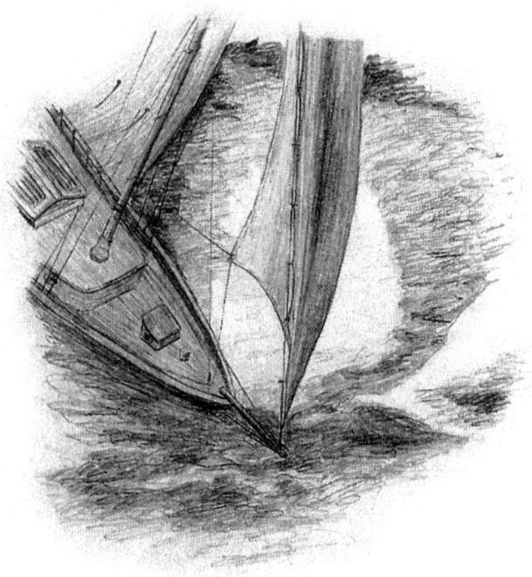

Dangerous rocky islands and point are called *no'mas*, Old-Man. In passing . . . in rough water, the traveler will pray, "Look at me, Old-Man! Let the weather made by you spare me, and, pray protect me that no evil may befall me while I am traveling on this sea."

—Franz Boas

We beat across the sound with all sails flying and a sky the deepest blue. The steep dark slopes closed in as we neared the pass. We were behind schedule for the slack but we couldn't run the engine, not on a heel, because although it worked fine bucking chop or running swells, when heeled for a time it sputtered, smoked like hell, and died.

Nello steered and trimmed the sails, softly singing a melodic *"Oi Vita, oi vita mia,"* while I, with binoculars, studied the water in the pass, suspiciously smooth with all this wind—the currents beneath much stronger than the blast of air above. Charlie was busy stitching an awning with even more dedication than normal, while Hay sat amidships keeping order in his life by making endless entries in his journal.

No one mentioned the dead man. We were all busy and intent, like schoolboys on an outing. Near the entrance of the pass, with small eddies forming around us, Nello asked if I would take the helm, went below, and came back with the fishing rod and cast off the stern into the current. "Hey, Charlie," he called out jovially. "I'll catch you big fish." He was trying to bring normalcy back to our lives. Charlie knew, and his eyes showed gratitude. The reel whined. "The pail, Charlie! Bring the pail!" Nello reeled slowly but evenly, keeping the pole bent tight, loading the line, not letting the fish throw the hook. Just a few feet from the stern the fish jumped, but Nello whipped the rod so hard it hit the mizzen shroud, and kept the hook in him. Anxious to get the pail under the fish, Charlie threw himself on the stern rail, and might have gone overboard if Nello hadn't grabbed his belt and pulled him back. To keep him safely there, he placed his bare foot on Charlie's butt. For a moment he seemed distracted and almost lost the fish, then he reeled in, dipping the tip of the pole in the water to shorten the line and not let him jump again. He maneuvered the shiny salmon under the stern, and Charlie, feeling safe under the foot, blabbered an excited stream of Chinese as he slid farther overboard, his feet churning the air. They got the thrashing fish into the pail. I was watching them so closely I nearly ran us on the rocks.

The first great whirlpool, maybe fifty feet across, surged from below us and swung us toward the shore.

We were late.

This close to land, the wind eased and we sailed upright. Nello went below and turned over the engine shattering the quiet. With its two-cycle throb—the dull explosion, then the long uncanny silence—the Easthope, seemed a tired heart that you could never be sure would ever beat again. With the added push of the engine we surged toward the narrows. The current pulled us in.

Charlie was too busy with the fish to notice, but Hay, sensing a turn in our lives, put away his journal, went below, and came back with his jacket buttoned tight and a pistol in a holster on his belt, as if that would somehow safeguard him from the pass ahead.

Nello came up content with the engine, looked at the languid eddies in the pass, and announced, "Charlie, my little pal, I hope you like dancing, 'cause we're about to shimmy and shake. Cappy, give us our orders."

I sent Hay up to the bow to watch for logs and deadheads, and Charlie to the portside shrouds to watch for rocks.

Eddies now formed everywhere, so there was no way to read the wind in the pass, and with the cold water rising from the sea bottom, and the islands blocking the outflow from the fjords, what the winds would do in there God only knew. On the rocky crags above the tree line, a lodged cloud spewed a misty breath—up high there was wind, but we were here below. The starboard telltale flung itself about, pointed to port, pointed aft, pointed up and down. The port telltale had given up and hung limp. The jib luffed, then collapsed, then back-winded, and slowed us. A deep, hard eddy flung the ketch aside.

"We're late," Nello said so softly only I could hear.

"How late?"

"Late late."

"Maybe we shouldn't go."

He looked at the shore speeding by. "We should never have *come*."

"Well, it's too late not to come."

The current and a whirlpool flung us forcefully ahead. He smiled a bitter smile. "And now it's too late not to go."

"Play the jib, would you?"

He hurried to the mast, uncleated the jib halyard, and let the jib crumple lifeless to the deck, flattened it to keep the windage down, then stood by with the halyard in hand and studied the currents in the pass. Bits of driftwood and some logs moved about and gulls rode the eddies, waiting for the stream to build and drive the fish to a frenzy. "The portside is with us," Nello called, and I let her drift closer to shore. A cool gust slapped my face. "Hoist her," I snapped, and Nello hauled the jib. I called Hay back to take the jib sheet and play it carefully, letting out a few inches, hauling in a few, then throwing it off completely when Nello had to drop the jib again. I had Charlie take the slack sheet and bring it in fast when I yelled, "Charlie, haul." I uncleated the mainsheet but left it under a horn and played every gust.

We passed the mouth; we were in the pass.

There was little change on the surface—the whirlpools had grown but were still lethargic, the gulls circling as before—but below, felt only as a firm push against the keel or a quick kick of a spoke against my hand, a great force began to move.

"Charlie, haul! Mr. Hay, throw off!"

A whirlpool and the wind hit us all at once, and the boom flew hard and checked to starboard, and the jib swept the deck, tearing the sheet through Hay's hand.

He yelled out in agony.

"Grab the fish," I snapped at him. "It's cold."

"Rock at ten o'clock!" Nello roared. A mound of white foam swirled up ahead.

"Charlie, throw off!" I had to haul the jib; Hay held the fish before him as if to fend off evil.

The gust held steady. In the middle of the pass the whirlpools swelled enormous—some two boat-lengths across with dark, deep centers, and we weren't even halfway to turning the corner. Silky, sloping water ran along the shore at maybe four knots, with another silky stream—only a bit higher—running faster right beside it; but in the opposite direction. Suddenly the inner stream reversed and coiled up like a snake.

The logs and gulls were now swept in all directions. Hay wrapped an arm around a shroud. Charlie took no clues from the world, only from Nello's face. When it showed satisfaction, Charlie beamed; when it showed apprehension, Charlie looked terrified.

Nello hoisted the jib for the third time, muttering *Porca Madonna* and *Dio-cane*, but, upon seeing Charlie's worried eyes started singing, *"Oi vita, oi vita mia, oi core chistu core, se stato prim'ammore—Whore-log at two o'clock and coming right at us!"*

It was a small log, maybe twenty feet long and a couple of feet across, but it was spinning in a whirlpool, so it would hit us like a hammer. We were pushing through with all sails and the Easthope, so there was no way to gain more speed unless we threw the anchors or each other overboard. To port was the shore, and to starboard a steep funnel, so I aimed for the end of the log that spun away from us, hoping just to skim it with the bobstay. I tightened the mainsheet until the blocks quivered. "Hold on!" I cried, and braced myself against the wheel, ready for the blow. But without impact the log vanished. In the long silence of the Easthope compressing, only the whirlpools murmured. Then the Easthope thundered and the log shot from the deep—vertically, right beside the hull—up into the sky. Its tip reached the spreaders, and it teetered, ready to crush us, but instead sank as it had come, back into the sea.

"Let out, Charlie! Let out!"

Hay stared hypnotized. "If that had come up under us—"

"We'd be a three-masted schooner instead of a ketch. Charlie! Haul!"

To port opened a gaping hole that belched the cold breath of the deep and smelled of all things alive and dead on the bottom of the sea. To starboard a wall of water rose and blocked the pass. Six feet tall, it didn't move; didn't change. Then, as suddenly as it had come, it sank, leaving a strip of foam that the currents tore to shreds. That was when I first noticed the din. Every whirlpool, every overfall, each stretch of current hissed or roared or gurgled.

"Down the next pass, Cappy!"

The pass seemed to be between a group of rocks and a narrow island, and I spun the wheel. "Let out! Let out!"

We swung. The current from the rocks shouldered us hard sideways. We hung on, all except Nello, who bounded aft, yelling, *"Past* the island! This is all rocks!"

I swung us north again.

Past the island we turned into a narrow cut. The water was smooth, unruffled emerald, but heaving fantastically, as if some giant were shaking an enormous bolt of silk. To the northeast, among some islets, there was no water, only foam. The current flung us viciously ahead. The shores flew by. The sails shook. The tip of the starboard island ended in a bluff, and the emerald stream heaved and swung around it, leaving a deep hole.

We were shot into a bay. There was no foam or heaving, but the entire surface was enormous swirling circles.

"That wasn't so bad," I yelled, and Charlie looked back with a frightened smile.

"Nothing to it," Hay said, brandishing his fish.

"We're through!" I yelled at Nello beside me.

"Through what?"

"Your killer pass! The narrows!"

He looked at me as if I had lost my mind. "That was the first rapids," he said.

"Well, they were easy. So why worry?"

"Because we're later than I thought."

"For what?"

He didn't answer; seemed to be counting circles. Then a wave slammed us broadside and spray shot over us. "For that," he said, pointing beyond the bay, where between black bluffs a dense fog oozed toward us. "Devil's Hole."

Beside us a wall of water rose, then spun.

"Hold on!" Nello yelled. His eyes were wild as he yanked the main hatch shut and held on to its grip. "Hold on!"

The world seemed to fall away around the ketch; the stern dropped, then, from behind, the wall of water came. It climbed aboard. The aft deck vanished and the cockpit vanished—only the mizzen mast stuck out of the water—the water that kept climbing up over the cabin.

As if rising from a grave, the ketch rose, bit by bit, out of the sea. The cockpit slowly drained. Nello released his grip. We crabbed toward the shore. The waters all around us took up a louder roar.

"There, Cappy!" Nello howled, pointing at a long green river that cut a path among the circles clear across the bay. I steered toward it and caught the edge, and it tried to spit us out, rush away, leave us behind, but I held her in, and we lurched and yawed, at terrific speed, ahead. I heard a roar and spun to look, but the roar was all around us. The great circles swelled, their walls sloped down, and they spun, whirling clockwise, whirling back, whirling all to hell, but the long green stream, like some wondrous locomotion, swept us on. To starboard the sea was a hillock, to port an overfall. We clutched lifelines, grabrails, shrouds, anything we could, looking no less bewildered than if we had awakened on the moon.

It came from the northeast islands through the foam: the black, ungainly tug. Its great, log-pushing teeth chewed through the swirling seas. Her soot-smoke rose, fell, then turned against itself. It had trouble holding course. It seemed headed for Devil's Hole, but then a whirlpool shot it sideways and it headed straight for us. Someone stuck his head out the pilothouse window, another stood on the bow with his head a glowing red. He held a stubby walking stick, like a gentleman on a stroll. I stared so hard I steered us off the stream.

We fell off the bluff and landed with a thud. "Hold hard!" I roared, and swung the bow into the wall. The wall exploded. Green water buried us. I couldn't breathe. It hit me that the cabin was being flooded through the cowls. We were sinking. I felt no fear, only disappointment.

Then the darkness lightened and we climbed out into the sun. Water poured down from the booms. The decks were still under, but Nello and Charlie and Hay were there, holding on to whatever they had clutched before.

The tug was much nearer, and coming right at us.

I swung her west.

Nello pulled Charlie to the mainmast, wrapped his arms around it and roared, "Don't let go! Don't let go!" He fetched the binoculars and steadied his elbows on the bed-logs, pointed at the tug. Then he handed me the binoculars and said, "Sayami."

They were ten boat-lengths away, rolling and wallowing, dark and menacing, half buried in the foam. Sayami, his red bandanna glowing in that colorless world, unwrapped his rifle, folded the rag, knelt on it with one knee, and leaned against the coaming for a brace. As I stared at him through the binoculars, he pointed the rifle right between my eyes. But he didn't fire; we were bobbing, yawing, plunging much too much. Hay stood up with the pistol in his hand, seeming so nervous I thought he'd shoot us all. Sayami just knelt there.

Five boat-lengths.

Hay said in the surprised voice of a child, "He's going to ram us."

We stared. Couldn't believe our eyes.

Three boat-lengths.

A great log shot at us but I couldn't avoid it; it skimmed the bow, then was at once sucked under. The tug steadied; Sayami aimed.

The tug's iron teeth headed for amidships where Charlie hid behind the mast, where Nello dove for him, where Hay, undecided, stood with trembling hands, and the tug gave a roar, a belch of smoke, then made its final lunge.

Sayami lowered his rifle. Three shots rang in quick succession, and the world went mad.

As if a volcano had blown below us, the ketch flew into the air and the tug reared, its bow blocking the sky. Then the bow came down with the sound of splintering and grinding, and the air was filled with shards of wood and glass and the stench of gas.

The ketch fell on her side, the masts in the water, the house half sunk, and the tug rammed our keel, trying to plow us to bits before we drowned. Charlie fell. He'd clambered across the cabin top and reached for Nello, but Nello was falling headfirst in the sea. Charlie grabbed air and fell backward off the deck. He went under. The tug hit again and turned us farther over.

Even underwater I hung on to the wheel.

When my head came above water, the ketch lay on her side. Circling. The waters around her empty. The tug floated behind us peacefully in the current, smokeless, its engine silent. Sayami was crumpled in the bow, the Dutchman outside, staring aft. Only when the tug turned did I see why he stared.

His aft deck was swept clean, the house gone, and through the shattered plankings of her deck, the great log towered, pointing at the sun. A fountain of water gushed around its base.

The Dutchman picked up a broken oar, then laughed. I had never seen him laugh before. He waved to me with his pipe. The whirlpool churned, sloped, and the stern of the tug went under. Sayami slid—a red blotch on his white shirt blooming like a rose—slid off the steep deck, and the whirlpool sucked him down. The walls of the whirlpool fell ever steeper, and the tug now sledded sluggishly down its side, then, with a last flash of its teeth toward the sky, vanished in the gurgling darkness of the chasm.

"Nello!" I yelled. "Nellooh!"

17

Canoe

Every living creature has a *himanoas*, one part of which urges him to good, another to evil.

—Franz Boas

The keel finally outweighed the current, and with unhurried deliberation the ketch began to right, the sails rising from the sea, shedding long cascades of water. I bellowed Nello's name so loud my lungs hurt. But he was nowhere. Charlie was gone, there was only Hay hanging upside down with his legs trapped in the halyards. We righted some more. A wave broke over us.

I stood in the flooded cockpit. "Nello," I said so softly I barely heard myself. The jib rattled madly in the wind. Its sheet had slipped the cleat and pulled through the blocks, and now it rattled irretrievably overboard with both its sheets trailing in the seething water. The waters tossed us, sometimes sideways, sometimes in an arc, pitching, never still, rushing at Devil's Hole.

I steered numbly, and the ketch barely responded. We were edging toward the shore. I had to tack, but I had no will, had never felt so tired in my life. Or so alone. Nello was gone; and she was lost with him. Where could I look for her now? Which of a hundred islands; a thousand nooks? I felt like lying down, just wanted to sleep. And I wanted to be on land, as far as I could be from the murderous, bloody sea.

That's when I heard the shout.

It wasn't a word—more like a gurgle. At first I thought I dreamt it. Fine, I thought, fine, and didn't even look. Then I heard it again, and climbed onto the cabin, but all around the water boiled empty. Only a plank from the tug; a teapot. Empty. Then the shout. Very near.

I went to the port gunwale. Nothing. To starboard. The same. Then the shout, so clear; directly from the bow. I wrapped an arm around the bowsprit, and looked down. We plunged and I went under, and when the bow rose, hanging from the bobstay, the rest of him below, white with fatigue, pale without air, Nello.

He gasped, "A rope!"

I grabbed a boat hook, snagged the flailing jib sheet, and the next time he came up, I lowered it to him. Then I hooked his belt. I had him. He was tying the rope underwater when it flew out of his hand as if it had a big fish on its end. I pulled him up until his foot found the bobstay. He was exhausted, but hung on. "Let me rest," he gasped.

I held him.

"Charlie?" he groaned.

"I'll pull you up," I said.

"Let me rest."

"Sayami," Nello said.

"Gone," I said.

"On the rope," he said. "I just tied him."

I looked back. At the end of the jib sheet, Sayami bobbed, shot sideways, went under, bobbed again.

"Charlie." Hay called out.

"Shut up!" I shouted. I put down the hook and was pulling Nello on deck, when Hay called louder, "Charlie!"

We looked up. Halfway up the mast with every limb around the spreader, hanging like a baby monkey, was Charlie with his head back, staring at the sky.

"Charlie." Nello smiled. "You silly little fucker."

Nello steered while I shimmied up the mast, gripping the halyard, and slung an arm around Charlie's waist.

"Grab my shoulders."

He let go of the spreader but hung on with his legs.

"For chrissake, let go!"

He swung against me; I started to ease us down when Charlie whispered, "Cappy. Canoe."

On the northern rim of the bay, where a cluster of rocks and islets formed a refuge, a dark canoe eased itself along. It turned here, twisted there, picking its way through the jagged maze. In its stern, a bulky figure pulled long, powerful strokes; in the bow, a much smaller one paddled a steady rhythm.

"Nello!"

Nello had a foot holding the wheel while he leaned over the portside, trying to haul in the jib sheet and Sayami.

He looked up, saw me waving madly, and looked over that way but could not have seen beyond the overfalls and waves.

The ketch rolled; Charlie and I drew great arcs in the sky. I let us down. Charlie collapsed in a heap at the base. "Hug it," I said, and wrapped his arms around the mast.

"They're here," I wheezed.

"Who?"

"The canoe. In those rocks."

"Give me a hand," he said, tugging at Sayami.

"Fuck him. He's dead. Let's get the canoe!"

"He's alive. I tied him. For chrissake, give me a hand!"

"The hell with him!"

"We need the sheet!"

"Cut him loose!"

"Cappy!"

"We're wasting time." And I yanked out my knife and started slashing at the rope. He grabbed my arm.

"He's *nothing* to you, is he? We're all *nothing*! Stick figures. Draw us in, rub us out. Just so you get *her*!"

"Cut him loose!" Hay roared, still hanging in the rigging.

"Be selfish, Cappy! He'll tell us who sent him. Might help us survive! *Porca putana della troia*!"

The unattended wheel spun; a whirlpool had us, we were sailing fast away from the canoe. Nello grabbed the wheel to keep us from gybing.

"She's right there! Tack and we'll have her!"

Nello looked at me as if I were crazy. "Tack and we'll die!"

"You want me to lose her?"

"Can't get her if you're dead!"

"Across the bay. Ten minutes!"

"Cappy!" he roared. "In ten minutes all hell breaks loose here!"

"We'll go in those islands; it's calm in there."

"For a canoe! We have an eight foot keel! He skims. We die!"

"Cut him loose!" Hay roared, half out of his mind. "Kill him!"

That settled it. I grabbed the jib sheet and pulled. Sayami came and banged against the hull. We hauled him up. He coughed and spewed and bled. Hay struggled in the rigging; Nello cut him down. We were half a mile from Devil's Hole.

I climbed down into the cabin—awash with pots, cans, bottles—and got the rifle. Nello went to get Charlie from the mast. I spun the wheel and pointed to head off the canoe.

We buried the bow, came up, and surged across a funnel that flung us violently toward the rocks. The smooth green ribbon of the overfall was gone; there were only gaping whirlpools up ahead.

Nello charged furiously at me.

"You're being suckered!" he yelled. "He wants you in those rocks!"

The canoe popped up out of the foam; vanished, came again. I braced against the wheel, raised the rifle, took aim at the big shape in the stern, and waited for a moment of less motion.

"Go on, Cappy. He's just a goddamn Injun. Kill him! Shoot!"

His eyes blazed with rage.

"What's the matter? Can't shoot 'em? You can drown 'em alright; you're a master at that! But no balls to shoot 'em?"

I leveled the rifle at his chest.

"That's it!" he roared. "Shoot me too. Then kill Hay! Kill Charlie! Blast away! Make sieves of us all! . . . . Just to get your hands on a woman who might not even want you! What if she walks away? She's done it before!"

I squeezed the trigger. The rifle roared. Nello quivered. I had shot well past him into the sea. He shut up, but too late; Hay had heard it all. Sat wide-eyed, crumpled up, then he raised his pistol and aimed at me.

"I can't shoot the Kwak," I said calmly to Nello. "Because if I do, she'll drown in the next whirlpool."

"That's right, Cap. He knows that. You don't see him ducking, do you? He's in the open. Inviting all fools."

Hay tried to aim past him. I should have shot him then. Nello walked calmly over to him and knocked the gun out of his hand as if shooing away a fly. Hay reached for it but Nello grabbed him by the hair and yanked back his head. "You touch it and I'll kill you."

Dead ahead, a wall of water rose. It was too late to tack. "Hold on!" Nello roared, covering Charlie with his body and clinging to the rail. We went into it. For a long time. We surfaced in a sea of foam.

We were so close now I could see the whole canoe, pointing straight at us. Then the big one in the back gave a long, strong pull; the slight one in the bow joined in, and they turned the canoe back among the rocks, back into the bay.

I stood with the water trickling from the barrel of the gun. With the decks still under foam, we lunged toward the rocks. I turned the wheel and we hauled the sheets, heading toward the cliff of fog that hung in Devil's Hole.

The pass narrowed; the current was a breaking wave atop a raging river. The air was gone, replaced by streams of brine.

The canoe vanished in the vapors. Nello stepped into the cockpit.

"Fewer rocks along the south shore," he said.

I didn't care. She was back there, going the other way.

"He has nowhere to go, Cappy. This is his only way home."

The waves raged along both shores, folded, turned, and crashed against each other. We hurled ahead and I steered, without conviction, for the thickest part of the fog. Nello pulled Sayami's rope tight and cleated it to the mizzen, told Hay to lash himself to the shrouds, then sat against the mainmast, facing aft, and pulled Charlie close to him. He whipped the tail of the main halyard around them both twice—pulled it so tight Charlie gasped for breath—cinched it on a cleat and, just to be sure, wrapped both his arms around him. I put down the rifle and wrapped the mizzen halyard around my waist. The fog was so thick the shores were gone, the masthead blurred, and Nello and Charlie were smudges. The only things I was sure of were my hands on the wheel.

We fell. We rose. We yawed. We twisted and fell again, hurtling always violently ahead, into the deafening white roar, all that was left of the world. I hung on. Hands and the wheel. The water fell away like a bluff below us—we plunged into Devil's Hole.

And in all that noise came faintly, *"Oi vita, oi vita mia."*

I lay on one plank and pushed the other ahead. Fog above, mud below. When it got dark they started shelling. They always waited until dark with the shelling so the explosions would shine brighter, the creases of fear on the faces dig deeper, the torn bodies in the trenches look so much starker, the bared teeth and terrified eyes even whiter.

I lay in the creek bed on one plank and pushed the other ahead through the mud, then crawled onto it and pulled the other from behind. I had nailed tin cans on the tips to help the planks glide, to keep them from digging in. Some had tied a plank to each foot and strode along as if the mud were really snow. But then a shell would explode near them and the ball of hot air topple them, and they would fall sideways and sink and vanish headfirst into the mud with their feet securely tied above. They never made it out.

I rested. It was midnight. Shells burst, lighting the fog orange, yellow, pink. There were screams behind me and screams up ahead, then frightened encouragement, then more screams. Then, through all that barbaric noise, I heard a delicate sound, like a sigh from a life I could no longer recall. It stopped: I crawled ahead. One plank, next plank. It rose again. In that unremitting hell where all humanity had been abandoned, a voice that didn't scream, or weep, or plead, a gentle voice, singing. *"Oi vita, oi vita mia, oi core 'e chistu core, se' stato prim'ammore: o primo e ll'ultimo sarai per me."* I stopped.

He sang softly to himself. He was very near and with every breath coming nearer. Then we collided plank to plank. We lay there face-to-face, in the mud, in the light of artillery shell, him going east, me west. He held a pistol in his hand an inch from my forehead. "You can shoot me if you want," I said in broken Italian, "but you still sing way off-key."

He laughed. Softly at first, then, when I laughed too, he laughed so hard he gasped, laughed until he shook, laughed until he cried. The shelling stopped. The fog went dark.

"You German?" he whispered.

"No. You?"

We laughed again.

"What are you?" he said.

"Drunk," I said.

"Me too," he said.

We snorted.

"Are you on reconnaissance?" I said.

"No. You?"

"No."

Shells burst very near and all around us. The mud almost buried us.

"They don't like us laughing," he said.

"It's your singing."

Darkness and silence.

"Where are you going?" he whispered.

"Home," I said.

"Me too," he said.

He had shrapnel in both legs, bleeding badly; hurting. He wouldn't get far. I tore off my sleeves and bound him. We agreed it would be best if I were to bring him in. To his side. Him capturing a deserter or a spy, and me risking my life bringing in their own wounded hero. Looked good all around. Might get us both home.

The only thing that had kept him alive, kept him going these past two years, was her. Thoughts of her and a worn picture. She was with him day and night in the mud. When the war was over he took me to his new country where his half-brother lived, where *she* lived, to meet her. San Francisco.

I quickly got a job skippering a fishing schooner. One Sunday I took the three of them for a sail. It was warm and hazy. The fog waited out there just past the narrows. We were well out in the open sea when the afternoon breeze kicked up and the fog blew in. We ate and drank and laughed. There was nowhere to look but at each other. We drank some more. It didn't take me long to notice. He saw it too: glances, smiles, looks that lingered. A surreptitious touch. We drank more but he drank the most. Nobody noticed when he lowered himself into the skiff we towed, cast off the painter, and slipped away into the fog. We yelled. I rang the bell. The fog was so thick it sounded dull. I rang it until it nearly drove me deaf. We only found him because he had taken a bottle, finished it, and started singing, *"Primo e l'ultimo sarai per me."*

I hauled him aboard, his face awash with tears. He went and sat alone on a coil of rope in the bow. The wind was picking up; the spray washed over him.

The brother and she stood very close. She held him or he held her, I can't remember. I told them to go. I didn't threaten; just told them to get in the skiff. They went. I cast them off and sailed into the fog. We were only a few miles from shore. They had good oars. But they were never heard from again.

KATE
The Pass

All night we paddle through the stars, the water is so smooth, reflecting them. We're only two now. At dawn we paddle into a narrow pass and hide among small islands to wait. After a while there comes a noise of rushing water, but I can't see past the islands. Before noon it stops. We wait. Then it starts up again. I see the tops of the sails. I want to shout out but I don't; useless in the noise. When we come out from behind the islands, I start to laugh because we had come at dawn on water like a mirror and now we sink between waves so high I can see only the sky. Rushing mountains of foam come at us and I laugh and shout as I haven't since I was a child when lightning ripped the sky and thunder shook our house. I'm not a bit scared. There is an ugly black boat near the sails. Then it sinks. Somehow it seems right. The sails vanish in the fog. That seems right too. After that the sea goes crazy. So beautiful.

I thought I had gone deaf and senseless. I no longer heard the cataracts, no longer felt us falling, no longer felt the whirlpools tossing, flinging us about. We sailed slowly, upright and silent. The wind fell; the fog thickened. I was untying myself from the mizzen when into that ghostly world rose a cry, *"Oi vita, oi vita mia, oi core 'e 'chistu core, se,"* boisterous, passionate, full of hope. "Come on, Charlie, I'll teach you. *"Oi vita, oi vita mia."*

Nello said there was an island up ahead in the middle of the channel, he wasn't sure how far, so we had better drop the anchor before it was too late to drop anything.

We fed out twenty fathoms but the anchor rode just hung straight down.

"There's no bottom!" I yelled, and cinched the rode on the samson post.

"There will be."

There was. We caught and swung around in the current pointing back at the invisible pass, set the anchor hard so the rode no longer bounced, dropped the sails, and hung there on the hook.

I leaned against the mizzen and took my first deep breath in hours. Back in the narrows I had imagined the uncontrollable joy, the sense of conquest that would overwhelm me once out the other side, but there was none.

Then we bailed. We were all soaked to the skin anyway, so we waded into the flooded cabin. I manned the bilge pump, Hay and Charlie bailed with pails into the galley sink, and Nello dried out and cranked the Easthope. At first it wheezed asthmatically, then coughed, then started with its lonesome bang. He took off the salt water intake hose, tied the tea sieve on its end so it wouldn't get plugged, and stuck it in the bilge. The Easthope pumped, and we bailed, and stroke by stroke, pail by pail, we took the sea from the cabin and heaved it back into the sea.

When the water was gone, we wiped the cabin dry and tented an awning over the mizzen boom to cover the cockpit. We hung our wet clothes all around it, fired up the galley stove, heated up pails of water, drank some rum, then took turns sitting naked in the cockpit and dousing each other to get rid of the salt. Except Sayami, who we left tied up, barely conscious, in the shadows. And Charlie, who was too damn shy, so he went in the darkest corner of the cockpit, sat with his back to us, and only then did he let us douse him. Then he covered up and went below and came back wearing a clean white shirt and black baggy pants, looking even more innocent than before.

The night was dark and hushed; it was slack tide. Charlie fried onions and threw in oysters and they steamed and sizzled in the pan. We passed the rum and Nello kept singing songs from Naples and Sorrento, and Hay seemed to know a few and sang along with him in a dreadful accent.

The cabin grew stifling. We hooked the storm lantern on a boom bail over the cockpit; the wet clothes swung against the wall of fog like tired dancers at a carnival. Nello played his squeezebox.

Sayami lay tied up in his corner. The bullets had gone through him, one through his side and one through his arm, and the salt water had cleansed his wounds and stopped most of the bleeding, so we bound him up and he looked weak but alive.

Hay drank. When the bottle was passed to him, he filled his cup, and in almost the same motion emptied it and jumped back into one of Nello's songs.

When I was drunk enough I pulled out my harmonica and played along with the songs I remembered from the throaty Italians selling sweets in our street-fairs. We stopped only to eat Charlie's onions and oysters whose smell filled the cold wet air, and some slimy lichee nuts that I normally hated but was so drunk I actually loved, *"O sole, 'o sole mio, sta 'nfront a te, sta 'nfront a te!"*

Charlie threw timid glances at Nello, who responded, "I like your oysters, Charlie. You make us all fat like seals." But Charlie instead of smiling looked off into the night and the deep darkness. When I closed my eyes, I could see the dark canoe gliding silently north.

Nello stood as best he could, played a livelier tune, swayed from foot to foot so that bit by bit the ketch began to roll. Then he leaned down close to Charlie, who just took long sips from his cup of tea, which Hay had laced with rum.

"Non mange piu non dorme piu che pecunderia! Gue picceri' che vene a di 'sta gelusia?" Nello sang.

And when Charlie gave a faint smile, Nello, encouraged, swayed and sang louder, and Hay, drunk as a skunk, got up and did a little dance.

They were doing drunken dance steps up the side deck and down into the cockpit, and I blew my drunken lungs into the harmonica, and Nello spun, and Hay pulled Charlie up to dance. Charlie was timid at first, reluctant to move, but the rum got the best of him, and Hay did something like a Charleston with his knees, and that made Charlie laugh and follow, and they jumped up on the side deck and down onto the bridge deck, *"Comm'aggi 'a fa pe 'te truve? I' senza te nun posso sta!"* Again and again he sang the refrain, and Hay leapt and Charlie spun around and around, and the string in his hair came loose and his long hair flew about, and he spun on the bridge deck but spun once too often, slipped, and fell toward the rail, toward the sea. Hay made a deft lunge to save him, managing to grab only the long tail of his shirt, and Charlie's shirt ripped away and he fell back against the lifelines. Nello stopped dead as if someone had choked his breath. I was so shocked I blew a long single note. Hay swayed gently, holding Charlie's empty shirt, and Charlie stood half naked in the lantern's glow, hair plastered, and below the dark hair shone her pale flesh—her small but perfect breasts. She didn't move but her face changed and softened. All the tension drained away.

Nello squeezed the squeezebox. He looked at the night, then looked back at her, then began, almost in a whisper, *"Era la festa di San Gennaro, ll'anno appresso cante e suone... bancarelle e prucessione... chi se po dimentica?"*

His voice slowly strengthened, and I got enough breath back to begin to blow the tune. Charlie sat up. *"C'era la banda di Pignataro, centinaia di bancarelle."* She took back her shirt from Hay, covered up her breasts with her arms across them, tossed her hair off her face, and began to sway. *"Dove sta Zaza? Oh Madonna mia. Come fa Zaza, sensa sua zia?"* With her gaze at first on Nello, then away in some distance, she danced—no longer the stiff gestures of a child trying to please grown-ups, but the movements of a woman capturing a man.

I took the first anchor watch.

Hay snored in his cabin and I shut his door to drown him to a drone. The galley stove blazed; the cabin was steamy, and I turned down the wicks, snuffed the lamps, and climbed out into the mist. As I slid shut the main hatch, I glanced down through the skylight into the aft cabin, and saw them in the soft flicker of a lamp, Charlie, her white flesh aglow, and Nello touching her with incomparable carefulness and wonder, as if discovering a new universe, one star at a time.

I bundled up in the cockpit and stared at the wall of fog, beyond which I could envision nothing.

18

The North

When a shaman dreams that the soul of a deceased person is hungry, he requests the survivors to burn food and clothing for them. The souls or spirits of the dead can use only objects that have been burnt.

—Franz Boas

At dawn the fog changed from black to gray. The island was still obscured but a breeze stirred and the fog now thickened into banks, now thinned into tatters, revealed a point here, a bluff there, or a clump of cedars drooping over the sea.

There was a peace about this place that we were reluctant to disturb. We moved about quietly. I hauled up the main, Hay folded the still-wet clothes and the awning, and Nello began taking in anchor rode, while keeping a protective eye on Charlie, who helped in the cockpit then went down into the galley, softly humming, *"Oi vita, oi vita mia."* The space on the boat seemed much greater now—all of us remained a bit more distant, walked by Charlie with more care, addressed her more politely.

We sailed out the anchor, took the island to starboard, and edged along the shore out of fog bank into brilliant patches of light, then back into the gloom again.

Still tied to the mizzenmast, Sayami had come to. He huddled in the cockpit while Nello washed his wounds with warm salt water, hissing and twitching until Nello lost his temper and shook him.

"Maybe the water's too hot," Hay suggested.

Nello stirred it so it would cool. When he began wrapping the new bandage, Hay again advised. "Not too tight. You'll cut off the circulation."

"Here," Nello snapped, throwing down the bandage. "You shot him; you fix him!"

Hay took over timidly.

"What the hell you shoot him for, anyway?"

"He was going to shoot Captain Dugger."

"Going to, going to! The road to hell is paved with good intentions. He lowered his rifle."

"I was sure he'd shoot."

"Yeah!" Nello snapped at Sayami. "What the hell was that all about?"

Sayami looked insulted. "I was doing my job. I was told the captain was wanted for murder. A thousand-dollar reward."

I was caught by total surprise. "A thousand dollars? For me?"

"Paid by the state of California, for you alive. If you wound up dead he'd pay it to me himself."

"Hopkins?"

"Who's Hopkins?"

"So why didn't you shoot?" Nello snapped.

"Why have it on my conscience? The Dutchman was going to sink you anyway. Besides, I saw his face."

"I bet you saw my face; you aimed right between my eyes."

Sayami formed a sad smile. "That's just it," he said. "I can't shoot people once I see their faces. Especially fools in love. He told me about you and her. He knew all about it."

No one moved. No one spoke. Hay stared frozen. Nello leaned on the bridge deck in confusion. The fog opened and sunlight turned the mist around us golden.

"Who?" Nello asked.

"What?"

"You said, *he* knew, *he* told me. Who is *he*?"

Sayami looked quizzically at him. "*He*, the husband. *Her* husband. *Hay*. *Mr. Hay.* He would have paid me the reward. *He*. Who do you think?"

Nello spun and grabbed Hay by the collar. "You son of a bitch! You offered him a thousand bucks to kill Cappy?"

"No. Honestly. I..."

"He just said! Didn't you hear?"

"What do you want from *him*?" Sayami burst in. "*He* doesn't know anything."

Nello, without letting go of Hay, yanked out his knife and held it at Sayami's throat. "I'm not in the mood for this!" he hissed. "Who's bull-fucking who here?"

"He's crazy!" Hay yelled. "I never said a word of it!"

"It's true," Sayami said. "It wasn't him! It was the *husband. Hay!"*

Nello held the knife, trying to figure out who to sink it into. Then he lowered it. But he held on to Hay, maybe just to have something to hold on to. Sayami picked up the bandage and went on wrapping his own arm. "I let go a thousand dollars out of some sentimental crap," he said bitterly. "And another five hundred for him," he said, pointing at Hay. "Mr. Hay said he'd give me five hundred to kill that wimpy son of a bitch because he was after her too. I guess he doesn't like competition, our Mr. Hay."

Nello scooped some cold dew off the deck and rubbed it on his face. "What did you say?" he said.

"When?" Sayami asked, annoyed.

"You said Hay promised you five hundred to kill *him*. But *he is* Hay."

"He maybe *your* Hay, but he ain't *my* Hay."

"You sure?"

"Of course I'm sure," Sayami said. "I know Hay and I know *him*. He works for Hay. Olson. A professor, studies Indians. Gets paid to go collect things." Then he laughed, "Like his wife."

"This true?" Nello said. "You Olson? Work for Hay?"

"Yes."

"And love his wife on the side."

"I'm not alone in that."

"No," Nello said. "It seems to be the national pastime." He went below, and I heard him clang the bottle on his teeth as he took a slug of rum.

"Why didn't Hay come for her himself?" I said.

"Safer this way." Sayami shrugged, then winced in pain. "His fortune is from insurance. He loves insurance. He wanted to insure that he stayed alive."

We were so close to shore that even in the cold fog I could smell the cedars. We had to tack. The current ran strong against us now and although the wind had stiffened, we barely clawed along. Nello checked the jib, then came back to the cockpit, tidied up the sheets, and, holding a coil of rope in his hand, said mostly to himself, "I'll be damned if I close my eyes tonight; never know who the hell *I* might wake up to be."

He adjusted the main with meticulous precision. "Cappy, I know you're glad Hay isn't here. But if he's not here, then where exactly is he?"

I FELT MYSELF shivering, and not just from the cold. I could not conjure up the world beyond the fog, and now our world aboard was slipping into chaos. I closed my eyes to try to see her, but now that Hay wasn't Hay, she seemed just as vague as the faint shapes in the mist.

Sayami finished his bandage and now tried to tie it off. Nello had to help him.

"So I lost a thousand bucks on you and five hundred on him. I figure somebody owes me something for my human kindness. Something besides bullet holes."

We ignored him.

"Now I know Hay gave him five hundred spending money," he went on, pointing at Olson. "I think this is as good a time to spend it as any. What do you think, Mr. Olson? If I can earn five hundred by killing you, I think it's only fair I get that much to let you live."

"Shut up!" Nello hissed, and wrenched his bandage. "Or I'll let you bleed to death."

The wind hardened. The fog rent. We were beating nicely now because inlets opened both to port and starboard, causing the current to slow. I looked around for the canoe. Olson looked too. But there was nothing dark and flat at the edges of the fog.

Charlie, her face flushed from the heat of the stove, poked her head out the hatch. When she saw Nello she broke into a smile.

"Everybody hungry?" she said.

BY LATE MORNING the current slacked and we pulled long tacks between mountainous shores. The fog lifted but only to the masthead, leaving us with the sensation of sailing under a burden. Sayami slept. Olson went to take up his old post by the mast, then he seemed to remember something—perhaps that he was no longer Hay—and with his head down came aft and went below. I pitied him; he had lost a lot all in one blow, even his name. In a way he scared me more than Sayami; not only was he smart and a good shot, but he had nothing left to lose.

I was sitting in the cockpit filling the logbook with banalities—the only thing that really mattered were the engine hours to keep track of the gas—when I noticed Nello's hands grip the spokes hard. His eyes were tight.

"Besides the hangover, what's eating you?" I said.

"Nothing. Life's ducky."

"Come on. We're out of the pass alive; there's no one after us; you have the sweetest woman down there who'd walk on coals for you—"

"Exactly!" he snapped. "I always knew God had it in for me, but not this much."

"Don't kid me. You're in love."

"For chrissake, Cappy! Her age."

"You were made for each other."

"Except she was made twenty years too late. Look at my face! Looks like they fought the war on it, then went home and left the trenches."

"Come on, she worships you. And you care for her. Hell, you even cared for her before she was a she."

"That's just it," he said. "I don't want her to waste her life nursing an old man." He looked away.

"You poor bugger," I said. "You really got it bad. It's all right to have it bad, just so you don't float off and leave reality behind, 'cause then up it pops in front of you, in the form of a barely submerged rock that rips open the hull and sends us to the bottom. All because you didn't see the kelp bed that signaled a rock as plain as day."

"I see it, thanks." And he nodded past the port bow, where the floating fronds of kelp glistened more random than the ripples.

The wind cleared the fog, and after a few more tacks the sun beat down out of a pure blue sky and blazed blinding on the sea. The rail went under and stayed. She was struggling too hard—we had to reef. I kept the helm while Nello worked at the mast, easing the main halyard, hauling down the sail, cleating the downhaul, hauling the halyard with the sail now slatting, the lines snaking; then he tied in the reef lines one by one, cursing, pounding flat the sail, clawing. "Slack off, Cappy, I'm no fuckin' Hercules!" It took a long time. But now she kept her rail up and sliced well through the seas.

He came back to the cockpit, coiled the mainsheet, then slammed it on the bridgedeck. "The strait's blowing like a whore," he burst out.

"Let her blow."

"You kidding? It's blowing twenty knots in here, that means a gale out there! And it's so narrow you have to tack once a mile, and every time you tack you lose everything you gained. It'll take us a week to beat fifty miles."

I felt sorry for him; he had it bad; maybe worse than I. His movements were as hesitant as if he were doing everything for the first time.

"For chrissake, " I said kindly. "Jump in. When was the last time life gave you something to jump into?"

He didn't answer. Fussed with the sheets.

"Anyway," I said, "it'll eat you alive if you don't."

At the end of our inlet, below the island's mountains, we could see the strait, dense with marching waves. The gale blew their tops into a dense layer of mist.

Just off our bow, a glistening geyser shot toward the sun. When the wind blew it apart, a dark fin rose, carved an arc, and slid under again. Then others came, five or six at once, and more geysers. "Good omen. Killer whales." Nello grinned and pulled the tin bucket from the lazarette, leaned over the side, and carefully, so that the rush of water didn't snatch it from his hand, he skimmed the top off a wave. He brought it back to Sayami and shook him awake. "Hey. I'm trying to save your life." Sayami came drowsily to. Nello lifted the pail. "Put some in your mouth and spit it toward the whales. Move. The closer they are, the stronger the spell."

They were close, alright, but had spread somewhat, allowing the ketch in among them.

Sayami sat up grimacing in pain, cupped his tied hands, then spat like a fountain over the side.

"Yell, *'da'gibixla' ye'golemex, n'noalakwe!'*" Nello shouted.

"Great," I said. "Get him good and healthy so he can kill us."

"The sooner he heals, the less we have to nurse him."

"If you had let him drown, we wouldn't have to nurse him at all."

He watched the whales, watched them surface, arc, hang in the air looking at us with their great eyes, unperturbed, indifferent. Somehow I felt safer with them close. As soon as I felt safer, I sensed her again, nearby. I called Nello back, asked him where he thought they'd be.

"Depends," he said. "On how tired he is. How much she helps. He's so close to home now maybe he'll rush right through. Only thirty miles before he turns in."

"You just said fifty."

"Fifty for us, thirty for him. There's a canoe pass at high tide up a bay. We go another twenty."

The whales, as if dancing, leapt into the air.

THE STRAIT BLEW a gale right in our teeth, blew the words we uttered right back down our throats. The waves were dense, high, steep. The ketch bucked violently, endlessly, rose gallantly over one, but the next was right behind, and she slammed into its face as if into a wall. The ship's bell clanged fiercely and the spray felt like hail. Nello steered. I stood stubbornly by the winches; I'd be damned if I let some cranky strait keep me from going north. Charlie sang, and Olson turned a color I had never seen before. We beat through green water for two hours and ended up three boat-lengths farther north.

"I was wrong!" Nello shouted in a lull. "It'll take us a year!"

We pounded on.

"Over there!" he hollered, and pointed at a wedge of an island ending in a sandspit that sheltered a shoaling bay. At its marshy end, a float house listed in the mud.

It was late afternoon. "Fine," I mumbled. "We could use a rest."

We shot into the lee of the island, edged as close to the spit and the island as we dared, and dropped anchor. Even without the jib, the wind still blew the bow down and we dug in. It took two of us to wrestle in the main and lash it to the boom.

When Charlie lit the stove, the smoke blasted aft and swept down over the stern.

At sunset, the wind eased some and the water around us became calmer. Nello wanted to take Charlie for a row, show her the island and the tidal pools, but I guessed it was mostly to get her away from us. We launched the skiff and it danced at the end of the painter. Shreds of red clouds swept at speed overhead; the foam in the strait and the chop around the ketch turned red, and over the spit and the tip of the island a pink spray flew like horizontal rain. The black fins glided back and forth along the shore.

"Could that be a burial island?" Olson asked as Nello lowered the oars into the skiff.

"Could be," Nello said. "There was a summer village in the bay before the plague."

Olson hesitated then got up the courage. "Would you mind very much dropping me off there to have a look? It would be a great favor."

Nello must have felt sorry for him, because he said, "Sure," and while he helped Charlie down, Olson went and rummaged in his cabin. When he came up he was loaded like a pack mule. "Cameras, notebooks," he said sheepishly. They went.

With the three of them plus the gear, the skiff rode low—Olson in the stern with his gear in his lap, Nello at the oars, and Charlie huddling low in the bow. When a swell swung in from the strait and raised and rocked them, Nello yelled, "Duck down. Duck down!" and Charlie looked around, confused, having no idea what the hell "Duck down" could be.

They landed in the crook formed by the island and the spit, Charlie jumping out first to lighten the bow and pulling the skiff closer in. Nello held the skiff while Olson clambered out, leaving much of his stuff behind. Then they pulled the skiff up on the sand. The tide was rising; the spit shortening. Nello and Charlie clambered among the rocks at the end of the spit. Olson had vanished; must have gone up island. I pulled out the binoculars and looked out into the strait where the foam blew, looked up and down both shores for the canoe, looked slowly, rock by rock, tree by tree, and only when I heard the shouts did I spin around.

The two figures on the spit had separated, the small one standing still, the other running hard toward the island. I raised the binoculars—could hardly see in the dusk—but I saw Olson in the skiff, rowing with all his might, away from the spit, straight toward the bay. Nello leapt in the water and thrashed after him but Olson did well with long, hard pulls—he was already more than a hundred feet from shore. I cursed and yelled. Sayami awoke with a start. Nello was swimming hard after the skiff but with each pull of the oars the distance between them widened. He stopped. Treaded water. The fins of the killer whales arced in the fading light. He turned and looked at Charlie alone on the shrinking spit—then began to swim back. Swam. Stopped. He waved toward the ketch. It was a while before the wind brought his broken shout. He swam, then stopped again and waved. The shout—it could have been anything—but sounded like, "Kill him!" My first thought was, How? I could try raising the anchor and hoisting the sail, but alone? Olson would have by then skimmed over the bar, out of our reach, in the shoal bay. The tide rushed in. The spit vanished. Charlie stood in the sea.

I ran below. Olson had cleaned out his cabin, left only his rifle. I stuffed the Winchester full, running back up, then cut Sayami's hands loose and shoved it at him. "He's clearing out. Shoot him," I said. "But don't kill him. If you kill him we might lose the skiff. Shoot him and maybe he'll come back."

Sayami struggled in pain, sat back against the deckhouse, and, with his elbows on his knees, steadied the barrel on the lifelines. He aimed and waited for a lull in the motion of the ketch. "I can barely see," he mumbled, with the butt against his cheek. *Kill him,* said the buffeting wind. Sayami didn't blink; didn't breathe. Nor did I. Then a deafening thunder trembled the twilight. Olson clutched his arm. Sayami sat still. Olson struggled up.

"Don't fall in, you bastard," Sayami muttered. Olson had lost an oar, struggled to his feet, pulled out the other oar, turned toward the bow, and, with his feet astride, tried pathetically to paddle.

"What now?" Sayami said.

Kill him! the wind said.

"Kill him," I snapped. "He's almost in the bay."

"I'll stop him."

"Kill him!"

Thunder. Olson's left knee buckled and he fell onto the gunwale.

"I hit him low," Sayami said. "If I had hit him high, he'd have fallen in."

Nello had reached Charlie and was dragging her through chest-deep water toward the shore. The black fins shot toward them.

Thunder. Olson hung over the side but he still held the oar and pulled with his dying might when, with a corkscrew motion, he propelled himself sideways and plunged into the sea.

"You bastard," Sayami said.

The sky had grown so red it reflected on the glistening fins. They had turned and headed toward the skiff. Then they formed a circle with their heads close together, and tossed up an odd shape that flailed dark and frantic against the red glow on the sea.

The gale blew for two more days and nights, strumming the rigging, rattling blocks and hatch boards, and hurling endless chop against the hull that in the night sounded like slaps against your head.

The first morning we flooded the skiff until it was down to the gunwales and let the choppy water rinse away Olson's blood. Then we bailed it and rinsed it and wiped it dry. Below, we cleared away every trace of Olson, as if that would somehow help us forget we'd killed him. I went through his big bag: some clothes, a few books, but the money was gone. I suggested that Sayami take Olson's things to at least get something for his trouble, but he said he didn't like him, as if you had to like who you killed before you kept his things. I took the bag and rowed to the island. Nello said to burn it all so he could use it on the other side, but I couldn't be bothered. I shimmied up a low spruce and wedged the bag into a fork—as a memorial.

I was already back down when I thought about the journal. I started a fire and burnt it, page by page. The last entry was just after Devil's Hole. *Can't see a thing. This is a land of illusions.*

I threw it in the flames; for sure he'd want that with him.

We hauled fresh water from the creek in the bay and washed the salt from everything on board. We sloshed out the lockers that had been filled with sea, rinsed all our tinned food and wiped it dry, scrubbed the decks, washed the salt off the varnish, laid the sails out on the deck and rinsed the salt out of them—must have made twenty trips with buckets. Sayami rested, Nello and Charlie worked together and talked endlessly to each other. I worked alone and talked softly—to Kate.

There wasn't much to say, but still I couldn't stop. I went over things we said, laughed at some, regretted others, tried to attribute deep meaning to her simplest words, and invented things she *should* have said to me. I went over what I'd say when I found her; rehearsed everything, then changed it a dozen times. Finally I decided it all sounded stupid and it would be best not to say a word. Stand there; let her speak first.

The wind eased after midnight—the howling stopped. There was only the odd gust in the trees, and the lulling stroke of wavelets washing against the hull. I lay in my bunk and closed my eyes. "Stay close," I whispered. "It's cold against the wood."

I went on deck, well rested, before dawn. The moon had set and the sky swarmed with stars. The lantern glowed faintly in the aft cabin. We could have hauled anchor and hoisted sail right then but I didn't have the heart to interrupt them.

KATE
The Illness

I'm without strength of any kind. I stop paddling at midnight. I'm so cold. He carries me into the woods and makes a bed of branches, bundles me in a blanket and lays me on it. I sleep but dream violently. When I wake up he's leaning over me. When the sun is high he unbundles me, lifts me up and takes me to a place between two rocks where the small stones of the beach are warm from the sun. He lays me down. They feel so warm. His big hands are very gentle as he takes off my pajamas, and I don't resist. He unties a coil of kelp that has been in the canoe, pours fish oil from it, and rubs it over me. He leaves me there in the sun and fills his shirt with the pebbles warmed by the sun, and piles the hot pebbles against my sides, against my arms and legs, between my legs. He returns with more until I am covered in warm stones. I can't move. I drift off in the heat.

The wind blows hard that night, and for the first time he builds a fire. He puts in stones to heat them, then he makes a bed of hot stones, covered with kelp leaves and tips of cedar. He lays me on it, then covers me with more hot stones. He comes back throughout the night to replace the stones, keeping me warm, and giving me water to drink. In the morning when he uncovers me, he laughs at my pale body in the sun. He rubs the oil from my skin with soft bark from a cedar, and covers me with a new coat of oil. He keeps his hands between my legs a moment, seems in thought, watches me, then he covers me in warm stones. I sleep all day. At night he moves us, but again the wind blows hard, and the waves are high, and we return to our hidden beach. He makes the hot stone bed with the kelp again. I fall into a deep, deep sleep. I awake pouring sweat in the morning. He rubs me dry and helps me dress. I am finally strong enough to walk.

19

Capsized

Ah, ah, ah, what is the reason, child, that you have done this to me? I have tried hard to treat you well when you came to me to have me for your mother. Look at all your toys and all the kinds of things. What is the reason that you desert me, child? May it be that I did something, child, to you in the way I treated you child? I will try better when you come back to me, child. Please . . . come back to me, child. Please, only have mercy on me who is your mother, child.

—Prayer of a Kwakiutl mother for her dead child

We left early and caught the best of the tide, which didn't turn and harden against us until midmorning. Then we hugged the eastern shore, where islands and points of land slowed the current's flow. The wind was cool but the sun warmed us, and Nello and Charlie sitting together on the foredeck, leaning against the house in the clear brilliance of the day, gave a peaceful honeymoon aspect to the voyage. Except for Sayami, bandaged and full of holes. In the mountains to the west, the lengthening plumes of fog poured thicker down the clefts, spilling ever farther over the cold sea. The wind brought tufts of haze and laid them gently over us like children lay angel hair on Christmas trees. Color drained from the world. Near me on the aft deck Sayami made a scuffling sound.

"What is it?" I said with little interest. "Fever?"

"Hell, no."

"Infection?"

"You kidding? He poured half the sea in them." He shifted around trying to get comfortable, then settled back and looked west over the mountains where the fog blew from. "I was going to go home after this," he said. "Get a small *ryokan* in the mountains where I'm from. You should see the colors this time of year. When a quick snow comes, the reds and yellows burn through the whiteness. Most people like to get married when the cherry blossoms bloom. Me, I'll take the snow. If she waited."

He swept water off the caprails.

"And now?"

"Ha! Now. I was going to get five hundred for him. That's gone. Five hundred for the masks. That's in doubt. A thousand for you. Hell."

"You could live on that?"

His face changed, became more businesslike. He looked at my face, my chest, as if he were trying to find a good place for a bullet.

"No," he said flatly. "Not on that."

"What, then?"

"Her."

I must have looked horrible, because he quickly looked away.

"What about her?" I said.

He looked away at the mountains again as if they were about to tell him something. "He promised me ten for her."

I didn't say a word. Just tried to gauge how much strength was left in him, how much greed, what kind of hardness.

"Alive," he said, almost reprimanding me. "Alive."

"You could kill me after I find her," I said. "Then you could get it all."

He laughed a sad, embarrassed laugh. "I'm not good at my job," he said. "Wolves, bears, cougars, sure. In the war, sure. They had me snipe. Good eyes, calm hands. From far away, but close up? I have trouble killing flies."

"Especially those in love."

He laughed.

"You can wait till I walk away," I said. "Then shoot me from a distance."

"Too late," he snapped. "I've already seen your eyes."

"You'd seen Olson's."

"But I didn't like them. I owed him a couple of bullets anyway."

Off the starboard bow rocky shreds of islands broke out of the mist, with wind-tormented trees jutting at the broken angles the gales had left them, only their evenly shorn tops rising toward the east. I glared into the rifts among the rocks, for any movement, for the dark line. "There's a good chance she'll go back with you," I said. "Just shake my hand and go."

He looked past me into the distance to the west.

"Last night," he said. "The stars. Everything so perfect. A thing like that can't happen."

From behind the last island discernible in the mist, where I couldn't be sure if it was a rock or a shadow or my imagination, came a long, flat shape; like a canoe. It stopped, then drifted silkily ahead.

"Nello," I called softly. I looked through the binoculars. We were heading away from the islands, amassing more and more mist between us, and what had been to my naked eye a shadow of a line became, through binoculars, a diffused stain. Nello came aft, looked through the binoculars, then handed them back to me.

"It's them. Right?" I said.

"Jesus, Cappy. I don't know. Could be them. Could be anything. Could be nothing."

"But you said they'd turn here."

"Cappy . . . ."

"Why would they stay out in the open? Way out of their way?"

"I told you: he was raised to deceive. Whatever you think he'll do, he'll do the opposite. Wherever you think he'll go, he'll go the other way. And when you think you figured him out, when you expect him to do the opposite, he'll do the opposite of that."

"But he let us see him. Was that on purpose, do you think? Is he trying to draw us in there among the rocks?"

"I don't know."

"What's your gut feeling?"

"My gut's in knots."

The rocks of the islands blurred; only the dark spruce trunks twisted, crippled in the fog.

"And if I follow him in there?"

"There is a short sound with a channel at its end, but I don't know it well. We'd have to hit it at high, high tide. At dusk. Maybe that's fine. Maybe we'd get through. But if we run aground, we'll be there till April."

"That's what he wants, isn't it?"

"You think so?"

"Sure."

"Then probably not."

The last twisted spruce trunk paled, then vanished. We sailed placidly through the fog; the western shore we saw just before tacking; the slopes of eastern forest, warmed all day by the sun, emerged as we neared in layers of rounded hills.

By dusk the air had cooled, but the wind remained. The eastern shores suddenly steepened, darkened, then split and, with two small islands marking an entrance, opened into a narrow sound. It reached fogless but dismal, twisting at the feet of rocky bluffs, as uninviting as a grave. We turned. The wind rose and pushed us in. The bank of fog towered behind us pressing us into the gloom.

The closeness of the place was suffocating. Out in the strait, in the fog, I could at least imagine open water around us, but here—trapped by the bluffs and brooding cedars and black water still as glass—I had the sensation of falling down a well in a dream.

"Five miles to the village," I heard Nello say, and all the time I kept falling.

Slivers of islands—reduced to forms of least resistance by the relentless back-and-forth scouring of the tides—shot by us. Twilight fell. The wall of fog closed in from behind, then, just as it buried the stern, it burst, shooting plumes among the trees and over islands. We glided in silence. The fog filled every indentation, every hollow. There was something unspeakably foreign about the place; the strange bittersweet smell of the evergreens, the riddled fog, the uncertain light that now grew dim, now brightened, as if even the sun wasn't sure whether to stay or go. The silent current carried us with an eerie lack of movement of the ketch. The sails stayed full yet the wind seemed to come from nowhere. According to the compass, we were heading south, which made no sense—not much did except for the smell of fried meat from the galley.

Sayami was behind me on the aft deck, oiling, cleaning, adjusting the Winchester for the hundredth time in two days, wrapping it in a grease-soaked rag to keep the fog off it, coddling it with the tenderness of a lover. Nello sat in the bow, his legs crossed, leaning slightly forward, motionless, like a watchful Buddha. Patches of fog drifted over him, buried him, then flew off, and he and the bowsprit stood out starkly against the black water.

I heard Kate whisper, *Then what?* And I could see her walk away.

Nello tensed. He was staring to port, off the bow, into the shadow of the hollow bluff. I looked until my eyes burnt but saw nothing. I heard Sayami breathing behind me, then a soft sound, the cloth sliding from the rifle onto the deck, and the sound of the rifle being pumped, slowly and as silently as possible.

We all saw it at once. The killer whale's back was as black as the sea, but sliced the water into a sinuous wake with its tall fin. He dove with a violent splash of his tail that shattered the stillness until the last echo was swallowed by the gloom.

The pass narrowed; there was less light. To be safe, I edged the ketch into the center. Sayami stirred. He had risen to one knee and, with an elbow on a stanchion, held the Winchester.

Charlie popped out the hatch. "Cappy," she said with her warmest smile. "Eat now?"

"Shhh," Sayami whispered. "Shhh."

He raised the rifle and aimed. Nello spun around and looked at me, hand questioning. I thought they had both lost their minds; nothing moved anywhere. Only the dusk thickened. A breath of wind swirled the mist. I heard Sayami stop breathing. Ahead, the mist solidified, and there, where Sayami was aiming, was the dark canoe. They were maybe ten boat-lengths ahead, close to shore, moving in the slower part of the current, and I could make out the Kwakiutl's broad shoulders, slowly leaning, pulling, leaning, pulling. He was on one knee in the stern, paddling on his right side, full strokes but jagged, as if his strength had ebbed. She was slumped in the bow. We closed in. Sayami, aiming, whispered, "Do I shoot him?"

I couldn't answer. Suddenly all I wanted was to turn the ketch and go home.

"If he turns around it'll be too late," Sayami pleaded.

"You might shoot her," I snapped.

"How bad a shot you think I am?"

He was right. The canoe was off our bow quarter, with a goodly space between the Kwakiutl and Kate.

"Would you shoot if you were me?" I whispered.

"I don't know," he said.

We couldn't have been more than a hundred feet away.

"Last chance," Sayami whispered. We were so close we could see the Kwakuitl's muscles bulge as he pulled the paddle trough. "Damn you!" Sayami hissed, as the Kwakiutl turned. He must have sensed us, for we made no sound, and he turned and looked at us, unsure but unafraid. Then he pulled ferociously. And pulled. They were getting away. Kate raised her head, as if awaking from a dream. Her face was drawn, barely hanging on to life.

"Kill him," I whispered.

"Damn you!" Sayami hissed.

"Kill him!"

"You kill him," and he thrust the rifle at me.

All in one mindless motion I spun, raised the rifle, barely aimed, and fired. The bluffs thundered back the sound.

The Kwakiutl lurched forward with his head thrown back, his back arched, but still he plunged the paddle in and tried to pull; but then, as if possessed, he rose, twisted, teetered, stumbled. "Jeezus," Sayami whispered—as the Kwakiutl plunged his paddle again and again, madly paddling air. Finally something inside him must have broken, because he stopped, then slowly, like a falling tree, tumbled over the side. With his foot caught under the thwart, he flipped the canoe on its side. The canoe filled and the current sucked it under.

The water was empty.

"Nello!" I yelled.

But Nello was flinging the skiff into the sea. Then he was in it and rowing like a madman. I spun the wheel. The ketch turned, the sails slatted. We headed after him—toward the empty water.

Nello was halfway there when the water near him burst, and out popped the oily bottom of the overturned canoe. Nello lifted its side to look below; then lowered it. And kept rowing.

I felt Sayami gently take the rifle from my hand. Charlie buried her face in her hands. "Poor Cappy," she sobbed. "Poor Cappy."

KATE

The Burial Cave

I'm sure I'm dying. Everything seems so very far away: the canoe, my hands, the broken shells next to my face as I lie on the beach. Even the tiny, transparent fish that skitter across the water and up onto the rocks. I paddle only once, then stop, not because I'm tired, but because it seems silly to try when the sea is so unreachable. I felt better for a while after the hot stones, but through the cold fog, hour by hour, I feel myself slip away. We are in a long, dark passage when I hear a noise, I turn, and there float tall sails against the hills, like great white wings of the Angel of Death. There's a terrifying boom, and then I'm under the black water. So silent. He pulls me out into a dark and sloping tomb, with just a cloud of light in the water at my feet. So cold. He lifts me on top of him and wraps his arms around me to keep me warm. Slowly, the water recedes, until on its surface shines a brilliant moon. Its light dances on the ceiling of our big, big tomb. He picks me up and sits me against the wall. On either side of me sit a row of dead. Some just bones, others shrunken flesh. So quiet. All in a row. On the far wall are piles of boxes and baskets and some canoes. He pushes a canoe over the sloping stones into the water, shattering the moonlight. The tomb goes dark. With all of us dead.

20

The Village

The whole ceremony to me was almost as impressive as the pipes over a grave, and I came away with a profound disgust for our so-called civilization, which is so intolerant, that it tries to stop such rites. Pagan they may be, but what right have we to say that therefore they are wrong, and what right have we to abolish, with them, the rich life of a people whose only crime was that they lived in a country which we want?

—T. F. McIlwraith, Anthropologist (1922)

I remember Nello passing me the bottle, saying sit down, sit down. Then him turning the ketch, working the sails, while Charlie held the wheel. I don't remember anything else until I awoke on deck.

A sky full of stars hovered over me. We stood so still that the tip of the mast pointed frozen at a star. A moon sat above a wooded hill and, below it, a curved beach glowed in the moonlight with enormous windowless houses, their gables facing the water, ringing the shore. A cloud of sparks shot from a roof and smoke wafted in the night.

I felt no sadness, not even loss, just a hard, deep cold I had never felt before, as if, somewhere deep inside, the fire had gone out.

THE HALYARDS HUNG as if painted on the mist. A timid dawn came without color, lighting up a scrub islet next to us that closed off the cove. The crescent beach curved between rocky points, with dark canoes lying at odd angles in the sand, and the houses of the forlorn village in a line above it. The cove was so still, the reflections so perfect, that the tall carved poles, the skeletal posts of houses, the pilings that supported rough shacks on the shore, all seemed twice as long, twice as delicate.

The cold from inside had overtaken me. I was too numb to move. Why would I? To go where? Do what?

Among the reflections of the cove, something moved. With long limbs like a water bug, it glided over the sea, coming slowly, carefully, until I recognized Nello's flat hat, and the oars. He rowed to where I lay in the stern, took in the oars, turned, broke into a drunken grin, and, blowing a cloud of rum into the dawn, proclaimed, "She's alive."

I WARMED THROUGH as if the noonday sun had blasted down on me. I helped Nello out of the skiff, as if he needed it, then went below and started breakfast, as if Charlie had wanted it; woke up Sayami to change his bandage and he cursed me for it. I ran around putting things in order, recoiled lines, refolded sails, scrubbed down the decks, then stood in the cockpit out of breath and the sun hadn't yet risen.

Nello brought out steaming plates and handed me one. "Your favorite," he said.

They were the best flapjacks I'd ever had. I chatted away about everything, anything: checking the level of the gas, whipping some lines, retying baggywrinkles, greasing through-hulls, maybe even giving the skiff a coat of paint if we—

"Cappy?" Nello cut in. "We can't see her for four days."

I calmed down.

"She's sick," he went on gently. "A *pexala* is with her; a shaman. A very good one who can cure anything."

"But four days," I objected.

"That's how it's done when you lose your soul."

I must have given him some kind of look, because he reddened and snapped impatiently, "When you have a terrifying fright, you lose your soul and get sick: that's life. Your soul escapes through your breath. If it can't get back in, the *pexala* comes to catch it."

"And if he can't?"

"It's worked for eight thousand years, Cappy. Why would it quit today?"

At the edge of the village, against the dark forest, someone hung a red blanket on a line.

KATE
The Shaman

In the night they carry me into a dark house with a fire in the middle of the floor. They lay me naked on a mat beside the flames; I see white eyes in the shadows. I am too weak to move; my chest is so heavy I can only take tiny breaths. A painted face is thrust into mine, with bloodshot eyes among the creases. His jaw trembles as he contorts his naked, painted body, a ring of branches around his neck and a crystal in his hand that throws beams of light into the dark. He writhes, possessed, lunges at me, then lifts me up and at once there is deafening drumming and women's voices droning an endless "eeeeee."

He carries me around and around the fire, places me back on the mat, trembles, and then bends so far forward that his head almost touches the ground. He runs his hands slowly down my head and down my sides, then he throws himself beside me and squeezes my head, my breasts, my belly, down. He grunts, his head touching my breast and then his mouth is sucking just below my breasts, until he lifts his head, pulls what looks like a thick, bloody worm from his mouth and throws it, with a cry, into the fire. I'm drenched in sweat; a woman with large naked breasts comes and wipes me dry with something coarse, then throws it into the fire along with some small fish and my pajamas, and they all smoke and fill the house with stench.

The other grabs for something among the flames, then he cries out and jabs it into the base of my skull.

The woman takes off her cedar-bark skirt and lets it catch fire, collecting the ashes in a pot. She stirs in fish-stink oil, then spreads the muck all over me. Many hands pass me four times through a ring of boughs, then hold the ring into the fire and take it flaming out into the night. I'm left on the mat alone with sparks flying through the roof to the stars.

21

Waiting

Sick people are required to wash every evening at dusk; therefore, their small houses are near the water. Most of them receive their songs from the noise of the water. They will hold a stone near the surface of the water and listen to the noise that it makes. They are quite naked when doing this.

—Franz Boas

The tide had come in, setting some canoes afloat, and stocky forms in blankets or trousers ambled down the steps in the bank, pushed off, and vanished among the rocks and reefs and islets of the shoals.

The village awoke slowly. Smoke rose in patches through the long planks of the roofs as if each house were smoldering; doors slammed and the sound echoed on the waters; kids ran along the wooden walkway before the houses, weaving among teetering carved poles that dwarfed them all; and old men came and sat around the great platform that jutted out over the water on pilings. Women came down to the beach and raised their skirts to pee in the sea. Someone hung laundry on the salal bushes.

I couldn't sit still, so I untied the skiff and set the oars.

"Don't go ashore," Nello said. "Not today."

I headed for the island. A canoe passed close by me with a man and woman paddling, their reflections so perfect that it looked as if water spirits mimicked their every move. Near the point, an old man gutted fish, spread them flat, held them open with sticks, and hung them on a rack over a smoldering fire.

In front of the houses, the enormous carved poles stood out against the sky. The largest, a long-breasted woman with puffy lips and eyes, reached her arms in a frightening welcome. A life-sized killer whale stood on its upturned head, its tail high, its mouth opened wide. On the biggest house was painted the image of a bird with its wings spread, head raised. Its monstrous head and beak—carved from a single log—burst seaward beyond the walk, its shadow reaching out over the water. The carved figure of a man, set in the bank, held it up. Farther down, a halibut the size of a canoe, harshly carved and painted in black, red, and white, seemed to float in the air, its tail on the edge of the walk, its chin, over the midden, supported by a pole. And where the walls no longer stood and roofs no longer hung, wide-eyed bears and solemn eagles and bent-kneed giants with their paint worn off long ago stood rotting in deep bramble. No longer frightening, the bear paws seemed to reach out for company.

I was at a respectful distance from the shore when the sun came over the forest slope and lit the beach and walk. All at once the village filed out and sat on the great platform or the steps, soaking up the warmth of the sun.

But by noon it had started to rain.

It was a misty, drifting rain that settled like a fine frost on the ropes, on our coats, in our hair. We stretched the awning over the cockpit, but the slightest breeze brought the rain in our faces and fogged my binoculars as I surveyed the shore.

Work in the village went on through the rain. Canoes came and were unloaded of stacks of blankets, boxes, and cedar baskets. Fires were started on the beach under the smoke racks near the rocky point and women wrapped in blankets squatted on their haunches, boiling clams before laying them, skewered, over the smoke racks. And the carved giant holding up the bird's beak was getting a fresh coat of paint.

"It'll be the biggest potlatch ever," Nello said. "And probably the last. The police are bound to show up sooner or later."

The sick came down to the water's edge and splashed handfuls of water at the sea. I watched the shore and the village all day but she was nowhere.

Darkness fell slowly in the rain. We ate in silence and drifted away to bed. I lay in my berth listening to the rain dripping from the rigging, and when I heard snoring from the bow and long breaths from the stern, I went out and silently pushed off in the skiff. The shore was dark, only the embers below the smoke racks gave a glow, and threads of light shimmered between house planks. I knelt in the bow and paddled to the point, then, circling through the woods, came into the village from behind. All silent.

The houses towered over me. I laid my ear against the planks but heard only snoring. Above me a crack spilled light, so I clambered onto a woodpile and peered in.

The interior was an enormous open space ringed by a double platform like an endless two-tiered stage, each platform chest-high and a couple of strides deep. In the center of a vast dirt floor, big logs flamed, and through the smoke-hole in the roof, the rain misted down among dangling ropes and racks. Across the way, steps led up to the only opening; on either side of it, colossal carved beasts with crazed eyes and sickle-length teeth held up the giant ridgepoles of the roof. On each upper platform stood a tiny, open-fronted house in which, beyond partially drawn curtains, dark forms slept. All was still; there was no sign of her.

The other big houses were pretty well the same except the last one. It was much wider and higher than the rest and the floor was dug deep into the ground, making the roof higher still. And it was empty. The two tiers of platforms were without the little houses, no signs of life apart from an old man sitting by a fire in the middle of the floor, nodding off but shaking himself awake as if he were guarding all that empty space. He must have heard me rustle, because he lifted his head and stared in my direction. I slipped away into the darkness to the shore. The tide was in, so I had to keep to the narrow strip between the midden and the sea, passing the smoldering smoke racks, heading toward the shack of the sick that stood on pilings at the water's edge. The rain hardened; shells crunched underfoot. A fire's glow and soft moaning came through the planks. I climbed the steps.

The fire burnt on a thick bed of sand over the floor-boards, and under blankets lay shapes so frail they barely made a ripple. Only one rocked lightly in rhythm with the moaning. The wooden latch was tight with rain and gave a thud as I slipped it, and as I stepped in, a floorboard creaked so loud I expected everyone to jump. From under the first blanket an ancient, cracked foot stuck out; I moved on. The moaning grew. A clump of long, tangled hair stuck out from the next. I reached down to lift a corner but lost my balance and pulled back half of it. A girl lay there: oval face, straight nose, sad eyes, and fleshy lips cracked from fever—closed tight as if holding secrets. She had no fear. I looked at her, pleading for silence, and her eyes softened for a moment before sinking deep and distant again. As I moved on, she grabbed my ankle. The frail hand had surprising strength, but her gaze was so uncertain I couldn't tell what she wanted. I pulled away and stepped gingerly ahead. It might have been the rain on the roof or the wind in the trees, but the moaning now seemed plainly, clearly to whisper, "Please. Oh, please." I leaned down. The form under the blanket seemed shapeless. I lifted a corner. As if blown by a blast of air, the blanket flew back and a naked, ash-covered woman—grayer than the dead—bolted upright. Her crazed eyes glared through paste and matted hair, the dark of one eye in the corner near her nose, her mouth open round, forming an ugly hole. "EeseOeese," she moaned. "Oeeeese." I ran. Missed the steps, crashed onto the beach, then scuttled through darkness to the skiff.

Can't be her. Can't be.

The rain strengthened and clattered on the shells.

22

A Dream

All nature, the heavenly bodies, rocks and islands, waterfalls, animals, and plants are beings of supernatural power whom man can approach with prayer, whose help he can ask.

—Franz Boas

I stayed in the skiff all night, adrift on the shifting currents. Twice I pulled ashore and went back to the shack to look through the cracks, but the fire had died down, and the moaning woman, sitting up, her mad face staring at nothing, was even less definable than before. I didn't dare go in, afraid she might cry out and wake the village, but neither could I go back to the ketch and leave her. I drifted, dozing, letting the current wash me past the point into the kelp beds, where the rattle of the oarlocks would wake me, and I'd row back past the village again. Just before dawn, when the night seemed darkest, the water murmured under the bilges, and I felt my head slump forward. And dreamt.

She stood on a long sand beach in a turquoise lagoon, beyond which waves crashed on the reefs, murmured as they died, and left a white line below the deep blue sky. I walked toward her but as I neared she turned away. And began walking. I ran after her and she walked slowly, unhurriedly, but the harder I ran, the more distant she became, until she was just a faint shadow on the horizon. And I was no longer sure if she had ever been there at all. I felt tears on my face. I awoke. The night was dark with rain. The dark sea glowed among the darker islands. The current flowed by the kelp, the skiff, the oars, outlining all with beads of phosphorescence.

At dawn, the clouds slumped heavily across the wet boards of the roofs.

KATE
The Cure of Death

I awake to a deserted house and silence, with the fire down to coals and dawn in the smoke-hole above me. There is the pleasant smell of fresh-sawn wood, and when I turn my head I see a coffin lying near me, new and clean: the most inviting thing I have seen since I left home. The door opens, steps approach softly, and the great painted face hovers over me. It's too dark to see his eyes but his hair glows like a halo. He pours something in the fire and when flames fly, he comes back and looks into my eyes. He seems puzzled, sits down on the coffin, pokes the fire, his gaze following the sparks as they rise. He drags the coffin next to me, looks at me again, then pushes it resolutely into the flames. As it catches, sparking and crackling, he lifts what looks like a skinny doll as tall as he, into his arms. He brings it slowly, stands over me, then lowers it toward me. Oh, no. No, no. The lips are gone, the eyes, just old skin cracked and tight. A corpse; long dead. He holds the empty head, and puts it on my breast, again and again, growling a song. Then he lays the corpse on me. Oh, no. Dear God, no.

23

POTLATCH: THE FIRST DAY

To attempt to describe the condition of these tribes would be to produce a dark and revolting picture of human depravity. The dark mantle of degrading superstition enveloped them all, and their savage spirits, swayed by pride, jealousy and revenge, were ever hurrying them to deeds of blood.

—WILLIAM DUNCAN, Anglican Missionary

One of the chief characteristics of the Indians on the B.C. coast is their hospitality and I have never known of a single instance where anyone was allowed to go hungry while an Indian had food near him. This hospitality has been regardless of race or color.

—W.M.HALLIDAY, Indian Agent (1918)

Is it not a beautiful custom among these savages *(wilden)* that they bear all deprivations in common, and are also at their happiest best eating and drinking together. I often ask myself what advantages our "good society" possesses over that of the "savages" . . . . If this trip has for me (as a thinking person) a valuable influence, it lies in the strengthening of the viewpoint of the relativity of all cultivation, and that the evil as well as the value of a person lies in the cultivation of the heart.

—Franz Boas

I awoke in my berth to thunderous drumming.

"Cappy, you're wanted," Nello called from above.

I climbed up into a day as gloomy as the dawn; the chill in the air warned of snow.

A boat-length from the ketch were four canoes full of broad-shouldered men, some moving their paddles to hold the canoes in the stream, others banging them against the gunwales in unison.

A magnificent man stood in the first canoe: head raised, wearing a carved eagle helmet, its wings spread toward the clouds. A dark blanket hung over one shoulder, trimmed in red, decorated with shells, but under it he wore a gold-trimmed purple coat that could have belonged to an admiral of some tiny landlocked nation or the doorman of a high-priced downtown hotel. Below it showed tuxedo trousers and bare feet. He carried a carved stick taller than himself, ringed with bands of hammered silver and topped with a brass knob from a bedstead. He spoke with proudly lifted head and raised right arm, his voice as lordly as a challenge, as emotive as an oration.

"He said he has paddled clean around the world," Nello translated.

"From where?" I asked.

"From the beach there. We like to exaggerate."

As he spoke, the man stepped gracefully from the canoe and walked toward us—ankle-deep in forty feet of water. He stopped with an arm raised, like some apparition, in the middle of the sea.

"How did he do that?" I whispered.

"Christ only knows," Nello said.

The man talked on, waving here, gesturing there.

"Is he threatening?"

"He's inviting us to his feast."

"As the main course?"

Instead of answering, Nello raised his right arm and, in a voice deep and stern, gave a long reply.

"What did you say?" I asked.

"Thank you."

WHEN THE CHIEF had walked back to his canoe and the canoes turned for shore, I pointed at the sick shack. "Last night, I saw a woman in there. Her eyes were deranged, her face so twisted I couldn't tell for sure but—"

"But what?"

"Do you think it could be her?"

"Do you?"

"Yes."

"Then it's probably not."

CANOES CAME FROM both north and south all day, some single, some rafted together to make a stable barge, bringing what had been secretly made or accumulated over years: masks, boxes, baskets, furs, enormous carved feast dishes the size of a small bathtub; piles of blankets, sacks of flour, pails, mirrors, bolts of cloth, washbasins, pots, pans, hats, braided wreaths of cedar, stickloads of bracelets.

Everything they brought was to be given away to celebrate the past year's big events: deaths, births, marriages, the raising of poles, the building of houses, the transfer of rights to fishing privileges or berry patches. "They come to feast, to sing and dance, Cappy. Tseka—Thanksgiving, Christmas, and Halloween rolled into one. Feasts and theater all winter long. We forget the world outside, just laugh and cry and frighten each other to death, and kiss each other's wives because there is no jealousy during Tseka."

At noon he rowed ashore and came back an hour later, excited.

"Come on, Cappy. I found a cousin married into this tribe. She'll show us around. We might just . . . ." But he stopped when he saw my eyes.

Charlie stayed aboard to look after Sayami, and Sayami to safeguard Charlie. We rowed to the north end of the beach, and landed near the brambles where smoke rose from fires that burnt in pits like shallow graves. Women tended them, putting a layer of stones over the coals, then flopping salmon and halibut onto the stones and covering them with seaweed to bake. Their movements were flowing, unhurried, the way small waves move as they spread over the sand. They watched me curiously as I said, "Good morning," but made no reply.

Where seals were being butchered out, a cloud of gulls shrieked and circled, then flew off toward canoes that came in, heaped with fish. Men were hauling great loads on their shoulders, and young girls worked an open fire ringed by skewers and roasting-tongs stuck into the sand—all with fish heads and slabs of fish and fish tails on them. The roasting fish smoldered when the girls watched the men more than the flames. They looked at us openly with dark, knowing eyes; one with a sensuous mouth and blanket open at her bare chest looked away, as if she knew men like us from before.

The village rose above us on the midden. From close in you could see its steep, eroded side and the dark layers of earth and white layers of shells where, over the centuries, the remains of old villages piled upon each other. Stairs led up the midden onto the boardwalk. Two strides wide, it ran the length of the village, covered with old and young: carrying or stacking high the arriving presents, or sitting weaving, or hanging hemlock branches onto housefronts. A raven cawed from a roof. We walked under fixed gazes and suspicious eyes, carved posts with monstrous heads towering over us. I stumbled over a loose plank and into the arms of an ancient woman. Her weathered skin hung in deep folds, her gray hair flew wildly, and her nose and jaw were as twisted as her feet. I apologized. She said something and laughed, and loud laughter rose around us.

"She said she'd keep you," Nello said, "if only you were younger."

We were stopped by two black bears beside a door. They were perfect but for their dead eyes and their angular human movements. Nello pulled me away like you pull a child. "That's the house of the Hamatsa, the Cannibal Dancers. If someone who shouldn't goes in there, he dies. And that's no theater."

A few houses farther on, we ducked through a yawning mouth into the gloom of a great house where the stench of urine mingled with smoke. "Don't stand there, Cappy, that's the pee box," Nello said. "We use it to wash blankets. And to wash our feet to keep away ghosts."

Around a fire in the center of the house, women squatted on their haunches, taking hot stones with tongs and dropping them into wooden boxes spouting vapors that smelled of fish. A pretty young woman came toward us; pieces of abalone shells hung from her ears and played in the light. "My cousin," Nello said, then, "Captain Dugger. An old friend."

"My soup is almost done," she said in perfect English. "I will show you the village." And she went back to her box.

"She speaks well," I said to Nello.

"Best in the village," he said. "She learnt from the missionaries when they came a decade ago and took away the children. It was for their own good, they said; for their health. Like hell. It was to teach them to speak white, think white. Be good white Injuns to work in sawmills and canneries, not ones that quit to go feast and dance all winter. That's why they hate the potlatch, Cappy. It doesn't make good slaves. Anyway, the kids refused to learn."

"Except me," the cousin said. "I learnt. I wanted to know what they said behind my back."

She led us out toward the quiet end of the village and, looking directly at me, asked, "Are you her husband?"

I started to answer, but was stopped by a hardness in her eyes.

"I thought so," she said. "The *paxala* has many places: huts in the woods, caves. All hidden."

"She's not in the sick hut, is she? There's a woman there who—"

"There's just a girl and an ancient one, and a crazy lady. Nice but crazy."

"And in the Hamatsa house?" Nello said.

"Maybe," she said.

By the time we rowed back to the ketch, the air had chilled and the first flakes of snow ghosted over the sea.

At dusk the beach emptied, the canoes stood alone, and the embers of the fires glowed through the falling snow. Snow-blurred figures with blankets over their heads shuffled like humble faithful along the boardwalk, heading toward the great house at the north end of the cove.

A booming voice drifted across the water, muffled by snow.

"It's beginning," Nello said. "Dress warm; we could be there awhile."

"How long a while?"

"Hard to say. My uncle went to one for a day and stayed two years." And he folded two blankets for him and Charlie. "You coming or staying?" he asked Sayami.

"You kidding?" Sayami smiled. "You think I'd miss a party?"

With all of us aboard, the skiff had little freeboard, so I rowed slowly. We hauled the skiff up the beach to just below the midden, out of the reach of the rising tide. "Remember where we're leaving it," Nello instructed. "Below the killer whale pole. And remember where the stairs are. If we're separated—or if anything happens—we meet back here. If the skiff is gone—"

"Why would it be gone?" I cut in.

"I don't know. But if it's gone, just take the smallest canoe and get back to the ketch."

"And if that's gone?"

He ignored me. "Take it and don't wait. For anyone. They won't wait for you."

The snow had covered the midden and the houses, and hooded the eyes of the carved beasts as if putting them to sleep. The people filed by barefoot through the snow, some carrying twigs as torches, others holding dried eulachons with their tails aflame. They stopped at the big house. At each boom of the voice from inside, a man stepped from the line—always of noble carriage, richly dressed in furs or ornate blankets—climbed the short steps to the door, and stood with the light from inside throwing a glow around him; his tribe followed close behind.

"The chiefs are received in order of stature," Nello said.

When everyone else was inside, the name of the ketch, a bit garbled, was called.

"Go, Cappy," Nello said. "You chief."

I walked slowly up the steps.

24

POTLATCH: THE FIRST NIGHT

The missionaries have labored for years to convert the Indians to industrious white ways, but the results seem to be negative. Until the potlatch is eliminated, there is not much chance for any great progress. The potlatch takes so much of their time and so many hours are spent at it in laziness and idling that it does not produce energy and ability.

—W.M. HALLIDAY, Indian Agent, Alert Bay (1913)

Every Indian or other person who engages in or assists in celebrating or encourages either directly or indirectly another to celebrate any Indian festival, dance or other ceremony of which the giving away of goods or articles forms a part . . . is guilty of an offence and is liable to imprisonment.

—SECTION 149 OF *The Indian Act Statutes of Canada*

Towering flames leapt from the fire pit in the vast house, licking roof beams and igniting sparks in roof planks. Around the fire the floor was empty but the raised platforms against the walls were dense with people sitting on their haunches, wrapped in their blankets, all watching me. On the far wall above the ramps hung torn sails painted with monstrous faces blinking and snarling as they moved in the fire's breeze, and far above them, catwalks, trapezes, and pulleys dangled from heavy ropes. Across from the entrance sat the chiefs, and at their feet sat the singers moaning a slow song, drumming on boards with long batons, or on skin drums that they held out to tighten near the flames. Only then did I notice the pack of carved beasts around me.

Enormous crude snouts encircled the door opening: a wolf with its head raised and teeth bared, standing on its tail; another with its neck twisted, snout down, jaws awry, the eyes wide open as if frozen in horror; and one, lying horizontally overhead, had its paws dangling near my shoulders. The flames died down. The two bears that had guarded the Hamatsa house, guided me down the steps, along the edge of the floor, up to our seats, on the top platform, in the shadows of a corner. Nello, Charlie, and Sayami came close behind. Near the singers, a row of solemn figures sat as still and dark as tombstones. "The family of those who died," Nello whispered. "A mourning song for them." It was a stumbling song, erratic like the beats of a frightened heart. The drums rolled softly as if from a place far away.

I searched every face, but the flames danced and shadows flickered and faces burst out for a moment, only to vanish in the darkness. Over the moaning a few clear words were repeated. I nudged Nello. "They're asking, 'Which way is he gone?'"

"Who?"

"The one who died."

One by one more voices joined, wistful, questioning. The

smoke burnt my eyes so I closed them, and with the drumming and moaning I drifted off. Tum, ta ta tum, ta, ta, tum, tum.

At a distant raven's call, I awoke. The fire was down, the smoke hung in flat layers drifting on the currents. A solemn sitter rose and began to dance, head down, arms raised and swinging while circling the fire, now and then shuddering the way cormorants do when trying to dry their wings. "Shaking off sadness," Nello whispered. One by one the sitters rose, all dancing the same way, as if feeling the same pain, shaking the same sorrow. Then the first one cupped her hands, drew water from a cedar box, and poured it over her eyes. The others did the same. The drums now beat louder, the voices grew stronger, the dancers moved freely. A bear neared the fire and hurled a pail of oil into the flames; the flames roared to the roof, and in that same instant the drumming and voices stopped.

The first great, carved bowl—in the shape of a reclining giant, bearded but with pendulous breasts—appeared in the doorway, and the fragrance of stewed meat filled the air. Four men hauled it to the chiefs, lifted the face, and served the first chief from the hollow head. The right breast was removed and the second chief was fed. They took her apart in pieces, finally scooping the contents of the hollowed trunk into small bowls and handing them to the crowd along with shredded cedar inner-bark to wipe our mouths. We ate a frothy mush that looked like melted soap that drooped when lifted with the wooden spoon.

"Seal stew," Nello offered.

"Boiled blubber," I said.

"Not to eat is a mortal offense. And we don't swallow the spoon; we eat only with the point. We're not savages."

A little boy ran down onto the floor but a roaring bear chased him back. Long trays arrived laden with hemlock boughs and seaweed that reeked of putrid fish and had clusters of tiny pale balls all over them. "Dried herring roe, Cappy. It's good, I promise." Sayami loved it, and Charlie didn't mind it, so I took a bite. The stench of it choked me and the brittle seaweed stuck in my throat.

"Dip in here," a soft voice beside me said. "It will go down more easily," and out of the darkness flashed the cousin's abalone earrings as she held out a bowl of thick liquid. "It's the most precious thing to the Kwakiutl," she said.

It ran thickly down my fingers, so I splashed it in my mouth.

"Water," I pleaded.

"No water," Nello said. "Water and oil don't mix. Make you retch." I couldn't answer, just tried to hold it down. The drummers started a rhythm and the cousin came back with a square wood pail. "Drink this," she said. I started to push it away until I smelled the rum. I filled my mouth with it, then swallowed it, then filled my mouth again. I must have drunk a mug. They all laughed, and they all drank. The fire was so low it barely lit our faces. I pulled Sayami to one side and before he could say a word I took my hat and jammed it on his head. With my hat here I wouldn't be missed. "Back soon," I said.

Nello grabbed at me but I slipped away along the dark wall and out the door into the night.

It was brighter outside than it had been in the house. Thick snow covered the walk, the beasts, the canoes; it stuck to the walls, molded the bushes into one, and weighed down their branches; the only thing it couldn't hide was the darkness of the sea. It crunched in singsong under my feet. When I heard voices behind me, I jumped between two houses and watched as young men came out with empty trays and walked away into the next house. I moved along in a deep crouch. When the rum hit me, I leaned against a wall.

I thought I saw the ketch through the falling snow, then it was gone and reappeared near the far tip of the cove, and at the end I wasn't sure if I had seen her at all. Perhaps she had dragged anchor and had been blown out to sea. Who knows, who cares? I thought, too drunk to give a damn. "Let her go, Cappy," I whispered. "Let her go."

A gust came through the trees and swept snow onto me from the roof. I got up to go but couldn't think of where to, until the snow melted on my neck and I remembered—her. I headed for the house the bears had guarded. In the next gust, an owl took flight and swept over the cove. "While the owl lives, the soul lives," I muttered, and pushed on. The drums behind me had faded to a drone.

With the bears gone, the Hamatsa house was unguarded, but its door padlocked. I tried forcing it with my shoulder; it wouldn't budge, but a barely perceptible moaning rose inside. I went between the houses to the back but there were no other openings and there was no way to the roof. At the house next door I climbed onto a pile of firewood stacked high against the wall, grabbed a roofboard and pulled myself up. But the Hamatsa house was a good three strides away. On all fours, I scrambled to the gable; the gusting wind almost blew me down. With all the balance I could muster, I ran down through the snow and, spreading my arms and legs, hit the roof across the way. Splayed, I began to slide; I clawed until my nails dug into the wet roofboards and held. I slithered sideways to the back wall, trying roofboards until I found one that gave, and slid it aside. It was pitch black down below. Wedging my toes between the corner post and wall planks, I climbed down until I slipped and fell face down in the dirt. Light filtered feebly through the hole above, and I could make out shapes. Someone moaned close by.

Wooden masks with enormous beaks, and hemlock wreaths were piled around me. The moaning rose again and, with an arm extended, I moved toward it until I touched boards. The moaner seemed to have difficulty breathing. I was running my hands along the boards, feeling for an opening, when I heard footsteps in the snow. A key slid in the lock, then the smooth sound of the tongue sliding out, and a knock as it was lifted. Torchlight fell into the house and I looked for a place to hide, but there was nowhere, except a sheet covering long lumps on the floor. I crawled under it and tried not to breathe. The torchbearer took a few steps, slipped another lock, and at once the moaning became a menacing growl. The torchbearer gave gruff orders and the growling stopped. Then the torch neared and the sheet over my face turned bright and lit up the corpse that lay inches from my face. It was a dry, hollow-skinned, long-dead corpse, who stared curiously at me. The tip of his tongue stuck slightly out, as if, in the last moment of his life, he had been tasting something memorably good. I lay there in a drunken swoon, wondering if the deadman was me.

Doors thudded shut and locks slipped into place, but the torch remained. I pulled the sheet aside and raised my head. The main part of the house was empty, but inside a cage-like room something moved. Stepping among the masks and piles of cedar bark, I approached. Inside were two naked youths, their eyes wild, their carriages distorted, beastly. I started back toward the hole in the roof when, on an impulse, I stopped at the sheet, drew back a corner, and saw the other long-dead corpse: a woman. Her parchment-skinned face—salt-air-dried, wind-dried, sun-dried—had the eyelids drawn with deep folds as if she were dreaming. Her nose—a long miracle of rises and curves—was sculpted and delicate; her cheek bones were surrounded by shallows, and her eyebrows were raised, as if in surprise. There were swirls like whirlpools painted on her cheeks. She was beautiful; someone who must have loved and been loved all her life. The torch flared, then flickered out. Moonlight drifted in. I sat down beside her on the cold earth.

The snow had stopped falling. The moon shone bright on the edge of a cloud and threw dark shadows of the carved beasts on the snow. The ketch huddled white on the dark waters and the islands lay in paling layers until they blended together in the distance and the mist. I sneaked along the wall back to the big house.

Great piles of pots, blankets, pails, and mirrors were being carried in. Singing and drumming filled the air. The rum must have made its rounds, because many weaved and bobbed merrily as they sat, and others had bright twinkles in their eyes. Sayami's eyes were barely open, Nello wore a blissful smile, and Charlie too must have had her share, for her head lay heavily on his shoulders. No one seemed to care that I'd returned or even noticed that I had gone.

They had stacked all the gifts to be given away—bales of sea-otter skins, mink skins, and blankets, boxes of biscuits, pots, pails and kettles—in enormous piles on the ramps on both sides of the door, squeezing us farther and tighter in the corner, blocking our escape unless we descended to the floor. Trays of sweet steamed cakes of dried fruit came around: cranberries, crabapple, salmonberry—trailed by that cursed bucket of oil, of which I took only an empty spoon, but made up for it with long, long gulps of rum. I was handing the bucket back to the cousin when she leaned close and asked, "Where did you go?"

"The Hamatsa house," I said. "She wasn't there."

She smiled in case anyone was watching. "At dawn we'll find the shaman's shack. We can follow his footprints in the snow."

I took another slug of rum. People ate with fervor and no one seemed to notice that the beat of the drums had grown louder and as quick as the thumping of a heart.

Women pulled pails of ash from the fire and spread them around on the dirt, leaving a drifting ash cloud in their wake.

The mirrors, waist-high, dozens of them, had been put side by side all around the house, leaning against the lower rise around the floor, creating infinite images of flames. The ash cloud was settling when a wild cry from outside filled the night. The crowd fell silent, the drums barely thudded.

Across the way, a corner roof board was ripped aside and in glared flashing eyes. Then footsteps on the roof, and the roof board above us slid open. A low wail-like wind over a hollow log—surrounded the house. A gust of icy air swept through as a giant wooden mouth on the back wall yawned wide and into the house leapt—over the chiefs, landing in a cloud of ashes—one of the half-beasts I had seen in the Hamatsa house. He was naked as before, but now one side of his face drooped in a demented snarl as he crouched. People drew back from the edge of the lower ramp; only the chiefs managed to sit still. Near them, a man stood up, raised a white skull in each hand, shook them, making a rattling sound, took a step forward, and the half-beast stood still. The man climbed over the mirrors down to the floor. The half-beast cocked his head. Nello pulled Charlie close, turned her head away, and seemed to look around for an escape but we were blocked in by the mounds of gifts; the only quick way out was the hole in the roof. "You might not want to watch," Nello whispered. "Hamatsa. Cannibals."

"You said it was theater."

"Some is. This isn't."

The man shook his skulls, and the Hamatsa, coiled low, howled. The man made a triumphant half turn to the crowd, and in that instant the Hamatsa flew with jaws open wide and knocked him to the ground. He sank his teeth deep in the man's neck. Blood squirted in an arc and splattered in the ash. Screams rose from the crowd. Men leapt to the floor with sticks, yanking the Hamatsa back, while others forced a stick between his teeth.

A woman appeared, her bare breasts glowing crimson, her

skirt stirring the ashes, leaving low clouds in her wake, and she danced toward him, her palms up, as if she held some power. He grew calm.

Then, with great effort and a howl, he tore out of their grips and leapt into the crowd, clawing, biting bits out of whoever he reached. In the doorway, shrieking, *"Ha ap, hap hap,"* the other Hamatsa appeared. He was much older, fined-boned, light-skinned, almost white, with a limp, frail figure slung over a shoulder. He stopped on the steps.

"Half English," Nello whispered. "He helped Boas collect things—like corpses."

The white Hamatsa descended with his load—the long-dead corpse of the man I had seen before. He brought down the corpse—all dark, the skin shrunk into the hollows—and flung it to the floor. The first beast came and sniffed the thin legs, then leapt to a mirror. Awed by his own face, he glared and then smashed it with a violent blow. He watched the blood drip from his knuckles, then took a long, curved piece of the broken mirror, wrapped some shredded cedar bark around one end to make a handle, and waved it in wide arcs in the firelight. Staring at his splintered reflection, he came back to the corpse, lay the shard like a long blade on its chest, and then he sliced. He held up the long piece of flesh like a trophy in the light. The crowd gasped. The other grabbed it from his hand and they fought, snarling, like starved dogs feeding.

Their struggle fanned the flames and churned the ash until they vanished in a cloud of dust and smoke. When it thinned, the floor was empty; only the shard of mirror lay there, throwing a jagged reflection into the darkness.

25

Snowy Night

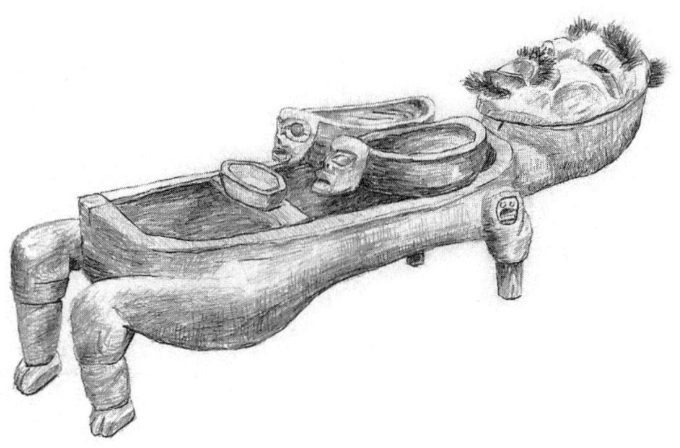

In the special house used for winter dances, secret tunnels were dug, and overhead mechanical devices installed . . . . Artificial limbs, guts, seal eyes and seal bladders filled with blood were used for gory effects . . . . Many of the torments however, did actually occur.

—Franz Boas

When I felt a warm breath on my neck, I thought Hamatsa, and I yanked out the pistol, fell against a mound of biscuit tins, and aimed squarely at the cousin's face. I was glad she couldn't see me go red in the dark. She glanced around to see if anyone had noticed but the fire was low and no one looked our way. Frightened groups broke up and people returned to their places, but the few raised voices were hushed as if one loud word would trigger the Hamatsa's return.

An old chief stood up, raised both arms, and in a voice so calm and melodious he could have been inviting us for tea began an interminable speech. The cousin leaned so close I felt her breath again and whispered, "The *paxala* left. We follow."

It was well after midnight but nowhere near dawn; the hole above us still yawned black. "In the dark?" I asked.

"The moon," she said. She turned and whispered something to Nello, then with quick motions climbed up the carved corner post and pulled herself through the hole into the night. I followed.

Below us, the islands and the village, snow-clad in the moonlight, seemed the most serene, peaceful place on earth. She scrambled up to the gable, where the open arms of the bear of the entrance pole towered over her. She grabbed the bear's arm, swung out, then, groping with her toes for footholds on knees and in open mouths, she climbed slowly down. We sneaked along the walls to the end of town and stopped near the shore. She leaned down in the snow and pointed to where small feet had left sharp-edged hollows. When she rose, there was a fierce look in her eyes that would have unnerved me even in broad daylight, but here, at the end of the earth in a half-light more eerie than darkness, I involuntarily grabbed her arm and she stiffened but she didn't look afraid—just defiant.

"Why are you helping me?"

"I'm not," she snapped. "I'm helping me. Find your stupid

woman and go. This is *our* Tseka." And she pulled away with force. "Ours!" she said, stepping backward in the snow and swinging her arm wide to include the village, the woods, the islands, and the stars. Then she strode off into the woods without looking to see if I would follow.

The paxala was either very old or very drunk, because he dragged his feet so much his toes rarely left the snow, and his path made no sense at all: weaved here, swerved there for no apparent reason in this open woods with gentle rises. He seemed to walk in arcs: one to the left, one to the right, then another to the same side. I lowered my feet cautiously so as not to crackle snow.

She walked slightly bent, nimble as a child, looking for the footsteps, which grew less distinct now in the tree-filtered light. Just ahead a big bird, roused, took flight, shaking a tree limb, and the snow drifted in sparkling clouds and thudded down in clumps. She stopped and knelt, but the clumps had cratered the snow over a wide patch and the footprints were gone. I looked for them where the craters ended, but there was only virgin snow.

"Go right, I'll go left," she whispered.

I had taken but a few steps when a hard gust shook the treetops and clumps thudded all around. I looked back; my steps were gone. Nothing moved in the moonlight.

"Calm down, Cappy, calm down."

Someone touched my shoulder.

The old paxala fanned the coals with drunken determination, until they flared and filled his small cave with light. He and the cousin talked in low, warbling sounds, patiently, waiting until the other had his say, then the *paxala* looked at me and launched into an oration. When he finished, the cousin said to me, "Very beautiful."

Quietly, I said, "Thank you."

"Not you." The cousin laughed. "Your woman."

Maybe it was the rum, or just the nerves of long days, but I laughed too. After that, I felt no need to be polite.

"When will I see her?" I asked.

The *paxala*'s reply was long. The cousin's face grew taut.

"He said," she began, and stumbled, "that she will come at midnight. With the ghosts."

The cave started tossing like a skiff in a storm. I put my hands on the ground.

"Alive or dead?" I blurted.

The *paxala* flung a log into the fire and sparks flew in the air. He spoke but the cousin said nothing, just looked at my face, as if what she saw there would in some way determine what she'd say.

"You white people," she began, then stopped as if the words defied continuance, then said simply, not accusing, "Have a simple world: day or night, alive or dead. What about in between? You have few words for rain, and few for the sea; we have them without end."

He stirred his fire, then spoke in rhythm with his stirring. The cousin spoke so softly her voice blended with his, and at times I couldn't tell whose words they were, or if they were at all.

"We have killer whale ancestors, and other ancestors that return as ravens. Live ones die, then come back: come and go like the tides. Dead, half dead, many times dead, many times returned, never-born, part-born, part-died. I was dead once," the *paxala* went on. "I died and they wrapped me in blankets. There was heavy snow falling, more than tonight, so they just took me to the end of the village and left me in the snow. They heard wolves howl there all night and in the morning I was gone. Many nights later they heard me singing. When the moon rose, I was on the point with the wolves around me . . . I don't look so bad, do I?" He stirred his coals to an unhurried time. "The Tuxwidl had the water of life."

A chink of light glowed beside the door: the moon, or the dawn, or something in between. The cave rolled again; this time putting my hands on the ground didn't help. I reached into my coat, pulled out the gun, but wasn't sure where to aim it, so I pointed it at the ground. He didn't even look up, just stared at the coals.

"Are there fences on the sea?" he asked. "Or borders among the stars?"

Then he said something with a sigh, and the cousin smiled.

"He said to pass you the rum."

I followed the setting moon among the trees out to the salal that blocked the shore, then turned north toward the village. The drums and the singers' voices were dampened by the snow. At the house of the Hamatsa, there was no lock on the door, so I stopped and tried it; it opened. There was silence inside. I left the door ajar. The long-dead woman lay there as before, only alone; she was even more beautiful now with the stray light from the moon. I thought of saving her; wrapping her in the sheet and carrying her down to the sea and the skiff. The tide had come in; I wouldn't have far to push. Then row out to the rocky islet just beyond the ketch and carry her up, shuffling through the snow. There was a cleft in a rock; I could lay her there and let her bask in the moonlight.

As I neared the big house, children's laughter rang out and echoed over the cove, again and again mingling with their shrieks, drifting over the snow like Christmas morning joy.

The big house was filled with that uncertain gloom of firelight and dawn. Overhead, dangling from ropes, a huge bird—a chaos of feathers, human limbs, and a great carved head with coppery eyes—fluttered and circled. On the floor, a black-bearded giant with long wooden breasts threw glittering dust from a basket over the crowd, and children leapt and grabbed for it amid long shrieks and laughter. Later a chief spoke but by then few listened; they leaned against the walls, or lay in each other's arms, and slept in the warmth of those around them. And the voice of the chief was a distant drone. We drank more rum. When no more came, we rowed back to the ketch, blinded by the sparkles of the low sun on the snow.

The ship's clock struck eight bells. I awoke with a start, not knowing whether it was morning or midday or late afternoon. Only when I saw the sun through the portlight did I realize it had already crossed the sky having left the snow in the trees and a pink glow in the clouds. The fragrance of roasted meats drifted from the village. I saw Charlie's tiny feet sticking out from the covers, saw the space beside her empty, saw Sayami in the cockpit, oiling the Winchester, and the sun sinking behind him. I came fully awake only when the skiff bumped the ketch. It was Nello, with a weary look in his eyes, not just fatigue but resignation, as if something was now unfolding with nothing to be done. He held on to the gunwales and stared at the sea.

"A canoe came from the south," he began. "They paddled all night. There's a big boat coming. Fancy, lots of windows. Slow, sticking its head into every nook; but coming."

He looked up at Sayami.

"It could be anyone," Sayami said, pumping the lever and sighting a tree top.

"Sure," Nello said.

The ship's clock struck twice. Seven hours till midnight.

When the drums started again, we wrapped ourselves in blankets, hid the rifles beneath them, and rowed ashore. Nello stared at the pass leading to open water.

"Whoever it is can't get in here in the dark. We're safe until morning."

When we landed on the beach, they stepped one at a time

from the bow to keep their feet dry, and then they were all ashore, getting the gear comfortable in their arms, ready to haul the skiff up high, waiting for me to follow. But I didn't. I just sat there. The dark current caught the skiff and washed it south toward the mouth of the pass that fed into the strait. I glanced up at the three of them standing there, then I looked over my shoulder. I felt an irrepressible urge to row out and get help from some of my own kind—whoever they were, the church boat, the police, even the bloody yacht—ones who would understand, intervene, set things right—against the savagery, the barbarity, the phantoms in the darkness. And I lowered the oars into the water and set the blades upright. And the village? The hell with them! Don't they do the same? Aren't they driven by a madness they cannot see? And if they perish—these half-beasts, dead-eaters—what of it? Didn't they exterminate whoever was here before? Why should they be spared? It's just their turn to go and ours to conquer. As it will be for those who exterminate us.

The smoke from the village spread like a veil over the waters; bloodthisty savages—let it all burn to the ground. But I held the left oar still and pulled hard on the right. The skiff turned around. Back toward the cove.

They stood on the shore, said nothing, showed nothing. The skiff ground the shells and I leapt out and began to haul, then let the bow down.

"I'm not hauling it. I'm not the bloody crew."

They pulled the skiff up, poor Charlie struggling, and only when they moved past me did I see the man standing in the sea. I recognized his shoulders, his carriage, the sharp lines of his face—the Kwakiutl who took Kate—and then he turned toward us and even in the dusk I could see his steely eyes. He was thigh-deep in the water with his arms out, walking slowly deeper, until the water reached his chest. He stood there with palms down as if blessing the waters, then, lifting his face, basked in the twilight.

"Cooling his skin to dull the pain," Nello said, pulling the blanket tight around the rifle. "You'll see."

"*He* must know where she is," I blurted. "We can make him talk."

"And start a war? You said she'd come at midnight anyway."

The pink glow had faded from the sky and left the colorless cold of winter. A hollow whistle blew.

"Let's go have some rum," he said. "And some eulachon oil. Your favorite."

As if some inexhaustible horn of plenty had opened, laden trays kept coming in through the door and were passed around the fire: deer meat in long strips, whole roast duck, roasted eagle that Nello said was best at this season when nice and fat on salmon, whole roasted perch, bear steaks, thin-sliced halibut, skewers the length of swords packed tight with smoked clams, a mud-looking thing that was *migwat*, or seal-blood soup, and seal tongue, curled fern shoots, sweet hemlock-bark sap, and berry cakes of every kind. And rum. The smoke thickened. We ate for hours.

Then came the announcement of the gifts, all that we had seen before plus rifles, chisels, axes, all given by the chief to the other chiefs in order of importance, and with all drums and rattles thundering, each chief danced wearing the great wooden masks of wolves, eagles, bees, unrecognizable birds, and unimaginable beings. Some danced with the solemnity of priest, others wildly like children, and some—singing softly to themselves—moved with a lulling motion, like a canoe on a rolling sea.

The flames were low. A belligerent banging on the outside walls circled the house. Nello covered Charlie's eyes. The Kwakiutl burst in, his wet body gleaming in the firelight, a knife flashing in his hand, and abalone shells dangling from wires through his skin. There was no sign that he had been hit by my bullet. He came down the steps, circled the fire, and all the while, with short quick swings, he slashed his forehead with the knife.

One of the chiefs came down, laid the tip of a knife against the Kwakiutl's back, and, sliding down, cut a deep slit. Blood ran. Then he moved his knife a few inches and cut again, and again, four times in all, then knelt and cut the back of his thighs and calves the same way. The Kwakiutl shook his head to shake the pain away. The chief lifted the skin away from the flesh and ran long stripped branches under the skin and out the other side.

Nello leaned close to me. "Maybe he'd talk if I threatened him with a slap."

The chief took ends of ropes that dangled from above and tied them around the branches, made sure the lengths were even, then the ropes were hauled tight. The Kwakiutl stretched his arms as he had over the water, and with his head back and face basking in the darkness, he was raised slowly toward the roof. The ropes were swung in circles and he began to fly: over the fire, in and out of the light, until a bear threw a bucket of oil and the flames roared in twisting columns and engulfed him. When they ebbed, the ropes dangled empty.

I heard an aberrant sound in the distance: like anchor chain clicking when it's fed out with care over a roller. Then it was gone.

All was still.

26

Midnight

And so, after eight thousand years of dreaming a world full of legend and myth, making it real through careful ritual; after all this time, perhaps the longest period in man's time on earth in which a culture was allowed to develop uninterrupted by massive warfare or other destructive forces . . . it all came to an end.

—Bill Reid

The floor was empty, the house nearly dark. There was no movement and no sound but for a wet log hissing in the smoldering fire, when, from far away, over the still waters of the cove, the ship's clock chimed eight times.

It was midnight.

A cool draft passed through and an ash cloud drifted low over the floor. A faint call, like a mother beckoning a child, came from a distance but not clear like the chimes—muffled—as if coming from the bottom of a well. It came again, not through the door or through the walls, but from right below us, near the fire—from underground. The draft strengthened and the ash clouds stirred in eddies. As the voices neared, a spot of ground before us swelled, cracked, and then a hand burst through, turning and reaching out as if waiting to be held. Beyond the fire, the earth now bulged and, with a sudden thrust, the top of a skull popped through, then the forehead, then the eyes: dark holes, and a long crimson tear on an ashen cheek. It looked around. All around the fire, the earth heaved and buckled, and a knee burst through or a leg kicked out, then an arm, a face; and they clawed their way out of the suffocating ground.

Four naked bodies, as gray as ghosts, erupted but remained hunched, unsure of the place. They turned a hand, raised a shoulder, twisted at the hips, as if they hadn't made these movements for a long time. They went to the fire and pushed coals with their hands, feeling, trying to remember, then they fanned the flames until a column of smoke spiraled up. Something stirred in the middle of the flames. Amid the smoke, an enormous form emerged from the ground; its great arms held out a naked woman, her head and frail limbs dangling lifeless. She was well off the ground when the smoke parted and a flame flared and lit her face, *her* tall forehead, *her* cheeks, *her* stubborn chin: Kate.

I started to get up but Nello pulled me down.

The ghosts walked through the flames, lifted her off gently as if afraid she'd fall apart, and, making sounds like killer whales' cries, brought her out and laid her on the ground.

Lightning flashed through the holes in the roof, then a sound like thunder, and a sinewy woman, naked except for a patch of cedar apron, landed in the doorway. She stood, knees bent, arms cocked—all angles—with a kelp tube over her shoulders criss-crossing between her breasts. As she came down the steps, the people drew back. Nello buried Charlie's face in his shoulder.

The woman danced, uttering sharp sounds. "Tuxwidl," Nello whispered. "She says she cannot be killed. In that tube is the water of life." Some people began audibly to cry.

Kate didn't stir.

It was either the draft or a wind change, but the smoke no longer rose in a column but swirled to the side, circled the walls, and shrouded over us, darkening the gloom. The woman neared Kate. She knelt, laid her palm flat on Kate's stomach, then her chest, put her head between her breasts, listening to her heart. She took the bulbous end of the kelp tube, untied the stopper that plugged it, and, with utmost care, dipped her fingers in and rubbed the moisture onto Kate's brow. She was carefully sprinkling Kate's chest with the water when, behind her, the ground violently ruptured and a powerfully-built man burst through, sword in hand, and pointed it at her head. She turned "Wina'lag," Nello said. "Warrior of the World." The ghosts scattered. Still down, the Tuxwidl plugged the kelp tube, slipped it from her body, and shielded it behind her back. The sword shone like a rigid flame in the firelight.

She half rose, backed away circling the fire, her left hand out searching, grasping air, then slapping it on her heart, her head, her belly. She stopped defiant before him, arm to one side, her body unprotected. He held the blade parallel with the ground and she lowered her hand, palm up, to her side, when he struck. The blade went straight at her chest, but in the last moment, as if hit by some enormous blast of air, it flew aside and the man lunged, stumbling, into the emptiness beside her.

He struck and missed again. Then, with a quick jab, he shoved the blade into the fire. When he pulled it out, its tip flamed. She watched the flame. He lunged. The blade plunged deep above her apron. She grabbed it. When he pulled it out, blood fountained. She stared at the blood gushing down her thighs and spreading in the ashes. She fell to her knees. With her last strength she nudged the kelp tube to her mouth and bit it. The man yanked it away. Her head fell forward and her hair hid her face, then she folded onto herself until she was no larger than a seal. People shrieked. Women came down and crowded around her and covered her with a bright-striped blanket. The man slipped the coil of kelp over his head, clutched the sword with both hands, then raised it high over his head. The women scattered. Then such stillness. With a glitter, the sword sliced the air and landed with a thud. He sliced again. Under the blanket something fell to the ground. He leaned down and reached under and pulled out her severed head. He walked with it around the fire then lobbed it in the flames. Clutching the kelp tube, he took two steps back and was swallowed by the ground.

Red spread on the blanket like on a blotter. Women wailed. Two men brought a big wooden box, lifted the Tuxwidl into it, closed the lid, struggled to haul it near the flames, and flung it into the middle of the fire. The bears threw buckets of oil, and the flames roared so high they set the roof ablaze, and men had to clamber out the corner holes and pull the burning boards apart to douse them in the snow. When the flames ebbed, the box still burned, then its sides crumbled and the striped blanket smoldered. There was a sound like hot oil sizzling until the blanket fell to ashes and only a heap of bones now glowed in the dark.

Kate didn't stir.

The floor was empty.

I had pulled out of Nello's grip and started down when, with a cry, a naked form shot from the flames, all angles. The Tuxwidl. She raised her bloodied head, threw back her hair, and her eyes shone with a weak smile. With the blood caked on her belly and thighs, she struggled back to Kate. She felt the earth where the man had vanished with her kelp and, with the sword, jabbed the earth. She dug a shallow hole, then, dissatisfied, she dug another. After a few tries she stopped and fell to her knees. Lifting her apron, she leaned back, arched her spine, and her stomach rippled in contractions. She thrust her pelvis forward and gave birth to a frog.

Sensing the fire, the frog stood still, then leapt from one hole to another, until, close to Kate, it stopped and burrowed. The woman helped it dig. When a good depth down, she reached in, searched, and pulled out the kelp tube. She was backing away when a hand shot up and grabbed her ankle. She thrust the sword with ferocity into the ground. The hand let go.

She untied the kelp and sloshed water on herself, rose stronger, then sloshed water onto Kate. Kate trembled. The woman knelt astride her, took a deep breath, and held her mouth to Kate's until Kate's chest heaved, then with a cry and an arching bound, she vanished in the flames.

Kate sat up—all angles.

That's when I heard the first click of a rifle bolt above.

27

The Choice

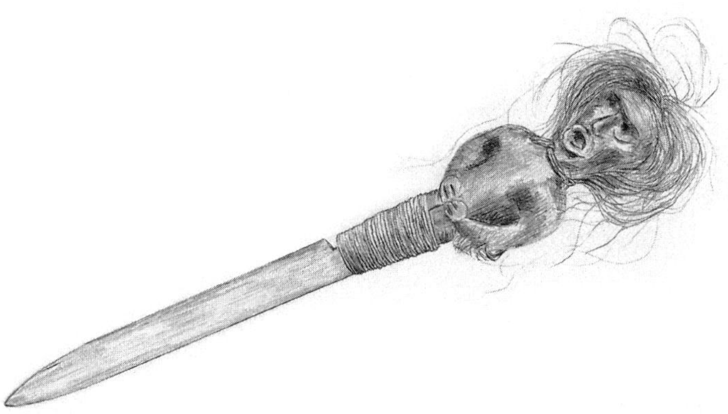

Much of the old way of life died with its followers, and the customs of the newcomers were forced in to take its place. It is one of the world's greatest tributes to the strength of the human spirit that most of those who lived and their children after them remained sane, and adapted in part at least to the strange new world in which they found themselves.

—Bill Reid

Kate stood mesmerized by the flames. Another rifle gave a sharp, hard click, this time close by, then another and another from every corner of the roof.

The first worn boots came down through a roof hole, awkwardly, searching for a foothold, then the rest of them dropped in through every corner: rag tag, scruffy white men holding guns. They spread out slow and silent on the catwalks that swung and swayed, dangling from the ropes.

I clambered down the ramps onto the floor. Nello, rifle in hand, headed for the door, but too late, because two more men burst in, leaving the door ajar. They nervously raised their guns but, seemingly unable to make out anything past the firelight, leveled them at Kate.

From the darkness above, and in a near deadfall, the Kwakiutl flew down. The twigs no longer tied, he let go of the rope.

He kept looking at the gun barrels while circling around Kate as if trying to anticipate the first shot, or trying to shield her on all sides. But they were everywhere now: on the steps, up behind the great house-poles by the door, some kneeling, some sitting on the swaying catwalk, their rifles pointing indifferently down. When the Kwakiutl saw me approach, he stopped and, with those piercing eyes leveled at me, tried to guess my intent; then he moved to Kate's far side, leaving me this side to defend. Her face was calm, the eyes alert as when I had taught her to sail.

Into the darkness of the doorway stepped an impeccable uniform, so white against the night that it seemed to glow—the captain of the yacht. He looked about, must have judged things safe, because he leaned out the door and said in a respectful voice, "All clear, sir." And stepped aside to make way. A tall, heavy man stepped in. He seemed embarrassed but his eyes hardened when his glance fell on Kate. I remembered the head, the breadth of his shoulders; it was Hay.

Sayami made his way through the mountains of gifts and went and spoke respectfully to him. They exchanged some words, then Hay took a step down. The rest of the house was motionless; watching. Somebody sneezed loudly and kids snickered.

Hay, reassured, began to descend. The Kwakiutl moved closer to shelter Kate and instantly there was movement on the catwalks up above. Hay shot out his right arm, palm down, calling for calm, and the movement above stopped. The Kwakiutl moved so close to Kate they touched, and Hay's hand trembled, then—as the Kwakiutl pushed her down to the ground—with a move as quick as the striking of a snake, Hay dropped his hand. Two quick shots rang out. The Kwakiutl's head fell forward as if in deep thought, he fought to keep his feet but his legs no longer held, and he went down on both knees, one arm holding him off the ground. He clawed the ashes. No one moved.

Hay's voice rang out, self-assured and loud, "Thank you, Captain Dugger, for a job well done."

I looked at Kate. She was still on the ground beside him and I couldn't see all her face, but I was sure I saw disappointment. Hay took another step and talked on but my head swam and I only heard how, "you more than earned your wages." Kate tightened. I took a step toward her, and, as my shadow fell on her, she grabbed the shard of mirror the Hamatsa had left behind. At the same moment there was shifting on the catwalk, but Hay's arm shot out and the shifting ceased. Hay, with his arm extended, walked down and talked on, about how not only had he taken the liberty of paying off all my debts, but he thought "a further ten thousand is in order."

He was talking to me but glaring at Kate, who now looked up at me, not reprimanding, not questioning—just waiting to see. And I watched her for a sign, a spark, a softening around the eyes; but she gave nothing. She rose. She looked back down at the

Kwakiutl still braced on his arm, then she made a small move—toward Hay. I blocked her path. Hay began to lower his arm and I braced myself for the bullets, but he held his arm steady and said softly, "Twenty thousand, Captain Dugger. In Tahiti that will last you twenty years."

Without looking up, Kate started to walk. I stepped out of her way. She walked toward him, getting smaller and smaller as she had in my dream, and Hay, smiling, reached out his other arm in welcome. She was near him, so near I had to take two steps to the side as I pulled out my gun and fired. Hay staggered; his hand went down. Shots rang out, the ash blistered around me, and something slammed my leg and threw me forward, then I felt a hammer hit my shoulder and I slumped down near the flames.

Kate looked back but seemed to have trouble remembering. She looked down at her own reflection in the shard of mirror in her hand. Hay, clutching his arm, laughed out loud, then he called to Sayami, who helped him off with his coat and looked at his bleeding arm. Kate walked steadily now, and Hay, with his good arm, reached out and laid the coat on her bare shoulders. But she let it fall; then turned away, leaving the shard of mirror in his heart.

Hay teetered; the red spread on his shirt. Sayami raised his rifle toward me, but hesitated and yelled out, "Nello! The door!" He pushed Kate down between towering piles of blankets, leapt clear, dropped to one knee, and fired and fired up into every corner of the darkness.

As the unarmed captain hid, Nello ran among the sacks, his rifle blasting at the gunmen at the door.

The catwalk erupted in gunfire, but Hay's men had to fire from the swinging boards and they shot wild, hitting the ash around us.

"Idiots!" Sayami roared. "Round-eyed morons!" And he timed the catwalk's swing and shot a man, who fell into the sails and brought them billowing down.

We edged toward the door. Nello hit a man who—now bent over—ran up a mound of pots, but the more he climbed, the more the pots slid down.

Hay had slumped to his knees. Sayami pulled him onto his haunches and used him for cover. A man on the catwalk steadied his aim by wrapping his arm around a rope, but Sayami shot first and the man flew off and, with his arm trapped, swung in lazy figure eights over the flames.

One was shooting through the smoke-hole in the roof but he was shooting almost straight down at Sayami and managed only to pump bullets into Hay. I emptied my gun into him, and he plummeted into the fire, sending a burst of sparks into the gloom. And under the shower of sparks the Indians sat astonished. The chief clutched his carved stick and watched in open admiration the spectacle of the white men falling—like dead birds—from the sky. They fell from the smoky darkness into the ashes; onto mounds of splintering boxes; onto exploding sacks of flour; and onto a row of mirrors, launching shards of glass glistening through the flames. And a twinge of jealousy seemed to glaze his eyes, perhaps envy for their performance, forgetting for the moment that they wouldn't rise at midnight.

But we were still pinned down. Two men behind the tops of the house posts were well hidden. Then Sayami cried out, "Nello," and, while Nello gave covering fire, he dashed into the open and shot one, who tumbled down and clattered among the pots. But shots came back and Sayami's coat rippled. Nello bounded up the sacks and fired along the wall. Black boots slipped out of the bear's mouth, but the big teeth held the rest.

The great house fell silent.

I pushed myself up but the house started spinning. Then everything went dark.

28

To Ashes

We will dance. We will dance when our laws command us to dance, and we will feast when our hearts desire us to feast. It is a strict law that bids us dance. It is a strict law that bids us to distribute property among our friends and neighbors. It is a good law. Let white man observe his law, we shall observe ours.

—Kwakiutl Chief to Franz Boas

A woman's voice hummed softly as if in a dream. I opened my eyes. The big house was empty. Only the dead lay about, in odd shapes where they'd fallen, with Kate rolled up like a sleeping cat beside me.

Nello was gone.

In the middle of the floor sat Sayami: legs crossed, hands on knees, back bowed as if from fatigue, his head fallen forward, lifeless, on his chest. His rifle lay before him on the ground.

The dead were everywhere, dangling, twisted, crumpled, or splayed like children playing angels-in-the-snow. And one, as in repose, before the shattered mirrors with his head cocked to the side, eyes wide open, staring at the glass as if he just couldn't get enough of seeing himself dead. And, in all that silence, an old woman hummed as she swept the platforms with a slow and even motion, sweeping around the edges of the dead as if they would—like the stairs and walls—remain there for a long time.

There was movement at the top of the steps, and I could make out, standing there, the captain of the yacht. He slammed his shoulder against the door twice, but to no avail, then yelled something incomprehensible at the planks. When there was no reaction from outside, he came down and sat on a sack of flour beside Hay, who was slumped dead on his knees with his forehead to the ground.

There were voices outside. Chains rattled and a key turned in a lock. The door swung open and let in moonlight and a flickering red glow as if from a fire. One by one the chiefs filed back in, Nello's cousin among them, then came men carrying two big wooden boxes, and others dragging weighty boom chains on the ground. At the end was Wina'lag with his sword in hand, leading Nello tied at the wrists with a cord.

The chiefs all took their places as before; only the one who walked on water and the cousin remained standing. He held up his right arm as he did in the sea, and began. At first the cousin didn't translate, but then started with, "We do not want anyone interfering with our customs. We were told that a man-of-war would come and destroy our villages if we should continue to do as our grandfathers and great-grandfathers have done. By what right? Is this the white man's land? Where was the white man when our God gave this land to our great-grandfathers? Do we ask the white man, 'Do as the Indian does'? Let your king rule with his laws; we will rule with ours. We don't want your man-of-war to stop our dancing, or stop us giving away what our hearts want to give; to hoard is a shameful thing among our people. And we don't want your man-of-war to tell us how to punish those who killed. We have our fathers' laws for that. There has been much death today, much sadness. May what we do now ease the long sleep of the dead."

He lowered his arm. No one moved. Then he gave a quiet command. The cousin didn't translate.

The men with the chains turned and walked toward the captain of the yacht. They held him down and began wrapping the chains around him when Nello yelled out, "Leave him alone; he only hid," then broke into Kwakiutl, but Wina'lag yanked the rope and pulled him to the ground. The chiefs conferred; the chain-wrappers slowed. A short command rang out. The chain-wrappers looked up. They unwrapped the chains from the captain, turned, and started toward me.

At the yelling, Kate sat up; all angles. I tried to reach out to touch her, but my right arm wouldn't move and I was lying on the left, so I struggled to one knee just as Nello jerked the rope loose from his keeper and lunged toward us. He was nearly there, ready to help, when Wina'lag caught him, and I saw a cold glitter as the sword blade shot ahead and plunged into his back. Nello stopped. His arms flew toward me as the blade came out his chest, tenting his shirt, and, as if a rain poured down on him, it turned, dot by dot, a somber red. He fell to his knees.

The men wrapped the chains around me, and I fought with one good arm, kneeling on one good leg, but they held me down with their feet and wrapped the chains tight and hooked them tightly together. Then they carried me like a dead man to the steps. My head dangled; the world was upside down. They dragged Kate, shouting, and bent her over a wooden box. The chiefs gathered around her. The sword went up and came down like a scythe. Her voice fell silent. We went jerkily up the steps as they threw a blanket over her and stuffed her in the box. Then the box into the flames and poured the oil. As we turned out the door, they dragged the other box to Nello.

My head dangled in the moon-filled night.

There was a steady banging that I remembered from long ago and I could smell the tide. We were in a canoe in the center of the cove and there was moonlight on the village still covered with snow. People lined the beach, some holding a flame, but there was a great red glow on the houses behind them. I twisted around; near the island, her masts against the sky, stood the ketch. On fire. The foredeck was aflame and there must have been a fire below, because the portlights, like blazing eyes, glowed yellow in the dark. With her anchor line burnt through, she was drifting out to sea.

They lifted me wrapped in the chains, shouted, held me up for all on the beach to see, then threw me with a great splash into the black water. I sank.

29

Dawn

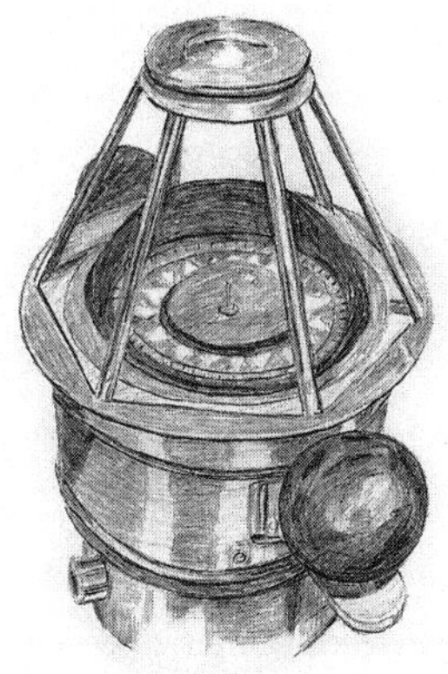

Play me a fiddle tune, sing me a song, banish misfortune, my time is not long.

—Gaelic boat song

I dreamt I was back in school with the pool of water on the roof rippling in the sun, then it glowed red and up leapt flames and it burnt, the roof burnt, and I could never dream again.

I opened my eyes. The sails were set, even the mizzen, and I saw the fog, swirling, thinning as we sailed over long hillocks of smoothly heaving sea, then a faint light coming through—the break of dawn. And from far, far away, as faint as a song remembered from the cradle, half hummed, half sung, came *Oi vita, oi vita mia.* I turned my head. Nello stood at the wheel, his coat flapping, his shirt caked with dried blood. He leaned down and let out on the mainsail. He must have heard me stir, because he turned to look, and seeing my eyes open said, "Morning, Cappy," in a whisper as if not wanting to wake me. "How about I make you a lovely heap of flapjacks?"

The wind pushed us on a reach but the ketch had a strange motion: long calm runs, descending, descending, then slower, gentler risings as if we were sailing in long swells. I pushed myself up. There was no land in sight, only the empty waters of the open ocean. On the starboard cockpit seat, bundled in blankets as in a cocoon, with only her auburn hair sticking out, was . . . and I couldn't breathe. Then Nello leaned down and whispered, "She's asleep."

He saw me staring at his blood-drenched shirt, and he laughed a silent laughter. "We're all dead," he said. "The ketch burnt. The yacht's captain saw it. The whole world knows we're dead."

Then the wind gusted and he closed his jacket against the cold. "Give us some credit, Cappy," he said. "Eight thousand years of long winter nights."

I tried to get up but everything was stiff, everything ached. My arm and a leg were bandaged. Nello looked concerned. "Those are real," he said. "But you'll be all right."

The ketch ran down the long back of a swell, her tall rig catching the wind even in the trough, then she rose and sailed with an exuberant surge up the face of the next hillock. I struggled across the cockpit and pulled back the blankets an inch at a time. With deep even breaths, as calm as a child, Kate slept. She was as pale as the dawn, the hollows of her cheeks deeper than before. She shuddered slightly, opened her eyes with a start, then, seeing me, the unease left her face.

"Good morning," Nello said.

The wind picked up, the mist thinned, and the sky and the sea filled with that all-deluding pink light. Kate sat up, rebundled her blankets, and looked around, but there was nothing to see but water.

"Where are we headed?" she softly asked.

Nello looked at the sails, then down at the compass, then, without looking at her, said, "West."

Kate smiled. She reached out her hand and cupped my face. "What's west?" she asked.

Nello eased the jib before he answered. "The East."

THE QUOTATIONS

CHAPTER

1. Joseph Conrad, *Youth* (1902)
2. James Boswell (1759)
3. Claude Levi-Strauss, *Gazette des Beaux-Arts* (1943)
4, 20. T.F. McIlwraith, *Field Letters* (1922-24) Franz Boas, *Kwakiutl Tales* (1910)
6, 28. Franz Boas, *The Kwakiutl of Vancouver Island* (1909)
8. Franz Boas, *The Social Organization of the Kwakiutl* (1895)
9. Franz Boas, *Ethnology of the Kwakiutl* (1921)
10. Franz Boas, *Kwakiutl Tales* (1910)
11. Aldona Jonaitis, *From the land of the Totem Poles* (1988)
12. James Teit, *The Lillooet Indians* (1910)
13, 25. Franz Boas, *The Social Organization and Secret Societies of the Kwakiutl* (1895)
15, 16, 17, 21, 22. Franz Boas, *The Religion of the Kwakiutl* (1930)
18, 21. 23. Franz Boas, *Ethnology of the Kwakiutl* (1921)
26, 27. Bill Reid, Courtesy of The Royal British Columbia Museum

NOTE ON THE ILLUSTRATIONS

The drawings at the chapter heads, by Candace Mâté, are mostly based on exhibited pieces, or historical photographs from the archives, of the Royal British Columbia Museum, Victoria, Canada

AUTHOR'S NOTE AND ACKNOWLEDGMENTS

My most profound thanks to the Kwakiutl Nation in whose islands and ancient villages I spent so much time, and from whom I learned so much. Their lives and traditions inspired a large part of this novel.

This book would not exist without the thirty years of field-work (1886 to 1930) and the many volumes of scholarly tomes by anthropologist Franz Boas. His *The Social Organization of the Kwakiutl Indians, The Kwakiutl of Vancouver Island, Kwakiutl Tales, Ethnology of the Kwakiutl, The Religion of the Kwakiutl Indians, Kwakiutl Culture As Reflected in Mythology,* and *Kwakiutl Ethnography,* edited by Helen Codere, make up the ethnographic core of this novel.

Other contributing anthropological and ethnological works were: Clellan S. Ford's *Smoke from Their Fires,* Jim McDowell's *Hamatsa,* George Clutesi's *Potlatch,* Aldona Jonaitis' *Chiefly Feasts* and *From the Land of the Totem Poles,* Bill Holm's *Smokey Top,* Audrey Hawthorn's *Kwakiutl Art,* Claude Levi-Strauss's *The Way of the Mask,* Pamela Whitaker's *Kwakiutl Legends,* and Hilary Stewart's *Indian Fishing* and *Cedar*.

Most helpful were important Nothwest letters and narratives such as Wolfgang G. Jilek's *Indian Healing,* Hughina Arnold's *Totem Poles and Tea,* T.F. McIlwraith's field letters *1922-4 At Home with the Bella Coola Indians,* Carol Batdorf's *Northwest Native Harvest,* The U'mista Cultural Society's *The Living World,* and *Tales from the Longhouse,* by Indian children of British Columbia.

The soul of the book came from one of the finest Kwakiutl wood carvers, Sam Johnson of Health Bay. Without his long days of companionship and story telling, these pages would have no life. The personal help of Alan Hoover and Dan Savard and many of the staff of the museum and archives of The Royal British Columbia Museum, New York's Museum of Natural History, New York's The Museum of the American Indian, and the University of British Columbia's Museum of Anthropology, were an indispensable contribution.

Authors traditionally thank their editors but this is a different thanks. Few authors can claim their editor as a dear friend; I have that privilege. Starling Lawrence, Norton's Editor-in-Chief, not only magically turned some of my phrases from Hungo-Saxon into English, but he also, most patiently, taught me how to get out of the story's way. And his merciless editorial comments had me in stitches when I most needed a laugh.

Then of course, there was always Candace, who for years sailed with me in the magical solitude of the Kwakiutl Islands. Her editorial criticism, her companionship, not to mention her steamed clams with wine and garlic, made life worth living. And our son Peter, who, from the age of five, rowed us tirelessly against tide and current to discover the mystical, long-abandoned Kwakiutl villages.